MAGE THRONE PROPHECY

JAMES A. HADDOCK III

WEBSITES:

Jameshaddock.us

Copyright © 2020

Author's note:

When you see this, "¥ and conversation, ¥" it means they are speaking Japanese. I hope it's not too confusing for you.

A routine physical shows Captain Ross Mitchell has a flesh-eating virus that specifically targets the brain. Prognosis says he'll be a vegetable by week's end. Having survived numerous incursions in combat around the world, he decides he's not going out like that. He drives a rented corvette into a cliff face at over 200 MPH. The fiery impact catapults him toward the afterlife.

Instead of finding the afterlife, he finds himself in a

different body with an old man stabbing him in his chest. He fights free, killing the old man before passing out. He wakes to find he's now in the body of Prince Aaron, the 15-year-old second son of the King.

In this medieval world, the Royals are Mages. The old man who was trying to kill him was a Mage "Vampire". Instead of blood, the old Mage was trying to steal Ross/Aaron's power, knowledge, and in this case his body. When Ross/Aaron killed the old Mage, his vampire power was transferred to him. He now has the memories, knowledge, and powers of the old Mage.

Ross/Aaron must navigate this new environment of court intrigue with care. His older brother, the Crown Prince, hates him. His older sister has no use for him. The King sees him as an asset to be used, agreeing to marry him to a neighboring Kingdom for an alliance. Before the marriage takes place, the castle is attacked. Someone is trying to kill him but is finding it most difficult. Where Mages fight with Magic, Ross/Aaron fights with magic and steel. It's hard to cast a spell with a knife through your skull, or your throat cut.

As Ross/Aaron travels with his fiancée toward her home for the marriage to take place, they are attacked at every turn. Someone doesn't want this wedding to happen. Ross/Aaron has had enough of people trying to kill him. With Aaron's knowledge, and Ross' training, they take the offensive. The Kingdom will never be the same.

CHAPTER 1

Head tilted back; I took the last long pull from the fancy whiskey bottle. I tossed the empty over the cliff, watching it fall until it shattered on the sea rocks below. It would be easy to follow the bottle over, but not much style in that. I sat down, feet hanging off the cliff in open air. I liked the feel and the smell of the ocean breeze, and the sound of the waves crashing. Looking toward the horizon, I watched as the sun edged up beginning a new day.

"Ya know Lord, it's always been just You and me. The military was my family, got no one else. With all the things I've done in my twenty-seven years of life, all the special ops training the deployments all over the world; All the fights, fire fights, crashes, explosions I've been through, to have You end me with a flesh-eating bacteria that eats brains, is kind of embarrassing. What kind of crap is that? Sorry, that's the whiskey talking. But, really. I mean I never wanted a blaze of glory, but my brain being eaten, and not even by zombies? Come on."

"Doc says I'll be a slobbering idiot in a week, laying in my waste. Well, I ain't going out like that. I'll fight You for it. I win I get to live; You win... well at least it will be a clean death... Nothing to say? Surely You have an angel trained in hand-to-hand as good as me, I'll fight him..." He waited, shrugged his shoulders, "It was worth a try. Ok, I'll see You in a few minutes."

I stood up, brushing my hands, and pants off, and walked toward the car. "Ya know, some cultures believe if they killed a horse at your grave, you'd have a horse to ride in the next life. Well, I rented me this new Corvette Stingray; it will be my ride in the next life." I laughed. "Don't worry I bought the extra insurance; they won't lose any money on it."

I got in the car and started it. I sat listening to the engine as I revved it a few times. I turned the radio on and turned the music up. Putting the shifter into first and eased out on the clutch. I shifted smoothly through the gears gaining speed with each shift. I took the curves faster than I thought possible. "Woo-Woo, Lord, this baby can hang the curves!" On the last long straight away I held the accelerator to the floor.

The cliff face grew larger and larger, filling the view through the windshield. I glanced down at the speedometer it read 205 mph. Oddly, I realized that Meatloaf's "Bat Out of Hell" was playing on the radio. I laughed, "Ready or not Lord, here I come." I heard God laugh. "*Uh-oh,*". The car went from 205 mph to zero in an instant. The inertia from the car's impact, and the exploding fuel caused the cliff face to collapse, closing the interstate.

***

All was darkness, but a pinprick of light. As I watched, it seemed to get larger. It was like a star in the night's sky. It was coming toward me or I toward it. I started hearing something. *"Wind noise? No, something else. It has a rhythm to it like music or singing. Chanting, that's chanting, I must still be drunk."*

The hole of light sped toward me, and I toward it. As I sped toward it, the chanting grew louder. I suddenly realized two things. God has a sense of humor; and be careful what you ask for, you might get it.

I was through the hole of light. There was a tearing pain in my right chest. I grabbed for the pain, my hand closed around someone's hand, and that hand was around the handle of a dagger. Time slowed; the chanting continued.

Another dagger descended from my left; I grabbed his wrist stopping it. My eyes focused on my attacker. It was an old man covered in blue, red, and black paint with gold runes all over his face and naked upper body. He might have been old, but he was strong, or I was weak. The dagger was coming down toward my chest, and I couldn't stop it.

I head-butted him in the face. The dagger's downward

pressure stopped, and so did the chanting. I forced the dagger from my right chest out and shoved but kept a hold on his wrists. As he fell back, he pulled me up from the table I was on, and we went over and onto the floor.

He was regaining his senses and starting to fight again, but I now had both dagger handles in my hands. He rolled over on top of me, but before he could do more, I slashed both daggers across his throat almost cutting his head off. His blood covered me, seeping into my cuts and stab wound.

His dying body lay on top of me, his blood draining out on to me. I was exhausted, I started to push his body off me but cramped and started to convulse. It felt like my flesh was on fire, burning me to the bone.

My mind was also burning, like someone was trying to rip it from my soul, and body. I fought to hold on. I fought like a berserker, screaming and tearing, holding nothing back. I don't know how long I fought, but I fought until blackness claimed me.

***

My eyes flew open. The old man was still on top of me. I was still holding the daggers, without thinking I reversed the daggers, blades along my forearms. I opened my hands, and the daggers sank through my skin, laying along the bones of my arms. I stared at my arms, then felt along them. I couldn't feel the daggers, but I knew they were there.

I closed my hand, as if around the dagger handles. They emerged from my arms, handles in my hands, ready to be used. I opened my hands, and they went back into hiding. *"How crazy is that?"*

I pushed the old man off me and realized I was naked. Not only was I naked, I was covered in blue, red, and black paint with gold runes all over my body. The runes weren't paint they were actual runes, made of gold, embedded into my skin. I looked at the old man, he no longer had any paint or runes on him. There was also no blood on us or the floor, neither were there any wounds on either of us.

I crawled over to the water pitcher and drank my fill. I looked around the old man's room; I knew it was his room we were in. My clothes lay on the bed. I needed to get this paint off me. I stood walking to the washbasin, wetting a cloth to wash. When I started, there was no paint on me nor any runes visible. The room spun; I sat down and lay back, washing my face with the cool wet rag.

That made me feel better. I crawled over to the wall and sat up leaning against it. I looked at the dead mage laying on the stone floor. "Mage?" Questions flooded my mind. Where was I that magic existed, or when was I? Why was he trying to kill me? Had this person, that I now was, been trying to kill him?

I felt weak, why was I so exhausted? I looked down at myself, this body. It, I, whatever, was young. I'd guess early teens. I would not say fat, but soft, out of shape. I leaned my head back against the wall. The question remained, why was the Mage trying to kill me? I realized that was what was happening; he had been trying to kill me. My head began to hurt like the worst hangover I ever had. I saw a memory through the dead Mage's eyes, like it was my memory.

***

I stood on the terrace overlooking the Royal gardens. The fresh fragrances opening my head, and the morning sun heating my old bones.

"Sir Mage." a servant called. I hated interruptions during my meditation time.

"Yes?" I answered.

"The King requests your presence." Which was the same as saying, drop what you are doing, he wants to see you now. I nodded and followed him toward the Royal chambers.

"Hopefully, the seeds I had planted have taken root."

We arrived at the Kings receiving room; they showed me

in. The King was sitting behind his desk looking out the window. I bowed, "Sire." He said nothing, I waited.

He turned and faced me, "I have reached a decision. You will give the boy the serum. He is fifteen Summers, and he has shown no abilities. It's time."

I nodded, showing no emotion. Inside I was elated. I had been working toward this opportunity for three years.

"When can you do it?"

"It will take me a day to prepare everything, so we can start tomorrow night. Then it will be three days before we know if it worked."

The King nodded, "do it."

"Yes, Sire."

He turned back to the window. I took that as my dismissal and left. It had been a long three years. It had been hard work holding the Prince back. Hiding and frustrating his power manifestations had not been easy. He was a powerful Mage in the making. He would make the perfect vessel for me, it would rid me of this old body, and get rid of the Prince at the same time. I would one day be king. I still had to deal with the Crown Prince, but I had plenty of time for that.

I must prepare everything just right. The blood magic spell was forbidden magic for a reason, it's very dangerous. This would be my ninth mind-body transfer; it was worth the risk.

***

My memory point of view changed to the Prince. "You will take the serum tonight." the King said, "It will shock your body and your powers will manifest."

"Or it will kill me," I answered.

"That is why the old Mage is giving it to you. He will help you through the transition. He has done this before."

"And all have survived?" I asked.

The King's face hardened, "You will take the serum tonight. We will talk again in three days." I followed him to the old tower where the old Mage's chambers were. The door was open, so we went straight in. "In three days then." the King said and left.

"Yes, Sire." The old Mage answered. "Come in Prince Aaron, let us prepare." He went to his worktable and got a vial of something. "Drink this." and handed it to me.

"Is this the serum?"

"No, that is to prepare your body to take the serum." I drank it. Things became foggy after that.

***

I opened my eyes and looked at the dead Mage. "Well, aren't I the turd in the punchbowl." I saw food on the sideboard and realized how hungry I was. I got some meat, cheese, and bread, sat down and began eating.

"Regardless of where 'here' is, or 'when' here is, the point is I am here. The question is what to do next. I'm in a young body, my father is king, our family is rich, but dysfunctional. I can work with that. The magic stuff may be a problem. The King is expecting me to be a Mage or dead. Though in rare cases the serum does not kill the person, and no power develops. I'll have to play this by ear. On the plus side, the King won't be back to check on me for a few days."

After I ate, I put the room back in order, as if no fight had taken place. I left the Mage's body where it lay. I'd claim ignorance of his demise. I drank more water, the pitcher always seemed to be full of water. I was still exhausted, so I lay down and went to sleep. I don't remember what I dreamed; I just remember dreaming. The memories were all mixed, ten others and mine.

I woke early and started what was my normal morning routine. Stretching, exercise, martial arts forms, and katas. I could not go running so I stayed with aerobic exercises. I had a lot of work to do to get this body into shape. I also had to concentrate more on my bladed weapons, as there were no firearms here. I started practicing with my forearm daggers and found them extremely sharp.

I had to do everything slowly, as I was not used to this body's coordination, and timing. I ate, drank lots of water, stretched, and rested. While I rested, I ran different scenarios through my mind, and how I would handle each. So far, I thought my safest bet was to say nothing, feigning amnesia. I'd let them make up a story they believed. In the morning, I expected them to come and check on me.

As the sun rose, I stood out on the balcony naked, as if in a daze. It worked better than I expected. They asked me nothing. They put a cover around me and took me back to my room. A short time later a doctor showed up and examined me.

"Do you know where you are?" I just stared at him. "Are you in any pain?"

I thought I might as well get something out of this, "hungry," I whispered.

"Hungry, you're hungry?"

This guy was quick. "Hungry," I repeated, and said no more. They started with desserts, Prince Aarons favorite. I pushed it away, "Food." They brought more foods. Out of the corner of my eye I saw the King at the door. I kept eating at the same slow pace.

The doctor went over to him. "How is he?" The King asked.

"He is still confused, but he asked for food, that is a good sign." The King nodded and stepped into the room. I kept eating.

He stood in front of me, "Aaron?" I kept eating. He reached and lifted my chin to look at him. I had to remind myself he was looking at a 15-year-old boy. "Do you know who I am?" I stared at him, as if thinking.

"King." I answered. He released my chin, I went back to eating, playing my part.

"He should be better in a few days Sire." The doctor said. The King nodded and left.

When I stopped eating, they took all the food and dishes away. When everyone had gone except the doctor, "bath." I said.

He nodded, "Good, very good." he said smiling. He had servants bring a tub and hot water. I bathed and changed into clean clothes. I thought I'd stick to single words for a while, it was working so far. They brought dinner to my room, which suited me. I wasn't ready to meet the family yet.

I rose early the next morning and continued my training program. I tied my small clothes, their version of underwear, on and worked up a good sweat. I washed off, put my clothes on, and waited for breakfast to be brought in. While I waited, I sat on the balcony meditating. The doctor arrived at the same time as my food did. I ignored him and ate.

"Prince Aaron, what happened to the old Mage? Do you remember?"

I did not look at him. Chewed my food a moment longer. "Died." I said and continued to eat. I'd let that mystery grow.

"How do you feel?"

Time to turn the game up a little. I froze with food halfway to my mouth and appeared to think. "Strange." I finally said.

"Strange how?" I said no more about it and ignored him after that. He finally left. This was getting boring fast. I left my room and headed for the training hall. Aaron had spent little time there. That was about to change.

The hall was empty, so I got a weighed wooden practice sword, and began to practice the sword forms taught here. At the very least it would strengthen my wrists and arms. I knew that the Weapons Master had watched me for a few minutes. Satisfied, he left me to my own devices.

I worked to near exhaustion, then went to the bathhouse, then back to my room. I slept better that night but was still having dreams. Crazy dreams where I was working magic.

The doctor and the King came with breakfast. I stared at the king. "Do you know me?" he asked.

"King." I answered.

He nodded, "what else?"

I stared at him seeming to think, "Father." I answered. That seemed to please him. "How do you feel?"

I squinted my eyes," Strange."

He nodded, "eat," and left. A man of few words. I sat

down and ate. Aaron speaking so few words was not his norm. Apparently, Aaron talked a lot. Oh well, not anymore. I have always kept my own council.

Aaron's new norm became early exercise, breakfast, training hall for weapons training, then back to his room for lunch, I added walking the castle walls and grounds to my routine. My body was responding faster than I would have expected. I suspected it had to do with magic and all the runes I wore just under my skin.

The Weapons Master started joining me. At first, he would make corrections, or minor adjustments. Then he started sparring with me. With his help I improved quickly. I had them make me a heavy punching bag and hang it in the back corner of the training hall. I started practicing my strikes and hand-to-hand when I was alone.

During a sparring session the Weapons Master came at me from an unexpected angle. I countered by dropping my sword catching his descending wrists, taking him around in the same direction; then reversing his wrists causing him to flip. We wound up on the floor with his sword at his neck.

I had done it without thinking. It was a standard defensive move to counter that kind of attack. I let go of him and stepped back. I expected him to be mad. "I'm sorry Master, I just reacted."

He jumped up, "don't be sorry, that was excellent, to defend without thinking is why we train. Where did you learn that, show me how you did it." So, I showed him how to reverse an attack like he had made.

"Where did you learn that move?"

"I don't know, it just seemed right." He didn't look convinced but didn't press me for more. That was the most I had spoken to anyone since I arrived in this body. Things were bound to change now.

Not everyone knew about the serum treatments given to Mage's children. They told everyone I had been ill and left it at that. No one questioned Royals.

CHAPTER 2

I continue with my strength training, this body definitely needed it. Many mornings the Weapons Master joined me in sword practice. I knew he watched me when I worked the heavy bag.

"Come with me," he said as I arrived one morning. I followed him out of the castle proper over to the guard's training area. "If you want to improve, you will need to train with others." I nodded.

"I would speak to you man-to-man." he said, I nodded. "These men are soldiers. While training one may get a bloody nose, or a bruise or two, you understand?"

"I'll try to go easy on them Weapon's Master." I said smiling.

He laughed, "You do that, lad."

We entered their training hall. It was more like a converted stable, but it was what they had. They continued to train. Some practiced swords, some knives, some grappled in a sand ring. We went over to the sand ring and watched.

"Corporal."

"Yes, Weapons Master?"

"Prince Aaron will practice with us for a time."

The Corporal cut his eyes at me then back at the Weapons Master but said nothing.

"Corporal, while I'm training in your house, I am a trainee, no repercussions. The battlefield will have no mercy on me."

He looked squarely at me. "Truly spoken M'lord. Trainee it is then. In the sandpit with ya."

I moved into the ring; the Corporal paired me with the smallest man there. Even at that he was a head taller and 50 Pounds heavier. We started slow, instructing me in the basics. I did not want to make them look bad, so I went along.

"Stop," the Weapons Master said. He pointed at me. "Stop wasting our time. Fight, or go back to the castle and train alone."

I nodded, "Yes Weapons Master."

The Corporal stared but said nothing. We started again. I countered his first hold and pushed him past. He came harder. I countered and tripped him. He was getting mad and came at me all out. I blocked his right blow slipped his left swing; I palm punched his diaphragm, and leg swept him. I waited for him to catch his breath from the diaphragm punch.

Everyone had gathered around the ring watching the exchange. "You could have done worse?" the Weapons Master asked.

I didn't answer right away. "One never shows all he's capable of, unless his life depends on it."

"A philosopher too?" He asked. I shrugged.

My opponent was back on his feet and came to me. "Show me." I nodded and walked him through the fight and my counters.

So began my training in the guard's training hall. As with most soldiers, what happened in the hall, stayed in the hall. My business stayed my business.

If anyone ever came to watch, we stayed with simple, basic sword practice. When it was just us, we went all out. If the guards were not on duty, they were training with me. The funny thing was no one ever asked where I learned my art. I guess it was their version of "don't-ask-don't-tell."

***

Afternoons I spent in the library reading. I read everything. Maps, magic, history, geography, if the book was there, I would read it. A few of the scholars thought to impose themselves on me. They soon realized I was far ahead of them in most areas. I didn't embarrass them or show off. After that they left me alone.

I studied and practiced magic at night. The hardest part was getting my mind to accept that magic existed in this time and/or place. Once past that, I began to improve. And because of the old Mage's memories I improved at an accelerated pace.

Maybe it was because of all the movies I had watched, books, and comics I had read. My imagination knew no limits as to what magic could or couldn't do. If Dr. Strange could do it, why not?

While I meditated, I levitated. I levitated objects and moved them around me like electrons around a nucleus. I teleported objects from one side of the room to the other, including myself. I learned to tell when people were near me, even behind a wall and could not be seen. I learned to eavesdrop at distances, and the list was growing. I was working on developing a 360-degree awareness. I still had a way to go before I became proficient.

The doctor still came to see me weekly. I'm sure he reported to the King as soon as he left. I went from feeling "strange" to feeling "fine". Most everyone left me alone, I was the "strange" Prince. That suited me, I doubted it would last though.

***

I borrowed six, baseball sized balls of yarn and took them with me to training. As I sat waiting for people to show up, I began levitating them and moving them around me. Everyone knew we were Mages, so it was no secret I could use magic. As far as they knew, I had always used magic. Royals kept secrets about their magic.

"What's this then, you going to teach us to knit?" the Corporal asked, everyone chuckled.

"I need help keeping track of multiple opponents and multiple weapons. I'm going to use these to practice. I want some of you to toss them at me while we train. Let's start slow until I get the hang of it."

After a week of getting beaned in the head, I started improving. After a month I was catching them spinning them in my atomic pattern, then throwing back to them. Once I had mastered that we changed to bean bags, and they came at me more than one at a time. I still missed occasionally, that kept me practicing.

***

Returning from the practice hall, there were servants waiting at the door to my quarters. "Yes?"

They bowed, "we are to measure you for new clothes Your Highness."

"Oh? What's the occasion?"

"They expect Emissaries from Shornwick at week's end, M'lord. You are expected to dine with them. They also expect you at breakfast in the morning in the family dining room."

"I see, all right let's get to it." They took my measurements; my body had changed a lot in the last few months. I knew this day was coming I just wasn't looking forward to it. "Suck it up, buttercup." I mumbled.

"Excuse me M'lord?"

"Nothing, please continue." They finished and left. I had better be ready for games in the morning. My big brother, Crown Prince Cain, would be on the prowl. He would start something, some prank to embarrass someone. More than likely that someone would be me. No problem, it couldn't be any worse than SEAR School. Two could play at that game.

Once all was quiet, I went down to the family dining room. I found Cain's chair and "fixed" it. I loosened the joints on one leg and used a spell to hold it into place until the time was right.

I was about to leave when I felt someone approaching. Without thinking, I levitated up into a dark corner of the ceiling. Two people entered. It was Cain, and our sister Celya. I smiled.

"This will be so funny," Celya said.

They went to my regular place at the table and pulled out my chair. "We'll see if the mute pup has anything to say when this goes off," Cain said. When they had finished, they pushed my chair back into place. They were both laughing when they left the dining room.

"What are we, in high school?" I chuckled. Once I was sure they were gone, I dropped down and traded my chair with Celya's. I returned to my room and went to sleep with a smile on my face.

***

I didn't want to be the first one in the dining room. Let them be first that would not arouse suspicions about me. Cain, Celya, and our younger brother Amos were already there.

I nodded to Amos, "brother," I greeted him.

He nodded in return frowning, "brother."

I was watching Cain out of the corner of my eye and knew the second he was about to spring his trap. I was ready to spring mine. There was a loud bang and a flash of fire came out from under Celya's seat. She screamed as it lifted her chair a foot off the floor. When her chair landed back on the floor, Cain's chair gave way dumping him on the floor.

It was quite the show, and I was hard pressed not to laugh. Amos didn't hold back. As my Grandpa would say, "He thought that was a knee slapper."

Celya was screaming at Cain, he was trying to untangle himself from his broken chair. Amos was laughing uproariously. I just watched the show like a good mute pup.

Cain saw Amos laughing and assumed he was responsible. He came across the room at him. "You did this," He shouted.

Amos saw how mad Cain was and stopped laughing. He was shaking his head, "no."

Cain leaned across the table reaching for Amos. "Leave him alone Cain," I said standing up.

Cain turned his head toward me, "So the mute pup speaks." He took Amos' plate and threw it at me like a frisbee. I caught it like a frisbee, spinning my body around, and launched it back at him. He didn't have time to react, the plate shattered against the side of his head, knocking him to the floor.

"This pup has teeth." I said.

Dazed, Cain staggered to his feet in a rage. He started conjuring a fireball to throw at me. I felt the King and Queen entering the room. Cain's fireball was the size of a volleyball when the King shouted, "Cain." That broke his concentration.

Timing is everything, I flicked a thought at the fireball. It exploded in Cain's hand setting his sleeve on fire and singeing the hair on that side of his head. The King flicked his hand putting the fire on his sleeve out. The room stank of burned hair.

The King looked around the room, "Well?" no one said anything. He waited a moment. "At least you stick together, when caught in your pranks. Get out, all of you. I don't want to see you again today."

As we left the dining room, "Thanks," Amos whispered, I winked at him. He smiled. All-in-all, I thought that went rather well for my first meal with the family.

***

Breakfast the next morning was a little more sedate. We ate in silence. "Aaron," The King said wiping his mouth with his napkin.

"Yes, father?" I answered. I felt sure what the next question would be.

"Have you shown any manifestations yet?"

I hung my head, acting the part of a remorseful child. "Not that I can tell, Father." He nodded. Cain smiled.

"Yeah, but he can throw a mean plate." Celya mumbled.

Cain's face reddened even more than his already sunburned color. The King ignored the comment.

"Are you still training with the Weapons Master and studying in the library?"

"Yes, father."

He thought a moment, "continue your arms training, your library studies, and add horsemanship to your training."

"Yes, father."

This was both good and bad. I could now do what I wanted training, but he was up to something. He did nothing without a purpose. He was planning something. He would use his perceived mundane son to further his agenda. And I probably wouldn't like it. I now had to consider whether I should manifest some small power, to throw off his plans, or let this play out.

The rest of the day went as usual, weapons training, lunch, library. I had finished reading another magic book and replaced it on the shelf. They were becoming redundant. One referencing another that referenced the first. I seemed to read in circles. I walked down the aisles browsing. When the aisle ended, I turned to go back, but an odd book caught my eye.

On a lower shelf were a few dust covered books pushed to the side and back. I looked through them; I saw nothing new. The last one, a small, plain brown leather-bound book. It was about the size of a small journaling notebook.

There was no title on the outside, the inside cover of the book read; Book of Thoughts and Memories. There were no pages in the book. I opened the book flat to examine it. It folded itself open into a larger book, doubling in size. It went from being pocket sized to a composition sized book.

Opening the larger book there were a few pages in it. Each time I turned the page there was another page there. It had been someone's notebook. A Mage's apparently, there were spells, descriptions, explanations and theories. It offered more sophisticated explanations than any book I'd seen since I had started studying. This would take time to examine. I closed the book to its smallest size and put it in my inside vest pocket. It was time for the evening meal with the family, and I didn't want to miss that.

I was first to arrive and took my seat waiting for the others to arrive. They brought me cool watered wine to drink while I waited. The others arrived shortly after that. The Queen who was usually quiet, was excited about the visitors coming to visit.

"I have seen no 'Genteel' Women in so long, it will be a refreshing change. I hope Margret and her daughter Regina comes with them. You can renew your friendship with her, Celya."

"Oh joy, I can hardly wait." Celya rolled her eyes.

"Mind your manners young lady, they are Royalty as well and our peers."

"She may be 'a peer' but she 'appears' to look like a sow."

"It's been five years since you've seen her, people change."

"For her husband's sake, I hope so," Cain said laughing cutting his eyes around at me. He had a new haircut, so both sides matched... Kinda. They had healed his face. Which was fortunate for him, as Mages that could use magic to heal were not all that common. Something tickled my memory.

It seemed the old Mage could heal using magic, which meant potentially, I could. The old Mage had chosen his victims based, at least partially, on their abilities and knowledge. The knowledge he had gained from each victim had given him a wide range of knowledge and abilities. Healing being one of them. There was talk of a ball and other gatherings. Most I let flow past me.

"Let's not forget, they are here primarily to discuss peace between our lands. I expect all of you to be on your best behavior." The King looked pointedly at each of us. "Don't mess this up."

"Yes, Father," came the chorus.

***

After my bath, I took my new notebook out and examined it. I opened it to a composition book size. The first two pages were blank, as I turned the page, words were on the third and those beyond. There was no telling how old this book was. From what I had seen so far it would take a while to read through it. "Too bad it doesn't have a table of contents." The page turned, and there was a table of contents. "No way." I started reading down the list and came to maps. "Maps, that should be interesting."

The composition book folded open twice more forming a large, old style, Atlas type book. Large pages of maps folded out. I heard my mother's voice, "close your mouth, you'll catch flies."

"Ok, a magic book, no problem." I looked through the maps. They were nicely done, but there was a problem. I didn't recognize any of them. No countries, no oceans, nothing seemed familiar. Small parts of countries, maybe. But the whole atlas? No. *"Ok, not in Kansas, got it. Doesn't change the fact that I'm here. Deal with it."*

I closed the atlas and opened the book before the atlas, and it held all kinds of drawings and diagrams. All perfectly done. I closed the drawings book and opened the composition book. I had my hand on a blank page, "I'm going to need a pen to add notes." I said.

The words, "I'm going to need a pen to add notes," appeared on the page. I stared at the words, and thought, *"Do I have to speak the words out loud to add them?"* Those words appeared on the page. I smiled.

I thought of a circle, not the word the object, a circle appeared on the page. I drew a happy face and a thumbs-up. Then erased them all with a thought.

I needed to keep this safe. A thought tickled my memory. I teleported to the old Mage's room. Even though the room was dark, I could see everything clearly. This was a new ability I had not noticed before. I looked around the room, going over to his work desk. There were a lot of notes and scraps of note papers there. I already knew what all those were.

I opened his wardrobe and found what I was looking for. There hung his Mage's Cloak. Not quite Dr. Strange's cloak but mine had a hood on it, and it could do some cool stuff too. Who knows, I may improve on it. There was also a leather belt with a pouch. If this had been D&D, it would have been a "blessed bag of holding". He called it a "pouch of gathering" it did basically the same thing. I put the belt and pouch on. I put my notebook in the pouch.

I gathered everything of any use and put it in my pouch.

Especially the rune scribing tool. It was used to scribe runes on to anything, giving the item magical abilities or powers. His, now my, Mage staff stood in the corner. It was a sad looking walking staff. At a thought it flew across the room to my waiting hand. When it touched my hand, it appeared as it really was, a dark Iron wood staff covered in mithril runes and engravings.

This was a Swiss Army Knife of staffs. It was a staff when held like a staff. If you put both hands at its middle and pulled apart, it became two fighting sticks. If you held it in front of you like a bow and made the motion of drawing a bowstring, an arrow would appear notched on a string ready to be loosed.

I had to try it to make sure it all worked for me, but I would need more room. I put on my cape, hood up, and stepped out onto the balcony. With my cape on I was part of the shadows. Using my Mage sight, I looked over at the guard turret, there was no one there. I teleported over to it.

I kept my cape on and ran through my staff kata. The cape flowed with me, never getting in the way. I separated the staff into fighting sticks and worked those. I put the two sticks back into a staff and tried the bow. I made the motion of drawing the bow, an arrow appeared as I moved my hand back toward my ear. I sighted down the arrow at a tree below and loosed it. The bow, nor the shot made a sound, but I heard the arrow hit the tree.

The arrows were made of mithril and wood, so they say, go through any armor. Once it hit its target, the arrow reappeared in the bow, like a magazine of arrows. You never had to hunt for arrows or replace them, as you never ran out.

I looked back toward my room, sending a "seeing thought" spell there. No one was waiting in my room, so I teleported back there. I thought of my cape, it changed colors, to a Royal Blue. It was finely made but did not draw attention. I hung it in my wardrobe.

The pouch became a nice black leather. I thought a moment. I took my notebook out of the pouch and held it against my left thigh. It sank into my leg, like my daggers had done on my forearms. No one could steal it from there. I rubbed my leg and could not feel the notebook.

I didn't want to leave my staff out in plain sight no matter what it looked like. I separated it into fighting sticks and put them back over my shoulders. They melted onto my back. I reached over my shoulders for them and they appeared in my hands. "That'll work." I put them away and went to bed, sleep came easily.

CHAPTER 3

Our visitors arrived, they brought quite a retinue. There were so many they took over the whole south wing. The Queens were cousins and had been close as children and teens. There was the usual "how the children have grown, you look great, I love your clothes," etc. etc.

Regina looked nothing like I remembered, other than her brown hair and bright green eyes. She had lost weight and didn't look bad. We were about the same age; I a few months older than her. She had grown to an average build and height, but she now moved smoothly, like a dancer or gymnast. What caught my eye was her bodyguard. He was between 25 and 30 years old. He wore a Katana, and a Wakizashi. He wore them in the traditional Samurai style, edge up. This is the first I had seen of Japanese weapons; he didn't look Japanese. Not Asian at all, more Italian or Spanish. I liked Japanese swords which was why they had caught my eye. I had studied in Japan and admired the culture. I was fairly fluent in the language.

We were not expected to interact, be seen and not heard. Except for Cain, as the Crown Prince he stayed close to learn the "ways of rulers." Better him than me. There was to be a dinner and a ball tomorrow night. They would rest from their journey tonight; we would meet tomorrow. I guess I was staring, Regina's eyes met mine, she smiled and nodded. I smiled and nodded in return. We had played together a few times as kids. I remembered little else.

I made my escape as soon as I could and went to the training hall. I had it to myself as all guards were on duty. I practiced with my staff as a staff, and as fighting sticks. I found that my daggers would fit on the end of the staff to form a spear, on both ends to form a bladed bo. They could also add blades to the fighting sticks.

Thinking of the bodyguard's swords made me realize I needed a sword, or swords. I'd save my daggers as my last line of defense secret. I'd have to think about it. I might go with a short sword and a dagger or sword breaker. No rush. There would be no horse training today the stables were a beehive, and I didn't want to add to their troubles. I practiced the throwing knives for a while, then went back to my room.

I got cleaned up and studied my notebook. There was a library's worth of books in the notebook. I found something new while looking at the maps. I asked for my location and the page turned, and a red dot appeared on the map. It would also give me pages of closer views of our area. I, that is Aaron, had been no farther than the surrounding city. He had not even been to the surrounding hills; I would change that before long.

"Show me my room on the map." the page turned, showing a map of my room, the hallway, and a passage on the other side of one wall. I laughed, *"Magic has its uses. Show me the castle layout, including all passageways."* the page turned, it showed me the blueprint of the castle. Including, I assume, all passageways. *"That might come in handy."* I went to the place in the wall the drawing said the door was. It took me a while, but I finally found the latch to the door, and opened it. It was stiff and hard to open but made no noise. It had been years since they had used it. I would have to put a warning spell on it, I reminded myself. I didn't want unannounced visitors at an inopportune time. Not only had this door not been used in years the passageway's floor was thick with dust. I'd have to explore this later; it was almost dinnertime.

When I arrived at the dining room, there was a crowd gathering. There had apparently been a change of plans. The Queens had decided that the families should eat together. Regina was seated across from Celya up the table from me. The kids kept quiet and listened to stories the Queens shared about their childhood.

Everything was going fine until Cain used this opportunity

to embarrass me. "I understand you've started manifesting your powers Regina." he said cutting his eyes my way.

She smiled nodding. "last month, I was wondering how long I would have to wait." she looked down the table at me.

"We're still hopeful Aaron will start soon." Everyone looked down the table at me. The King was not happy.

"Girls usually mature faster than boys I'm sure yours will happen soon." Regina said. Cain had an evil grin on his face.

"Actually," I started. Cain's grin dropped. "I have what I think maybe the beginnings. It seems I have an affinity for weapons, and I have been learning at an accelerated pace. Cain helped me discover it by tossing a plate at me." Cain's face reddened, Celya and Amos snickered.

"Good news then." Her father said raising his glass. "Here, here," the King said. I raised my glass at Cain, he clinched his jaw. The King steered the discussion in a different direction looking pointedly at Cain. I'm sure he'd get a butt chewing about that.

After dinner I found the Weapons Master. "The King will probably ask you about my weapons training, and how fast I'm learning. He may even ask for a demonstration. If he does let's not push things too far, I'll just match who ever I face."

"He's already been checking on you. I've reported that you are a quick study, and a diligent trainee. Which is the truth. I'll pass the word to the men; they'll be ready if it happens."

"Thank you, Weapons Master."

He bowed "Your Highness."

***

I slept for a while, then got up to check out the passageways. I opened the passage door and started inside but stopped. A memory told me to put on my Mage Cloak, it would hide my presence on different levels at different times. Donning my cloak, I entered the passage closing the door behind me. I levitated a few inches off the floor so I would not disturb the dust.

I could see everything as if the passage was fully lit. The passageway went through most of the castle, and as far as I could tell the dust was not disturbed anywhere. I stopped at peepholes along the way. I learned nothing other than everyone was asleep. I guess someone forgot to pass on the secret of the passages. Curiosity satisfied I returned to my room. This was good information to have, you never knew when you might need it.

***

When I returned to my room after breakfast, my new clothes and servants were waiting for me. I had to try everything on to ensure they fit properly before they would leave me. Most of the excitement was taking place in the women's quarters. They apparently were not satisfied with the fit of some of their new dresses.

The Queen was shouting, "I have not gained weight, you cut your pattern too close." I smiled, there were some universal constants.

I was changing into my training clothes when I felt a servant approaching. He knocked, and I answered the door. "Excuse me Prince, The King wishes your presence in the training hall."

I nodded, "Thank you, I'll be there at once." He bowed and left. I followed shortly after. No use putting off the inevitable. I arrived at the training hall to find the King, the weapons Master, and two of the King's guards. These guards were men I had not trained with. It seemed the King wanted an honest test with outside opinions. The Weapons Master brought me a wooden practice sword. He lifted an eyebrow as he handed it to me. I smiled.

We took our positions and started. The first guard started slowly with basic moves. I matched him move for move. They traded; the next man took me to the next level. I stayed with him going no further than he did.

They traded again, the other immediately attacked full on. Right behind him the other joined. I kept moving so I would only have to face one at a time. I was holding my own, when the King, literally threw a wild card into the game.

He threw a practice throwing knife at me. Time slowed for me, I saw aspects of the attacks; I saw where the King stood, where the Weapons Master stood, the position of my attackers and where I needed to be to defend.

I caught the knife and used it to deflect the left guards attack pushing him to the right blocking the others attack. I stepped behind the left guard and gave both "killing" strokes and backed away still on guard.

The King showed no emotion. "Bare steel, first blood." The Weapons Master looked at him but said nothing. The two guards traded their wooden practice swords for their real swords. The Weapons Master chose a good steel sword for me, but I shook my head. I went to the Weapons Cabinet and got two narrow short swords, one was a sword breaker. The Weapons Master raised his eyebrows at my choices.

I approached the two guards; I would have to end this quick. They were pros, and their reputation was on the line. Once this got intense, they would not hold back. The potential was there for someone to get hurt, and badly. I didn't want it to be me.

They attacked, I changed my tactics and attacked, forcing one in front of the other. Father wanted to see if I would shy away from naked steel. Well now, he'd seen. The attack I needed one of them to make came quick. One came in with a side slicing cut. I locked his sword with my sword breaker and continued his attack toward his partner forcing him to defend. When he did, I cut both men on the legs.

That's when dear old dad launched his attack. I had just enough time to turn and face him before the fireball was upon me. I got my swords up between myself and the fireball. The steel took most of the heat, but the blast knocked me down and slid me across the floor. No one was charging me so I stayed down.

I beat the fire out on my vest. I stood slowly, taking my burned shirt off. I had a nice sunburn on my chest and face.

"Couldn't stop the magic attack?" He asked chuckling as he approached.

"It appears not father, but I'll keep practicing."

"You do that." He pointed at the ruined swords I had been using. "Those'll need replacing." I nodded. "Weapons Master, take him to see the Old Armorer, buy the Prince the best he has."

"Yes, Sire."

The King left, the two guards stopped before me, and bowed. I bowed in return. There were no hard feelings.

The Weapons Master and I stood looking at the still hot swords. "You could have dodged that attack." he said.

I shrugged, "maybe, but he was after two things this morning. He wanted to see how good I was, and to make sure I knew he was still top dog. He wouldn't have stopped until he'd made his point."

He nodded looking at me, "You'll make a wise King one day."

"I'll be happy just to live long enough to become wise." We laughed. "Who's the 'Old Armorer' he mentioned?"

"He's an armorer and weapons dealer. He has the best weapons made from all over the world. You'll enjoy going there, and the King said buy you the best he had." he said smiling.

***

There was a large crowd at the ball. All the ladies dressed to the nines, or what passed for the nines here. The great hall was decorated, and a band played in the background. There were finger foods, and plenty of punch to drink. All the mothers brought their daughter to show them off to prospective husbands. It was at events like this where deals and alliances were struck, and marriages arranged. I'm sure my name came up occasionally.

They expected me to circulate, and dance, at least some.

So far, I had avoided the worst, which was being hemmed in by someone's mother and forced to attend to her daughters' company. I think my reputation of being the "strange" Prince was helping.

I was standing to the side of the dance floor sipping on a glass of punch, watching the dance. Celya was enjoying herself. She wasn't a good dancer, but she was giving it her all.

"There you are," I recognized Regina's voice, and turned. She looked lovely. Her bodyguard was close by, her father's doing I'm sure.

I bowed, she returned it, "Good evening." I said.

"And to you."

"Punch?" I asked pointing toward the punch bowl on the sideboard.

"Please." I filled her a glass and handed it to her.

She pointed with her chin, "Celya seems to be enjoying herself dancing."

I nodded taking a sip of punch.

"¥She moves like a wounded sow,¥" her body guard said. I shot punch out my nose and started coughing. Regina was looking hard at him, then at me.

"Sorry went down the wrong way." The bodyguard was looking at me, I ignored him. Luckily, I kept from laughing.

I put my glass down; she handed me a napkin. I cleaned myself up. When the next dance started, "May I have this dance?" I asked offering her my hand. She nodded and took it. She flowed more than she moved. She was a joy to dance with. Fortunately, Aaron was a decent dancer, and I didn't embarrass myself.

During our second dance, I noticed the Queens watching us, and their heads were together. "There's trouble brewing," Regina said.

"What, where?"

"Our Mothers." she answered.

"You think they are talking about us?" I felt sure they were.

"Almost certainly. Mother is looking for me a husband, and

father wants an alliance. And here we are dancing the night away. We are definitely on the auction block."

"It could be worse; they could auction off Cain instead of me." I said smiling.

"Nope, we don't have enough money or land to buy him. Mother and father think you are the best we can hope for." she said chuckling.

I laughed, "I don't know, that price, for that particular Prince seems kind of high for what you'd be getting."

She smiled, "I think so too, I think you're the better deal."

"Really, how so?"

"Well, if we got you, we'd take you home with us. If we got Cain, I'd have to stay here. I like my home better."

I nodded, "sound reasoning."

"I thought so. Besides, Cain has always been a mean, vindictive jackass."

"So, you have met him." She laughed; it was a nice sound. We spent the rest of the evening together talking and dancing. Her bodyguard keeping us separated from interruptions. As the evening ended, I kissed her hand, "Thank you for a wonderful evening."

"It was my pleasure."

I turned to her bodyguard and bowed "Thank you." I almost spoke to him in Japanese, but the time was not right. There were too many people around. Especially if Regina could understand us, and I suspected she could.

He returned my bow. "Prince Aaron," he said.

***

The Weapons Master and I left the castle early the next morning heading for the Old Armorer's shop. It was a good distance across town, but I was enjoying the outing. The sights and smells were familiar to me, as it would be to anyone who spent any time in a third world country. Most of the streets were unpaved, and the buildings were close together. It was the same with the open-air market area. Sights, sounds, smells, colors, this I enjoyed.

The store fronts were open with shutters they could close at night. Glass was too expensive to use for these people. We weaved through streets, and side streets. I kept my eyes moving trying not to miss anything. Which was ok, it was what any 15-year-old would do.

We passed a small armor shop, and something called out to my Mage Sense. I stopped and looked over a few of his items. This was a lower end shop, for those with limited funds. Been there done that.

I didn't know what I was looking for but there was something magical here. I had to dig through some used, very used, sheaths and harnesses before I found it. It was a throwing knife in an over the shoulder rig. The rig was like a figure eight, or infinity. The sheath off to one side of the crossover. There was nothing special about its look, but it was special, I could feel it.

I picked up a couple of other knives looking them over. The owner was watching me to see if I'd bite on any of his bait. I tossed them all aside except the one I wanted.

I looked at the Weapons Master, "This one will do for practice if I break it, no big loss," he nodded. I tossed it on the counter and walked out, as if not caring if he bought it or not. I waited outside while the Weapons Master concluded the dickering and purchase. The Weapons Master handed it to me as he came out of the shop. I dropped it in my pouch. We continued on our way.

The Old Armorer's shop was not what I had pictured. An old rusty sword hung over the door. That was all the advertisement the shop had. The shutters on the street weren't even open to show his inventory. We went inside.

The Weapons Master was known and the Old Armorer himself came out to assist us. "Good Morning, Weapons Master. How may I serve?"

"Good Morning, Arms Master, may I present Prince Aaron, The King's Second Son."

He bowed, "an honor Highness."

I returned his bow, "mine as well, Arms Master."

"We are here," the Weapons Master continued, "at the direction of the King. He has sent us to buy Prince Aaron a weapon. He named you specifically." The dickering had begun.

"I am honored that the King remembered his humble servant." They both stared at each other a moment, then burst into laughter. "Come my friend, let's see what we shall see, for our Prince. What weapon does he favor?"

"I will let you and he decide that." The Arms Master nodded smiling. We walked through what I thought of as a showroom. He didn't slow down but kept walking. We went down a back hall, and into what I guess was his private apartments. We passed through a large indoor, open-air courtyard, and into another show room. Here he stopped. Compared to these, that first show room was bargain basement stuff.

CHAPTER 4

"You may try anything you wish, look them over and see if anything speaks to you."

I walked among the weapons, swords, knives, spikes, weapons of all kinds. I looked at each one, all were impressive. But none spoke to me. I sensed there was more going on here. This was some kind of test. I reached out searching with; I guess I'd call it, my Mage Sense. There were more and far better weapons in another room. And some of those were runed weapons.

I walked back toward them, "None of these speak to me. Perhaps one of those back there will." I pointed with my thumb over my shoulder.

The Arms Master Smiled, "we shall see, hopefully one will." He led us deeper into his apartment. He showed us into a smaller side room. There were fewer weapons here but of a higher quality. He stepped aside and allowed me to enter. I walked among the weapons looking at each one. Some I would have loved to handle, but I waited until I had seen everything.

Once I had seen all, I stood in the middle of the room, closed my eyes. I listened, or felt, or maybe a combination of both. Nothing shouted out to me, but there was something. I turned back toward the far wall. I walked toward it looking at the swords on display there. But it was not anything on display.

"What do you have inside this cabinet?" He frowned and walked toward me. He opened the cabinet and there was something rolled up in a black cloth laying on the shelf.

"Ah, I have had this for many years. No one has ever taken a second glance at it." He unrolled it on the countertop, drew the sword from its plain black scabbard and lay it down, stepping back. Laying there among the other swords it looked out of place. I could see why no one liked it. It was too different for this time and place.

It looked like a straight Katana, but not as long as a standard Katana. The handle was longer than standard for that length of a sword, the blade was a deep dark gray with black patterns in the metal similar to a Damascus blade. The hand guard was a squared off "u" with the backside being a sword breaker type. It was not a "flashy" sword, but a warrior's sword.

This one spoke to me, "May I?"

"Of course, please."

I grasp the handle it felt incredibly light, like nothing was there. There was magic at work removing much of the blade weight. It felt like an extension of my arm. "Training room?"

He nodded and led us out and to the room. I stepped to the center of the room. Closing my eyes, I centered myself. I began slowly feeling its weight and its flow as I moved. Once I had the feel of her, I picked up the pace. It reminded me of dancing with Regina. She was smooth in my hands and held to me as I held to her. She was enjoying the dance as much as I was.

I was making sweeping turns and cuts, then my lower hand twisted the lower part of the handle, the one sword became two. The second being a shorter sword breaker, the length of the handles remained the same. I never slowed, this felt so natural, I didn't even have to think, we just danced. When the dance was closing, I slipped the second, shorter sword back together the two become one again. I stepped in the center of the room; myself centered again. Instead of being winded, I felt refreshed.

The two men were staring at me. "Cut the straw man," the Arms Master said pointing. I moved to the straw man, not hesitating I made a killing pass, the blade took off an arm, cut the man in half at the waist and took off its head before the body hit the floor. The blade was beyond sharp, it never slowed at any cut.

"I have had that sword for over 20 years. It has sat in that cabinet for probably 15 of those 20 years. I have been doing this for most of my life, but I have never seen the like of what I witnessed today. That sword was made for you. It will cost you one gold. I will not keep it from, it's owner."

I took a gold coin from my pouch handing it to him. I bowed deeply, "Thank you, you honor me." He bowed in return, "Then we are both honored."

***

As we walked back to the castle, a thought struck me. "Do you know of a leather worker shop that makes good armor?"

"I do." I felt my new sword pull me to the left.

"Is it to the left by chance?"

He nodded, "It is."

"Good, let's go see what they have to offer." I followed the Weapons Master, and my swords lead. It seemed everyone knew the Weapons Master. Of course, these people would, this was how they made a living.

"How may we serve, Weapons Master?"

"I would like to look around Master Armor." I said.

"Of course, M'lord, take your time."

"Thank you." I followed my sword's leading around and down a back aisle. It stopped me in front of a dusty, dirty, sweat stained set of black, well mostly gray from sweat, armor. I moved the pile around with my foot. It was a full set of medium weight leathers, with metal plate backing. Chest and back pieces, bracers, greaves, and skirt.

The Weapons Master looked down at the pile, then at me. "That?" I nodded. He shook his head; he was not impressed. "How much?" He asked the Arms Master.

"As is, or do you want it cleaned?"

"Oh, as is, I have a trainee who needs to learn how to take care of his own gear." He said smiling. I laughed.

***

Looking back, I shouldn't have laughed. It took me a week to get the set inspection ready. While cleaning the armor I found runes written on the inside of all the pieces. It would take me a while to figure out what their capabilities were and maybe improve on them.

The throwing knife and harness turned out to be another gift. I had likened the harness to an infinity sign, that turned out to be true... kinda.

The knife which was incredibly sharp. Like the arrows from my bow, when the knife hit the target, it reappeared back in its sheath for me to throw again. I would never run out of throwing knives. It also, when I wanted, could hide under my skin, and I could still throw from there.

Once my new armor had passed inspection, I started wearing it during training. The first day I trained alone. I needed to see how it moved with me and if there were any places that restricted my movement. There were none. Like my sword the armor was almost weightless and moved like a second skin.

While training I learned about my armor. The greaves once attached merged with my shoes, or sandals, becoming boots. The bracers covered the back of my hands, wrist, and forearms to my elbows, and became magic shields when needed. How big they became depended on the need.

The chest and back piece had high collars. The back collar raised like an accordion over my head becoming a helmet. The front collar raised becoming a throat guard and face shield. Magic made them all work together seamlessly.

The skirt protected my upper thighs and lower abdomen. I wore a type of pants or leggings under everything to prevent chaffing. I needed to add thigh shields to better cover my legs when mounted.

The Weapons Master instructed me to go armed and armored all the time until every movement wearing them was second nature. The first family meal I showed up to armed and armored, the King looked at me and nodded his approval.

"Expecting trouble?" Regina asked smiling.

"Yes, some mothers are becoming quite insistent about me dancing with their daughters," I answered.

"Shameful," she tsked, smiling at me. "Will you escort me

on a walk through the garden after breakfast?"

"It would be my pleasure." Breakfast passed quickly and Regina and I walked down to the garden and strolled along under the trees. Her bodyguard stayed close, but out of conversational earshot.

"Would you do something for me?" she asked

"If I can, yes."

"When we are alone would you call me Reggie, like you used to when we were children?"

I had forgotten about that. I smiled "I don't know, Reggie, that seems awful forward of me."

She chuckled, "let's risk it," she said. "What news of intrigue?"

"I'm not the one to ask. I don't have time to snoop around and listen from behind doors."

"Yes, I've heard you train a lot, and that you are quite good."

"I guess I'm ok for my age. I've still a lot to learn."

She cut her eyes at me, saying nothing. I changed the subject. "What intrigue have you heard?"

"You assume I have time to listen from behind doors?" Her hand covering her mouth in mock surprise. "lucky for you I do." she laughed. "Negotiations continue, father thinks he is making progress, mother is talking to your mother about wedding plans. We are just a commodity to be bartered."

"Well watch father, he's up to something, he had me training harder, as if preparing for something. It may be for show, but I don't think so. He'll try to get the most from the trade as he can. But he's always got a second game running."

"Doesn't everyone?"

"I'm not sure everyone does."

"Do you?"

"Mine are more of a tactical nature. What would I do if attacked, what are my enemy's weaknesses, where are the closes defensive points? That kind of thing. Well, that and escape plans."

"Escape plans?" She asked frowning.

"Oh yes, I've been stealing from the treasury at night, as soon as I have enough, I'm making a break for it."

"How much do you have?"

"26 coppers, I figure in another 20 years I should have enough to make my move."

She laughed, "What if you get a better offer?"

"Better than 26 coppers?"

She nodded.

"Wow, I'd probably have to take it." We laughed.

I found it unusual that I, as a 27-year-old man, was having so much fun with this 15-year-old girl. Rather young woman. This body was 15 also, and to do otherwise would be way out of the norm. To their way of thinking I was already strange. My "I don't remember," answer was still holding though.

"They made you take the serum didn't they." It was a statement not a question. I nodded, "What was it like?"

"Bad." I left it at that, she didn't push. She took my hand, and we continued our walk in silence.

When we arrived back at the terrace, "save a dance for me at the ball tomorrow night?" she asked.

"You can have them all if you keep the crazed mothers and daughters away from me."

"Are you ignoring the fact that my Mother got you and I alone in the garden?"

"Gullible men never have a chance, do we?"

She turned walked away laughing.

"¥Sometime that is a good thing,¥" The bodyguard said as he followed.

"Maybe," Nodding my head.

***

The rest of my day went as most days, training and studies. The families ate separately tonight. I guess everyone needed some "me" time.

"You and Regina seem to get along nicely," the Queen said.

"Yes, I enjoy her company, she has a quick wit."

"She's too much of a tom-boy. She works out with her bodyguard every day. She's learning to fence, and hand-to-hand fighting. I think that's very unladylike. But she dances well, I'll give her that." Celya said.

"Interesting no wonder she moves so well."

"Her father has made inquiries as to a betrothal. He seeks an alliance." The King said looking at me. "What are your thoughts on the matter?"

I looked thoughtful for a moment. This was a test; he was fishing for something. "We could do worse, they have good farmland, their capital is a major port city. They have a fair-sized army if we needed support. Trade would increase and we'd get free access to their port. Regina and I get along well enough." I made it all about "we" and "us", I think he liked that.

"You would have to move to their city become a Queen's Consort." the Queen said.

"True, but I could do worse." She nodded. Satisfied with my answers they let the subject drop.

After dinner I went back to my room instead of the library. I wanted to look nice in my armor at the ball and wanted to try something to make it look more "fancy". As it was, it was all black. *"It needs some bling."* I felt it could change colors to match my field camo needs. Would It change to match "dress occasion" needs?

I looked at myself in the polished metal mirror, which sucked as a mirror. I ran my hand over my armor, changing the black buckles to silver. I also changed the black eyelets to silver. I added silver inlay to the forearm bracers, and greaves-boots.

I attached my cloak to the shoulder epaulets, and it matched the armor's black and silver. I would still look less formal; everyone wore enchanted clothes like a bunch of peacocks. Still, I would not be embarrassed.

My sword, "Dancer" as I now thought of her, got into the act. She matched the black and silver motif. I liked the look. I took Dancer from my belt and lay her on the bed. I turned back to the wardrobe to get undressed and put away my things.

I froze, my combat senses came up, as did the hairs on the back of my neck. I reached back; Dancer had attached herself to my belt. Dancer and my armor changed colors to muted charcoal. I levitated up to the corner behind the door.

My door exploded inward as a fireball tore through. The shields on my bracers flared to covered me. The room dropped into blackness. My night sight could not see through it. I changed to infrared sight as I would have on my night vision goggles.

I instantly saw their heat signatures as they came through the door. Three came through fast. Soldiers. One held back, the Mage. I killed him first. My throwing knife went through the top of his skull, then reappeared back in its scabbard. I killed the three soldiers the same way. They were all dead before they realized they were in trouble.

I sent my Mage Sense out to see if anymore were coming in. I saw down the hall to Amos' door, another group was about to breach.

I saw Amos sitting up in his bed as if listening. I teleported in, grabbed him and teleported into the passageway behind his room. I had my hand over his mouth, as he was struggling. "Amos, It's Aaron," I whispered. "Keep still assassins have breached the castle." He stilled. We heard the muffled boom and felt the vibration when they breached.

"I'll be back, wait here." I teleported up into the ceiling of the hall behind the Mage. His soldiers were already through the door. I dropped behind him and removed his head with my forearm daggers. Then I was among the three soldiers. They got into each other's way and could not fight effectively. One took a dagger through his eye, the next a dagger up through his chin into his brain, the last took my blade through his heart. All were dead before they hit the floor.

I teleported back to Amos. he was sitting calmly with a glowing ball of light floating in front of him. "Dead?" He asked.

I nodded "Dead."

"Thank you for saving me."

"What are brothers for?"

"Cain would never have risked himself. You can do magic now?"

I nodded, "let's keep that between us."

"Deal."

I showed him where the latch for the door was to get into his room. "You wait here. I need to see how bad this is. I'll be back." He nodded and sat down.

I levitated and moved swiftly through the passageway. The rest of our wing seemed secured. I headed for Regina's wing. When I got to their wing, their guards held the hallway leading to their rooms. Roughly 20 invaders were about to make a push to get through.

I put my helmet collars and face guard up, and I gathered my magic, I made myself into a big flash-bang grenade. I drew Dancer, split her, and teleported into the middle of them. As soon as I landed, I set the flash-bang off.

They were all knocked to the floor, stunned, ears ringing. I killed them as quickly as I could. It was a meat grinder, cut, slash, stab, kick, and stomp. My shields took some hits covering me but nothing serious. When I was finished my armor was covered in blood. I lowered my helmet, looking around. None survived.

I walked to the corner of the hall. "Reggie?"

A moment later, "Aaron?" she called out.

"Yeah, we're all clear out here, are you ok?"

She and her bodyguard came to the front of the barricade, "father is wounded." She motioned me forward. I went to her.

She took me back into her mother and father's room. I knelt to look at his wounds. He had a nasty cut on his chest and a stab wound in the stomach. I lay my hand on him, using my healing magic I could tell he had a lot of internal bleeding.

"¥Can you help him?¥" The bodyguard asked.

Before I thought, "¥ I'll do what I can.¥"

I closed my eyes focusing on his stomach wounds and saw in my mind's eye the bleeding stopped and the flesh healing.

I did the same for his chest wound. Once finished I leaned back lightheaded. The Queen had tears running down her face holding her husband.

"You are a Mage Healer." Reggie's father said.

"No, I am not. You were never wounded, and I was never here." I looked at the bodyguard, "¥Insure none of your guards mentions me being here.¥"

He nodded, "¥You were never here.¥"

I nodded to Reggie and teleported back to Amos.

"Is It over?" Amos Asked

"I think so, let's get out of here and have a look around."

CHAPTER 5

Amos opened the door to his room, and we left the passageway, closing the door behind us. "Amos let's not mention the passageway or any of my magic. Just say, you didn't see what happened, and that I killed them."

He nodded, "You saved my life, I'll say anything you want me too."

I smiled, "just that."

"Ok."

I walked over and started searching the bodies. Amos watched me.

"I'm looking for information about our attackers." I said.

He nodded and knelt beside me. We found a few coins which I gave to him. "Put that away you may need some money sometime." He did. Their knives were decent, but not great. I left them laying on the floor.

I searched the Mage carefully, knowing my hiding places. He might have the same. He wore a few rings and bracelets, and a circlet on his head, all of which I put away until I could study the runes.

He had a good runed knife; it was better than Amos', so I gave it to him. "This one is better than yours, keep it." He took it and looped it onto his belt.

We moved to my room and searched the bodies. We found about the same, the few coins I tossed to Amos. He tucked them away. This Mage had also had rings, and bracelets, but no head circlet. Another good knife, I gave to Amos. He tucked it away.

"What are you going to do with the rings?"

"We will study the runes to see what they are capable of. If they are safe, we'll split them."

"Only you and me?"

"Yep, this was our fight, our prizes."

He smiled, "Deal."

We heard people approaching. I knew it was the Weapons Master and squad before they rounded the corner. Amos and I stood ready. Amos had his hand on his new knife.

He looked at us and smiled when he saw Amos standing ready. "Well met warriors, any trouble?"

"Nothing we couldn't handle." I answered.

The Corporal was looking at the bodies. "Same as the others, no markings."

The Weapons Master nodded. "The King is holding court in the great hall, taking a head count. Let's go see how bad they caught us." We followed him to the great room, the squad following us, there was a low murmur in the great hall. The wounded were along one wall being seen to by the doctor.

"These are the last Sire," the Weapons Master reported to the King. The King looked at us seeing we were not hurt, he nodded. Amos went and sat with the Queen, who hugged him. Cain was sitting by himself. He seemed jumpy.

I went to the sideboard and got a cup of water. As I drank, I surveyed the room. There were not as many hurt as I expected. It seemed the targets of the operation had been Amos, me, Reggie, and her family. Everyone else, though hurt, were collateral damage not the intended targets.

The King walked up behind me I ignored him until he spoke. "You protected Amos?" I nodded, turning to face him. "How many did you kill?"

"Six soldiers and two Mages."

He nodded looking around the room. "What do you see here?"

I looked around again, "This was a targeted attack, they were after Amos, me, and Regina's family. Everyone else were just people who got in the way."

"And what does that tell you?"

"Someone doesn't want an alliance to be formed between us."

"Why?"

"I don't have enough information to form a reasonable guess."

"Guess anyway."

I thought a moment. "Someone wants them to remain weak or not get our help. They have a port city and good lands, but their army is smaller than it needs to be. Perhaps a neighboring Kingdom is looking to expand. Or a foreign Kingdom is looking to use their port as a toehold. Way out on a limb would be both."

He nodded, "Good assessment." He turned and walked away.

Reggie and her bodyguard came for water, she looked around ensuring no one was near. "Thank you." she said.

"I'm glad I could help, how is he?"

"He says he's fine just weak. You speak Rodrigo-San's language."

"Some."

"No, I speak some, you speak a lot. Where did you learn it?"

"I told you the serum was bad." she nodded, "I don't remember how I know, I just know,"

"And your magic powers? Why keep that a secret?"

"My father, The King, is a user. He would use me, squeeze every drop of use out of me to further his ambitions. His ambitions are not my ambitions."

She looked around, licked her lips nervously. "If a deal can be made, would you still come with us, become my husband, and Queen's consort? This is me asking not my family."

I knew it had taken a lot for her to ask. She was clutching her hands together fearing the answer. "Yes Reggie, I'll come with you, be your husband, and Queens Consort." I surely didn't want to stay here. The "Aaron" in me said this was a good thing.

She let out a breath she'd been holding. She had tears in her eyes. "You won't regret it."

"Well, you had better have over 26 Coppers, that's all I have to say." Her tension broke, and she laughed. It was a nice sound.

"Celya would pay me at least that much to take you."

"Cain would pay you more, hit him up first," we laughed.

***

It was early morning before we got back to our rooms. I could not sleep so I levitated meditating. I don't know why I was not freaking out about marriage. I had come close a few times, but few can stay with a Spec-Ops guy long. Especially when you won't quit the team for them. But why was I so calm about marrying Reggie? I liked her, she's an only child, but not spoiled. If I stayed here, eventually I would have to marry someone for an alliance or have a knock down drag out with the King. This way at least I have some choice in the matter.

The castle was in lock-down, or their version of it. The King had called up some of the army. I doubted anyone was making a move against us, but better safe than sorry.

Out of boredom I took out the six rings I had taken from the Mages I had killed. I examined them. Four of them were basically batteries, to hold Mage power to use when casting. The other two did nothing. I guess even Mages or maybe especially Mages can be vain. I'd give the batteries to Amos.

I took out the bracelets. They were matched sets and were both batteries and shields. As the shields protected you, they would use the force from the attack to charge the shields, strengthening them. I'd have to study the runes. Maybe I could improve my shields.

The circlet was the same as the bracelets, but for your head. It became a helmet that protected your face and head. Well, unless someone cuts your head off.

I wonder. I took my notebook out and lay the bracelets on the page. The notebook copied all the information from them, all the runes, and their placements. I did the same to all the jewelry. I'd give one set to Amos. I put the other bracelet and circlet set away for now. I must fix the runes to cover my neck, so I don't lose my head.

I could finally sleep for a few hours, before going to breakfast. I was the only one who showed up; I guess everyone else slept in. I ate light and went to the training hall.

As a test I put the bracelets and circlet on a training dummy, I took a wooden staff and tapped a bracelet. Nothing happened. I took a hard swing at the dummy and the shields flared protecting the dummy. I swung at the head and the shield-helmet formed protecting the dummy's head. Satisfied I took the jewelry off the dummy and put them back in my pouch.

I started my workout, getting warmed up, working up a sweat. I felt someone coming and recognized it was Reggie and Rodrigo-San. I kept working when they entered and when I finished; I faced them.

"May we join you?" Reggie asked. Both were carrying bamboo Shinai practice swords.

"Of course." I continued to practice. They stretched and warmed up then practiced sword katas. That done they started sparing. I watched; Reggie was not bad. She had good form and flow. She was quick to adjust. What she lacked would come with time and practice.

She stepped back, bowed and took a few breaths. "Would you like to try? Or are you just going to watch?"

I smiled, "against you or him?" She laughed handing me her bamboo. I took it and stepped over to Rodrigo-San. I bowed and took my guard. He started slow testing me to see what my skill level was. Once satisfied be began turning up the heat.

I knew right away Rodrigo-San was a Master Swordsman. He was quick and tricky. He had a fluid grace; he was a wonder to watch. After an intense exchange neither one of us getting the advantage we stepped apart, sweating. I bowed deeply, "¥Master. ¥"

He bowed just as deep, as to an equal. He stood up smiling, "¥I must be getting old I thought a few times I had you.¥"

I laughed, "¥you are not getting old, if it weren't for my magic you had me. I have never faced a true master before. It was my great pleasure to do so.¥"

I suddenly remembered Reggie. I turned, and she was watching us. "That was amazing. I've never seen anything like that. No one has ever matched Rodrigo-San."

"If it had not been for me using magic, I would not have been able to match him. He is a Master Swordsman. You are lucky to have him as a bodyguard, and teacher."

She nodded looking at him, "I know."

"How close did they get to you last night?"

"Closer than I want to think about, only Rodrigo-San stood between us."

"Were you armed or armored?"

"Neither."

Making my decision, "I can help with part of that now, we'll work on the other later." I reached into my pouch and took out the bracelets and Circlet. "These bracelets are shields and the circlet is a helmet. When anything tries to hit you, they will stop it, just like a real shield." She allowed me to put them on her.

"Do I have to do anything to make them work?"

"Nope, they work automatically."

"Are you sure?"

I slapped her wrist. The shield flared stopping my strike. "Pretty sure."

Lifting her eyes, looking up, "the circlet will kind of stand out."

"Hide it, let it sink beneath your skin."

"How?"

"Just concentrate on it and tell it to go under your skin and hide." I took a ring out and put it on. I made it hide. I made it reappear and put it back in the pouch.

She nodded, closed her eyes and concentrated. They slowly sank out of sight.

She opened her eyes, looking at her wrists, "did it work."

I nodded, "now it always covers you, even when you are not dressed. I'll make you a dagger or a set that does the same thing," she looked at my hands. I just smiled.

Rodrigo-San watched all of this, "Good."

"I need to get cleaned up, see you at dinner." Reggie said.

"Yes, I need to get cleaned up too."

I found Amos on the way to my room and gave him the rings and the bracelets. I taught him how to "hide" things under his skin. That made his day. He now had new hidden shields. *"A Star Trek, or maybe Star Wars, fan in the making,"* I smiled.

***

They sent word that dinner would be a semi-formal occasion. Which meant dress nice, but not in your finest. I changed my armor and arms to the silver accents but left the cloak off. On my way to dinner the increased guard presences was noticeable. At dinner I saw that everyone came armed.

Cain and Celya looked like peacocks. I guess they liked to take advantage of every opportunity to show off. Everyone else was dressed nicely but not showy, which made those two look out of place. They didn't seem to care.

They held the dinner in the great hall, as there were more than just family here. They had invited nobles that attended the ball. There was no dancing but a lot of a cross table socializing. Reggie, once again sat across the table from Celya, so we really couldn't talk.

Amos sat next to me, so we kept each other company. "Do you think the Weapons Master would start training me?"

"I imagine he would, especially after the other night. The earlier you start the better you'll become."

"Cain thinks it's a waste of time."

"Cain relies too much on his magic. What happens when he faces someone stronger than he is, or has an artifact to counter his magic? He'll wish he had trained different then. Just think, you have your shields to protect you. That will allow you to get close enough to use steel, someone else can do the same. Never rely totally on one thing to save your life, even if the other thing is running."

"True, if you hadn't gotten to me, I'd be dead. I didn't like that feeling."

"Next time you'll be better prepared."

"Do you think there will be a next time?"

"Train like there will be, and you'll be ready. But at some point in your life, yes, there will be a next time."

He pondered that, nodding, "I'll talk to the Weapons Master tomorrow."

"Wise." I said, he smiled.

The Major domo thumped his staff on the floor gaining everyone's attention. He stood beside the King. Once all were quiet, The King rose.

"As you all know we were attacked. Assassination attempts were made against us, our family and our guest. We will find those responsible and deal with them. That notwithstanding we have a Royal announcement to make. Prince Aaron, and Princess Regina, come forward."

"Uh-oh, ambush," We rose and made our way forward. We met and stood in front of the two Kings.

"We and the Kingdom of Shornwick have formed an alliance. Sealing that alliance, Prince Aaron, and Princess Regina will wed." There was polite applause. "The betrothal ceremony will be in the morning at the Royal Chapel and the wedding will take place upon their return to the Kingdom of Shornwick."

"Someone's in a hurry." Reggie took my hand, and we bowed to the kings. She was better at the protocol of Kings than I was. She then faced us toward the crowd, and we bowed again. This time the applause was a little more heartfelt.

The rest of the evening was a receiving line where we were congratulated and were gifted with pieces of jewelry. This was apparently a tradition at surprise announcements like this. No one had brought gifts so personal jewelry was expected to be given instead.

I could tell that some, especially the ladies, were not happy at having to give their jewels. *"Note to self, always wear an extra ring or two."*

An elderly lady approached, she was dressed nice, but not

in the newest fashion. She started taking off her wedding ring, as it was all she had. Reggie placed her hand on hers stopping her. Aaron's memory told me this was our widowed great-aunt. I placed my hand on top of Reggie's.

"Aunt Maggie, keep your wedding ring, what we wish instead is a blessing."

The lady smiled, nodding. She placed hands on ours clasping them tightly and spoke in a strong voice.

"Father God, creator and giver of all good things. We ask your blessing upon these two young people. Grant them wisdom, knowledge, understanding, and discernment. Bless them with an abundance of wealth and many children."

I swear I felt a shift in the atmosphere. She put her hand out to the side and the Major-domo's staff leapt to her. Catching it she brought it down on the floor with a thump that was felt to the foundation of the castle. Her eyes took on a distant stare. The great hall was completely silent.

"In your time, you shall become known as the Good Queen, and Good King." She thumped the staff. "Your People will rejoice in the peace and prosperity of your reign." THUMP. "Your allies will be at ease with the peace your reign brings." THUMP. "Your Enemies will Fear you and flee before you." THUMP. "Your kingdom shall increase." THUMP. "Your children's, children's, children shall rule after you for six generations." THUMP.

Her eyes refocused, and she smiled at us. She kissed us both on our cheeks. "This is why you were brought here." she whispered in my ear. My mouth dropped open. She stepped back.

Reggie and I bowed deeply.

The Major-domo was at her side. She returned his staff and took his arm. She turned and walked regally toward the main doors. As she passed everyone bowed, even the King and Queen. Everyone remained bowed until she had exited the great hall.

The room seemed dimmer without her presence. I am a believer, but I had never seen or heard anything like that in my life. Aaron's memories told me she was widely known and respected as a prophetess. As far as anyone knew, all that she had ever prophesied had come to pass.

After that, everyone gave every piece of jewelry they were wearing. Even the ones who had been by us once, came back through. Whether it was to cover their bases, or because they were in Awe, I don't know. I, for one, was in Awe.

CHAPTER 6

After Aunt Maggie prophesied over us, the betrothal ceremony was rather anti-climactic. Word had gotten out about the prophecy and everyone in the city wanted to see Reggie and me. They moved the ceremony to the fairgrounds, so those who wanted to could come. The Kings were not ones to waste an opportunity to show magnanimity, especially when it cost little.

We rode in a wagon through the city waving at anyone. It seemed a joyous occasion, as parties were in full swing all over the city. It took us a half a day to get back to the castle, and I was glad to be back. This soon after the attack, I had felt too exposed up in that wagon.

As we parted, I kissed Reggie's hand. As everyone turned to leave, she quickly pecked me on the cheek, and hurried away.

The plan was to leave in three days. There was a lot to do in three days. Not for me, I could be ready to travel in half an hour. The logistics for them was more involved. They had wagons, horses, and provisions for their troops. The ladies had their own wagons and equipment for traveling. This was already turning into a learning experience.

The families ate separately after the ceremony, as was the custom. After breakfast father took me to the stables. "You'll need a mount, chose anyone you want, even mine if you desire him."

"*A parting gift.* Thank you, father," I bowed. He nodded. I walked through the stable, the Stable Master walked right with us to answer questions or help if needed.

I approached this as I had with my sword and armor. I kept my Mage Sense open searching. Nothing in the stables spoke to me. I walked outside to the paddock. There were over a hundred horses out here. I walked among them. The Stable

Master followed, the King did not. "If he does not find what he wants here Stable Master, take him to the market and see what they might have there. Buy whatever he chooses."

"Yes, Sire."

We wound up going to the open-air market, there was a livestock area, and they sold horses.

We walked among the dealers, and horses.

"What is it you seek M'lord?"

"I'm not sure, this is an, I'll know it, when I see it, thing."

He nodded his head.

"Young Master," a man called.

I looked at him.

"You seek a horse."

"How can you tell? Because we're in a horse market?" I said smiling.

"True, but you are not seeking just any horse, you are seeing a certain horse."

"Aren't we all?"

He shrugged his shoulders, "some more than others."

"And you would have a certain horse?"

"I would, but who can say if it is your certain horse."

"Show me your certain horse." he led us back to the stable area and in the back, we came to the horse. He was black with dark gray spots.

"That is a Chorton Cavalry Horse, they don't sell those." The Stable Master said.

"True, I found him wondering in the Outlands, he followed me. What was I to do?"

I laughed, "he followed you? That's the story you're going with?"

"Well, when you say it like that... He shrugged his shoulders. But I must warn you, he's mean, he bites, he steals, and he does not like other horses."

"And he has a split hoof." The Stable Master said.

"He heals quickly."

"He'll need too, that's the second time that hoof has split.

Sell him to the nackers, let them make sausage out of him."

"I could never do that; he is too good a horse."

"One time maybe, no more."

"How much would the nackers pay for him?" I asked.

"six silvers, maybe."

"How long before his hoof heals?"

"two months if he's lucky."

"I'll give you eight silvers; I can recoup most of my money if he fails me."

"Eight? he's worth golds, not silvers."

"If he was whole, maybe. He is not."

"Eight silvers, going once..." I waited a moment. "Going twice... G,"

"Wait... Eight silvers."

"Done." I paid him and he was gone as soon as the silvers hit his hand.

The Stable Master watched him fade away into the crowd. "You know he was probably a deserter."

I nodded, "Probably."

He turned back to look at the horse. "I suppose you have a plan?"

"Maybe." I said, the horse had been watching me the whole time, not looking anywhere else.

I ran my hand down his leg looking at his hooves. I used my Mage Sense and could tell all his hooves were weak. I concentrated on the split one, healed and strengthen it. Then I strengthened the others so they would not split.

I stood up, and the horse put his head in my chest. "Suck up."

The stable Master stared at me. I shrugged my shoulders. He shook his head. "I didn't see anything."

On the way back to the castle, we bought a black saddle, tack and light cavalry armor to match my armor. I would inscribe runes on them later. I spent the rest of the afternoon taking care of "Gray". I washed him, brushed him, had them put new shoes on him.

I inscribed his armor with runes. It was all shielded now, and anything he carried only weighed a quarter of its real weight. While I was at it, I added the same weight saving runes to my armor, I also added a rune to my boots so they would make no sounds as I walked.

***

I got back to my normal routine with my workouts. I woke early and went to the training room. I had it to myself. I worked up a good sweat, the weight saving runes on my armor made a world of difference. When I finished, I returned to my room and got cleaned up, then went to breakfast. Again, I had it to myself. After I ate, I went back to my room and got out the jewels that were given to us at the announcement dinner.

I laid everything out and looked the pieces over. Some were magical, some had sun stones in them, most were just ornamental, but it was all gold. I separated them into the three groups. Using magic, I separated the sun stones from the gold. I took the three largest sun stones and made an engagement ring of them. Then a wedding band with some smaller stones. I made a simple wedding band using the rest of the small stones for myself.

The rings were basically batteries, but I added runes to them so that each ring would know where the other one was all the time and the condition of the wearer. Like a tracking device. I then made two sets of bracelets and two circlets, these I inscribed with runes to make shields and helmets. These would be gifts for Reggie's mother and father.

The jewelry work had been intricate and had taken longer than I realized. It was late afternoon when I finished. I put all the jewelry in my pouch and started packing for the trip. We would leave in the morning and I wanted to be ready no matter what time we left.

I was up early and ate my last breakfast, at least for a while, with my family. It was sedate, no sentiment from this bunch.

Amos was the only one put off but tried not to show it.

A servant had taken my things and put them in my wagon. I didn't know I would have a wagon, and I didn't know what was on it. Apparently, a Prince was supposed to travel with a certain level of decorum. The King gave me a large pouch of gold. "Spend it wisely, use hers first." He laughed at his joke.

I just smiled, "Thank you, father." I said putting it to my pouch.

He nodded, "keep me apprised of events."

"Yes, father." I bowed. *"Not likely, or very little."*

I mounted Gray and took my place with the Royals. I rode beside Reggie's father. Reggie rode in the Royal coach with the Queen. Mother and father stood on the steps to see us off. With the clip-clop of horses' hoofs and the creaking of wagon wheels we pulled out heading south along the King's trade road. There was no fanfare as we left, we just left.

***

We moved slow to start, checking wagons and animals. After a mile or so, we picked up the pace but not by much. The plan was to make five miles today and tomorrow then increase the pace trying to make ten miles per day.

"Have you travelled the King's trade road before, Aaron?"

"No, Sire, I have not. Truth be told I have never left the city."

"It's beautiful country between here and home. I believe you will enjoy it."

"I'm looking forward to it."

"I noticed your father sent no retinue with you."

I smiled, "I'm sure he felt they were better used elsewhere. And I'm just as sure my brother, the Crown Prince, was behind it. He could not let me go without one last jab."

"You did not get along, then?"

"Not really, he is a king in the making. I am an underling, along with the rest of humanity." I laughed. "He actually did me a favor. Now I don't have to figure out which one is a spy or just assume all of them would be. The next question is what kind of useless junk had them packed in my wagon." The King looked at me thinking. "Of course, I'm not completely without blame. I did teleport a load of horse manure under his bed as we left." I said smiling.

The King burst out laughing. After a while, "so why keep your healing abilities a secret? Most would shout from the rooftops."

I nodded, thinking how to answer. "From what I've read, seen, and been taught there are important leadership traits. One of those traits is how you manage assets. Assets being people, food, equipment, money, etc. One type of leader will use his assets to his best advantage to accomplish a mission, to make the lives of himself, his people, and his kingdom better. The other will wring every drop of sweat, blood, and coin from them to further his own agenda, to prosper himself. I believe the old quote is, 'They'll ride a good horse to death.' I didn't want to wind up a dead horse."

He stared at me, thinking. "Wise young man."

I shrugged my shoulders, "just good teachers, who taught me to observe, and form my own opinions, and not to follow blindly."

We rode in silence after that, at the five-mile marker we stopped for the night. Wagons, and animals were checked, as camp was being set up.

I had to smile when I found the King waiting at my wagon. "Couldn't resist, huh?"

He chuckled, "nope."

I untied the cover and flipped it back. The wagon was full of camping gear. Tent, cooking gear, sleeping mats ground sheets, food, and other supplies. Everything I would need. There was a letter laying on top with a wax seal. I recognized the imprint from a ring I had given Amos. I broke the seal and opened the letter.

It read: *"Brother, I've learned to teleport objects. Eldest filled your wagon with junk. I practiced my teleporting using Items from the wagon he and father take hunting. Don't worry I won't get in trouble, I left them a note thanking them, and signed your name. What are brothers for?"*

I laughed and handed the letter to the King. he read it and laughed, shaking his head. "What are brothers for, indeed." Handing the letter back to me. I put it in my pouch.

"Your driver will help you set up your tent. You will eat with us."

"Thank you, Sire."

My driver, Trooper Oaks, and I unloaded and set up my tent. I noticed his limp, and he favored his knee. I didn't bother with most of the gear as I would eat with Reggie and family. "You'll sleep with the wagon, Oaks?"

"Yes, Sir."

"Then use the ground sheets or sleep in the wagon whichever you prefer."

"Thank you, Sir. Ground sheet, and under the wagon will be fine Sir."

Before I went over to the Royal's wagon, I used a spell that took all dirt, grime, and sweat away from me and my clothes. I felt as if I'd had a bath and smelled like it too. *"Magic has its uses."*

Rather than go straight to the Royals tent, I walked the camp's perimeter, fixing in my mind how things were laid out. And that everyone was being fed, and they posted a guard force. Some habits you don't get out of, and if you want to live, you never get out of them.

As I approached the King's Tent, He called to me. "Prince Aaron, please come and take a seat."

They had a table and chairs, but they were camp table and chairs, set up under a canopy in front of their tent. I could see the King watching me to gauge my reactions. *"Tonight, would be a test."*

"Thank you, Sire." and took the offered seat. He poured me a cup of diluted, or watered wine. Moments later, the ladies joined us.

We stood, the Queen and Reggie were dressed in leather

pants, silk blouses under leather vests. A long thin coat was over it making it appear dress like. They both looked very nice. I must have been staring.

"Does our attire shock you Prince Aaron?" The Queen asked.

"No M'lady, it's wonderful. It not only looks good, it's practical too."

"Practical?" she raised an eyebrow. I heard the King clear his throat. Reggie covered her smile with her hand.

I nodded, "If we were attacked, and you were wearing that, you'd be better able to defend yourself. And as I said, you both look very nice."

"Nice recovery," she said smiling.

They took their seats, and they served dinner. Again, the King watched me. We were being served the same meal as the troopers were having. No special privileges. I wonder if this was their common practice or just a test for me. It was good; I ate without comment.

We talked of small things. How long the trip would take, which turned out to be two to four weeks depending on the weather. They talked Kingdom business; I listened. They discussed trade, crops, cattle, sheep and many other topics, I found it interesting my mother and father never talked like this in front of us. Reggie was an intricate part of the discussion.

"How is your father's kingdom trade doing?" The King asked.

"I have no idea, mother and father did not discuss business in front of us."

"How will you learn?"

"we, now they, will not."

"Do you have an interest in learning?" the Queen asked.

"Everything I can." I said.

The King nodded.

"I read of a custom," I said. "In some countries, that the man gives the woman he asks to marry him a ring, they call it an engagement or betrothal ring. During the wedding they exchange Wedding rings. I liked the idea." I reached in my pouch and pulled out the engagement ring. I stood and walked around to Reggie. I took her hand and slid the ring on her finger. She jumped up and hugged me holding me tight for a moment then turned to show her mother the ring.

The King shook his head, "Now every woman in the Kingdom will want one." he said smiling. The Queen slapped him on the arm.

"Another custom is to give gifts to the mother and father of the bride." I took out the bracelets, and circlets. "These are enchanted, runed pieces that become Mage Armor when attacked. After our close call in the castle I felt we all needed a little extra protection. You wear these under your skin all the time, so you are never unprotected." I looked at Reggie, she nodded, and showed them hers.

Reggie and I helped them fit them. "Where did you get these?" The Queen asked.

"The first one was donated by a Mage that was trying to kill me and my brother Amos. He didn't need them anymore. Reggie is wearing that set. These I made."

They looked at me. "You made them? You inscribe runes?" the King asked. I nodded.

"Is there anything you can't do?" the Queen asked.

"I don't cook so well." we all laughed.

"When did you give Reggie hers? Before or after the betrothal announcement?" The Queen asked.

"Before." I said. "She told me how close the assassins came to her. She needed them more than I did." Both ladies had tears in their eyes.

"Do you wear a set?" The Queen asked

I held up my arms, "In my bracers, I plan to make me a set to wear under my skin later."

"Do it sooner, rather than later." Reggie said hugging me.

***

Walking back to my tent I picked up a twig that had a long sharp thorn on it. Looking at it I got an idea. I found the Captain of the Guard.

"Good evening Prince," he greeted me,

"Good evening Captain, I have read where some armies surround their camp with thorn bushes," I held up the twig. He almost rolled his eyes but not quite. Before he could say anything, I continued. "I realize it would take a lot of thorn bushes." He nodded. "What If I could use magic to make a thorn bush perimeter fence, would you be interested in that?"

He thought a moment. "Show me what you mean,"

We walked out to the perimeter, "do you need an opening, or do you want a solid wall?"

"A solid wall."

I concentrated on the twig and dropped it. It took root and grew four feet thick and six feet tall. I stopped it once it was ten feet on its way to encircle us. The thorns were from two to four inches long, sharp, and hard as nails.

He looked at it. "How will you get us out in the morning?" I waved my hand, and the bush went back to the single twig.

He nodded. "Do it." I dropped the twig, and it took off growing around our camp as fast as a man could run. We walked the perimeter. "Good idea, Thank you."

"Glad to help." I continued to my tent. Trooper Oaks was sitting by a small fire outside my tent. As I approach, he started to raise. I waved him off.

"How did you hurt your knee?"

"Horse fell on it, then tried to get up. Twisted me leg almost off, he did. Doctor did what he could, but it was bad. I counted oneself lucky to keep me leg."

I looked at it with my Mage Sense. He was right it was bad. I used his other leg as a guide and repaired it. He flinched as it slid back to normal. "See how that feels, I fixed it a little, maybe it won't bother you as much now."

He stood up flexing it, "it feels like it was never hurt. It feels better than the other one." He was grinning from ear to ear.

"The only thing is," I said, his smile dropped. "When the Sergeant hears about this, he'll want to put you back in the rotation."

He looked around, "Well now, we ain't got to tell everybody, now do we." We both laughed. "Thank you, Sir, this is truly a gift. Thank you."

"Glad to help Oaks. Good night."

"Good night, Sir."

"I now had a new loyal friend."

CHAPTER 7

I was up early, well before sunrise. I wanted to stretch and get some exercise in before we got back on the road. After my workout I practiced my blade katas, and hand-to-hand.

I was working up a good sweat when the morning peace was shattered by screaming. I stopped and waited. People seemed to move toward the Mess Wagon. Oaks came running toward me, "M'lord, Cookie is in a bad way." I ran, following Oaks.

Oaks cleared the crowd and got me through. 'In a bad way', didn't quite cover it. Cookie was still crying out. I'd seen burn victims before, but when they were this bad, they were usually already dead. I flung my hand at him, knocking him out with a spell. I waved my hand and the hot water became cool.

Cookie had dumped a large vat of boiling water on himself. His hands and arms were cooked and swollen like sausages. He had third-degree burns from the waist down.

I knelt putting my hands on his chest; I sent my Mage Sense into him. I was shocked at the pain that struck me. I pushed past it to his wounds. I stopped the cooking of his flesh the boiling water started. I started replacing the cooked flesh with new flesh. I repaired his arms and hands, and his fingers. The tendons where the hardest, they were a mass of cooked meat. I knew I was expending a lot of energy, but I couldn't stop. I was afraid if I stopped, he would lose his hands, and maybe his life. I don't know how long I was at it, but I felt my consciousness slip away.

***

I was swaying, like in a gentle breeze. There was a sound, a soft sweet sound. Humming. I listened then followed the humming up toward consciousness. I kept my eyes closed, enjoying the sound and the soft breeze. I realized my head was laying in someone's lap. That someone smelled good, and she was soft. I could lay here forever.

My mind began to clear and become more focused. "I must be dead."

"Why would you say that?" Reggie asked.

"Because an angel is holding me."

"You'll have to do better than that dear, I've heard that one before." The Queen said.

My eyes snapped open; my head was in the Queen's lap. Both ladies were smiling down at me.

"Relax dear, don't get up too quickly." I felt my face turning red.

"How long have I been out?"

"Three days. When you passed out saving Cookie, they thought you had died. They said you were crying tears of blood. You used too much power at one time. That can be dangerous. You must be careful of that in the future." The Queen kissed me on my forehead. "Thank you for the second life you have saved for us."

"I couldn't let him die when I had the means to save him."

"Even if it meant losing your own life?"

"I didn't consider that at the time. But it would not have mattered, I had to try."

"No greater love." The Queen said.

"How long before we stop?"

"Soon."

"Good, because I have to pee like a…" They both were staring at me smiling. I could feel my face turning red…again.

The both put their heads down on mine laughing. "You are priceless," the Queen said. All I could think was, *"they smell good."*

They sat me up slowly; I was a little lightheaded. It cleared quickly, and I felt fine.

"How do you feel?" Reggie asked.

"Ok, just hungry."

"Good," the Queen said, "That's a good sign."

From the noise outside I knew we were stopping. Once we had stopped, the Queen tapped a drawer under the seat. "Chamber pot," and they got out.

I relieved myself and got out of the coach. I took it slow as I felt weak. Reggie took my arm and walked with me. She gave me their version of a sandwich which was basically a hunk of bread with a hunk of meat and cheese in it.

"Cookie sent this over to hold you until dinner."

I devoured it. She was looking closely at my hand, "what?"

"I was just checking to see if you had eaten any fingers as fast as you ate that." She said smiling. She handed me a jug of water. The cool water was a relief, and I drank deeply.

We stayed by the coach and let the men set up camp. Once the Royal tent was up and the table and chairs were out, they sat me down with cool watered wine to drink. I sat watching the camp go up.

Rodrigo-san came by, "It's good to see you back on your feet."

"Thank you," He bowed then moved on about his business.

As I sat there, my mind became unfocused. I became aware of everything around me. The ground, and the life in it. The camp, the forest, and the life in it. The sky, and the life in it. Though I could not see any of it with my eyes, I felt the surrounding life from the smallest insects to the larger animals out in the forest. It felt amazing, the ebb and flow of life. I sat and watched in my mind's eye.

Someone's hand touched my hand, my eyes snapped open and my defenses flared. Reggie had her hands up backing away. Her shields were up protecting her. "Aaron, It's me, you're ok, it's me."

My bracer shields were fully up, and my daggers were in my hands the air around me crackled with energy. I shut it all down and folded the daggers away.

"I'm sorry, you startled me. I just reacted."

She smiled, "It's ok, I won't do that again. At least we know the shields work."

"Please, if I am asleep or meditating, say my name before you touch me."

She nodded, stepping back to me, she hugged me. "Were those the daggers you told me about?"

"Yes."

"They appeared so sudden; you must teach me that."

I nodded. "I will, but I'll have to make you a set first."

"Let's go for a walk until dinner is ready."

I got up; she took my hand, and we walked the perimeter. "Captain Motts said you were the one who thought of putting up the thorn bush barrier around the camp." I nodded. "We've been doing that every night since. That was a great idea. Everyone slept easier, and they didn't have to use as many guards."

"Who's been putting it up?"

"Mother, she has more of an affinity for Earth Magic."

"Earth Magic?" I stopped and looked at the ground. I felt the earth pulsing with life. "Is this a normal stopping place? A permanent camp site?"

"Yes, they have them every five to ten miles on the King's Trade Road."

I looked around, "Is there a well?"

"Not at this one, it would have been useful if they dug one though."

I looked around; we were on a high point of the clearing. I felt an underground stream here. I knelt and put my hand to the earth. I visualized a well opening lined with rocks. Rocks started raising from the ground forming a circle, then they lined the shaft as it went down. At ten feet we had water, cool, fresh, clean water. I raised a stone trough to water the animals, filled it, and put a spell on it to always keep it clean, and full.

"There, we now have fresh water."

She shook her head, "show off." She squeezed my hand. The men started bringing the stock to water almost right away.

"You should not be using magic so soon; you need to

recharge."

I nodded, but I felt the earth recharging me through my feet. It felt like drinking cool water. "let's sit down a minute."

"See, I told you."

When I sat down on the ground, my recharge rate increased. The earth was refilling me, soothing me. "I just wanted to sit with you."

"Whatever." She fussed, but smiled at me.

I saw they had set my tent up. She saw me looking at it. "The men set everything up every night, and had guards posted with you all night, every night. The men have started calling you Captain Aaron."

"Why?"

"Well, all Royals are Mages, and we have titles, some call Healing Mages 'Sir Mage'. In the army most of the doctors they get are mundane. They usually just call them doctor. If they are good, the men call them 'Doc'. They saw you save one of theirs. No one asked you, you asked for nothing, you just did it. They saw you crying tears of blood while you, basically, grow new arms and hands back on the least of them, a cook. They have claimed you as one of their own. You are more than a 'Doc', and in their eyes, more than a Royal Mage. They have named you, 'Captain Aaron'. For anyone to impress them now, they'll have to walk on water."

"I hope I can live up to their expectations."

"The fact that you are worried about doing that, says you will. Come on, let's go get you a change of clothes," we stood up. "Mother and I bathed you so you're clean." I stopped, she kept walking,

"Excuse me?"

"Someone had to, and you are mine now." She said over her shoulder.

"You're kidding right? Your mother?"

"I needed a chaperone."

"But your mother?" I heard her chuckle as she kept walking. "Don't worry, she said she had seen naked men before."

"That's not funny." I ran to catch up with her.

As we moved through the camp, everyone greeted me. "Good evening Captain." I was a Captain again it was a nice feeling, a familiar feeling. I was among my own, whether they knew it or not.

"We need to stop by the Mess Wagon to see Cookie. He has come to the tent every night to check on you and to thank you."

I nodded. "You always want to keep the cooks, medics, and paymasters on your side." She frowned at me. "I read it somewhere."

When we got to the Mess Wagon and the old cook saw me, tears streamed down his face. Holding his arms out to show me. "You made them new, not just healed, you gave me new." The new skin was red rather than tanned.

"How could I do any less, my friend? You had a need; I had the gift. How can I withhold something that God freely gave me?" He dropped to his knees weeping. Those around us all started crossing themselves and took a knee. I looked around and half the camp was kneeling.

I magically amplified my voice, "hear me. I am but a man, as you are. I have been given a gift. Do not worship the gift or the man who uses the gift. Rather worship the giver of gifts, and the only one who is worthy of worship, God the Father."

"Amen." Someone shouted.

"Amen," I seconded. Then everyone said Amen. Cookie came to me and hugged me. Thanking me.

As we walked up toward the Royal tent, "So, now you walk on water too." Reggie said smiling.

"Not even close my dear, not even close."

***

Our days fell into a routine. Up before sunrise to exercise, break camp, move ten miles, set up camp. I would put in a well and animal trough, the Queen would put the thorn bush barrier up. Wash, rinse, repeat. Hunting parties would kill deer and elk along the way to keep us in meat. I had started riding with the outriders, saying I needed the training. They took me right in. I also started training on how to fight from horseback. Grey needed no training, he seemed to know which way I needed to go.

When I was not riding with troopers, I rode with Reggie. I enjoyed her company. She had a quick wit, and an inquisitive mind.

I shifted to Japanese, "¥How many people speak Rodrigo-San's language? ¥" I asked.

"¥As far as I know only, he and I. He's been teaching me for about five years now.¥"

"¥So, if we wanted to have a private conversation this would be the way?¥"

"¥Yes, except for Rodrigo-San. Are you ready to tell me where you learned the language?¥"

I thought for a moment, I really wasn't ready, but I didn't want to burn any bridges. "¥It's hard to say where I learned it, my memories are jumbled, almost like some memories belong to someone else.¥"

She nodded, "¥It's the serum they made you take, from what I've learned it has some bad side effects, even if it doesn't kill you.¥"

"¥I suppose, I try not to think about it. I just accept it and move on. But speaking this language give us practice in it, and we will improve.¥"

She nodded, "But, only when we are alone or it's very important."

"OK." We continued to practice as we rode, it helped pass the time.

***

It was a dream; I knew it was a dream. I was back in South America. The Cartel had tried to surround our team and then drive us toward an ambush. Good idea, bad execution.

I came fully awake. My fingers were gripping the ground. I sent my Mage Sense out through the earth. A large force was moving into position to surround us. They weren't in position yet, but it wouldn't be long before they were.

I put my armor on quickly, including my cloak. I stepped to my wagon, "Oaks." I said in a normal voice.

"Sir." came the reply.

"Find Captain Motts, tell him we are surrounded. Pull everyone to the center of the camp to protect the Royals. Move quickly, but quietly."

"Yes Sir." He had dressed as I spoke, then was gone.

I needed to buy the Captain some time to prepare. I put my helmet up and pulled my cloak around me. I levitated and rose thirty feet up. I turned looking; I could make out the enemy moving into position.

I concentrated and called up a fog from the forest. I kept it out of our camp. I switched to heat signature vision. The cool fog made the enemy stand out like torches.

I felt magic being used, someone was trying to counter my fog. He wasn't having much luck so far, but I didn't want to give him time to figure it out. As I moved toward the place where the magic was being used; I took out my staff-bow.

I aimed and sent an arrow at his head. His shields flared, but the mithril arrow went right through his shield killing him instantly. His shields faded. my arrow was back.

"Ok sniper, time to go to work." I moved further back into the forest staying roughly thirty feet up. I found their rear most attacker, I aimed and put an arrow through the back of his head. The only sound he made was when his body fell. I worked my way around their circle. I put an arrow through the back of each one of their heads. None of them ever made a sound.

Once I was sure I had accounted for the men sent to attack us, I searched further back in the forest and then down the road. I found their rear guard, horses, supply wagons, and camp. There was an officer setting at their fire waiting. I killed their rear guard as I had the others, arrows through their heads quick, and quiet. The officer by the fire never heard a thing.

I landed out of sight and put my helmet back into my collar. I stepped out of the darkness and walked toward the light. When he saw me, he cut his eyes left and right.

"They're not there." I said. He seemed to relax and nodded.

He was drinking a cup of something hot. "share a cup?" He pointed to the pot over the fire.

"Thank you," I poured myself a cup, and sat down across from him.

"My men?" I shook my head. "The Mage?" I shook my head again. "He said you were good."

I took a swallow of the warm spice wine, nice flavor. "Who is 'He'?"

"For that information you'll have to work a little harder."

I nodded, "I hope they paid you well, and in advance."

"Yes, to both, very well actually. After I kill you, I'm retiring. I'll be rich enough I'll never have to work again." We stood and moved away from the fire. He removed his cloak, so I did as well. I could tell he was wearing runed armor and using runed weapons.

We drew swords; he didn't hesitate he came straight at me, hard and fast. I gave way, blocking each attack. I stutter stepped, changed my direction coming in low. The shields on his greaves flared. We separated.

"Nice armor, part of your payment?"

"Yes, and worth a fortune by itself."

"I'll take good care of your armor."

He laughed, "you do that."

He attacked, he was good, and his speed was magically enhanced, but so was mine. My advantage was 'I' was magically enhanced, where he was wearing enhanced jewelry. I could feel the earth recharging me. I don't think his worked that way.

I matched him stroke for stroke. Thrust, cut, parry. Attack, defend, attack. He was slowing and was dripping wet from sweat. In one exchange, I hit him on the side of the head, his shield flared. He was wearing a crown shield too. In a desperation move he came in close and pulled a dagger, trying for a side cut. I separated my swords and blocked both attacks.

We parted, he dropped his sword and pulled another dagger. I joined my swords and sheathed Dancer. I lowered my hands, and my arm daggers appeared in them. He was slowing. It was time to end this. I slashed at his face he blocked I stabbed his femoral artery and backed away. No armor down there. He staggered back, then sat down.

He didn't even look; he knew he was done for. I kept my distance in case he tried to take me with him. He sheathed his daggers, and I did as well. "Well fought, I guess you get Armor." He smiled. "I've never been beaten this badly, even discounting the fatal cut. It was humbling."

"They'll never stop coming after you. Your enemies are from your south, north, and from the sea. But the one you're interested in is..." He started convulsing and his tongue burst into flames. Screaming his head melted like wax. Someone had put a death spell on him to keep their secret.

CHAPTER 8

It was roughly one AM, and the fog I had called was still thick. They wouldn't lower the thorn bushes, to come out of the camp until after sun-up at the earliest. I had plenty of time to search the bodies, and their camp to gather intel. I started with their Captain.

I stripped him of all his weapons, armor, jewels, and set everything to the side. He was wearing a blessed bag. I'd search it later, I set it to the side. I searched his cloak and tossed it on the pile of his belongings. I picked up his shield bracelets and put them on. The circlet was somewhat odd. It had fine gold chains hanging down the back of the neck getting shorter as they moved around toward the face. The band was wider than I'd seen so far. *"I'm guessing that's for neck protection,"* I put it on. I made them all sink under my skin.

"I need a way to keep all this, or a way to fit it into my bag of holding." A word sprang to my mind. I took out my notebook and looked up "holding crystals." I found it and read. It was basically a marble that things went inside of. You first cast the spell to miniaturize everything, then they gathered inside the holding crystal. You could carry everything like a bag of marbles.

I fixed the spell in my mind, then waved my hand at the pile of goods. Everything shrank and became a holding crystal, about the size of a child's marble. I dropped it in my bag and continued my search. To save time, I cast a spell taking his dead body out of its clothes. I gave the items a cursory search, then cast the spell to put everything into a crystal, the crystal went in my bag. I'd search everything more thoroughly later.

So far, every man had been wearing a cloak, runed armor, carrying runed weapons, and shield bracelets. It seemed the shield bracelets were someone's calling card. Someone had paid a fortune to outfit these men. *"He said they had paid him in advance. Seems it's expensive to hire a mercenary company to kill a King, Queen, Princess, and Prince. I guess he could afford to retire after this job."*

There were three wagons and sixty some odd horses in camp. Two of the wagons held supplies. The food supplies were war rations. These men were moving fast, not in comfort with home cooking. The last one was a command coach with a side door entrance. I could sense magic on the inside.

I opened the door and came face to face with the biggest dog I have ever seen. He stared at me. I stepped back, "Alright, out. Go do your business, I don't have all night." He kept staring at me. "Out." I thumbed over my shoulder. He jumped down and trotted off. Presumably to take care of his business. "Thank God, he had to weigh 250 pounds."

I stepped up into the coach, there was a desk to the right. I sat down and started looking through it. There were a lot of notes. Our locations and destination, how many troops, and our descriptions. The coach shook as the huge dog came back in. I looked, he walked past me to the left and went through a curtain. I frowned; he came back out with his bowl in his mouth and dropped it by me. I looked at him; he woofed.

"Yeah, Yeah, I get it. You got a name... No way. Your name's not Armor by chance is it?" He woofed again, I laughed. "I said I'd take care of his Armor. No wonder he laughed."

I picked up his bowl and walked toward the curtain. I parted the curtain with my hand expecting a closet or something. What I found was another room. It must have been 20 feet square. "Pocket dimension" came to mind. I shrugged my shoulders, "Magic has its uses." Armor pushed past me and headed to a corner where a large barrel sat. I went over and filled his bowl and sat it down. He began eating. "I guess we're friends now." I made sure he had water.

I walked around looking. There was a bedroom area, with a real bed and clothes chests. A dining area with a table and chairs for eight. A sitting area, with a couch and chairs. An office area with a large desk, the desk out front must be for show. "Dude, you didn't tell me you had an RV." Armor cocked his head at me. I chuckled. It even had a bathroom with a type of commode, a tub and hot water. "Get out of town, I wish you hadn't made me kill you. Of course, then I wouldn't own this would I." I shook my head, "I'll take care of Armor."

It was now four AM; I didn't have time to search everything right now it would take too long. I stepped back outside. I fixed in my mind what I wanted to do, and cast the spell. Bodies and weapons began arriving in the clearing. I laid them out in neat rows, dress-right-dress.

I walked down the line casting the holding crystal spell, putting marbles in my pouch. With that done, I looked back over the dead. I had seen this kind of thing too many times. With a thought their remains sank into the earth. "Rest Brothers." I walked away.

With the horses hitched to each wagon, I climbed up onto the driver's seat of my new coach. I left Armor in the back of the command wagon. I chuckled again at his armor joke. I cast a spell for all the horses to follow. The sun would be up in an hour. I eased the team out onto the road and headed back to our camp.

***

By the time I reached our camp it was light enough to see clearly, I reversed my fog spell, and it was gone. I came to a stop at the thorn barrier. Captain Motts came out to see me. "You sent word we were surrounded," he said looking around carefully.

"We were, I took care of them."

He looked down the road at the wagons and horses behind me, and back at me.

"We'll talk later." I said.

He nodded, turned back toward the camp, "Prepare to break camp." He shouted.

I got down from my coach and opened a wider path through the thorn bushes and awaited the inevitable. I didn't have to wait long, here they come. I bowed as the King approached.

"Sire." He nodded looking down the road, then back at me.

"The report I received was that we were surrounded, to pull into the center of camp and prepare to defend."

"That was correct Sire, that was the worst case. I was able to take advantage of a vulnerability and stop the attack."

He looked back at the horses. "Any survivors?"

"None."

"Anyone talk?"

"One tried to, but someone had put a death spell on him attached to their identity. He didn't survive."

He nodded. "To the victor go the spoils." He chin pointed at my caravan of wagons and horses.

I bowed, he returned to the camp. As soon as he left Reggie walked up.

"You are well?"

"Yes, I'm fine."

I saw it coming but took it anyway. She punched me in the chest. "You went out in the dark woods, during a potential attack alone? Are you crazy?"

"That has been suggested." I smiled.

"Oh, I see, you think this is funny." Her hands on her hips, reminding me of a Tac-officer I had once. I expected to have to start doing push-ups any minute.

"Not anymore." I held my hands up. "look, I saw a chance to roll them up and took it. It was the easiest way for me to protect the camp, and you. I'm sorry if I worried you."

She looked at me a moment longer. "How many were there?"

"fifty...seven."

"fifty-seven?! You took on fifty-seven enemy soldiers by yourself. You are crazy."

"In my defense, I didn't know there were fifty-seven when it started."

She turned and stormed off. The Queen was next. "Are you ok Dear?"

I bowed "Yes M'lady."

"Don't be mad at her, she was so worried she'd lost you. We all were, and not because we would lose the alliance, but because we'd lose you."

"I'm sorry M'lady I'll try not to do it again."

She smiled, "see that you don't. You may not survive the next time. And I don't mean from the enemy."

I smiled, "Most definitely M'lady."

Oaks showed up with Gray for me to ride. He drove the new coach; Moss drove my other wagon. Before we started to move, I let Armor out. He ignored everyone, running along, staying close to the wagon, or me.

On one of our stops Armor walked to the side of the coach and pawed a board. A panel opened that held a food bowl and water bowl both were full. He drank his fill then put his head under the panel and lifted it closed. He lay under the wagon resting. I sat on the ground soaking up energy from the earth to recharge. I thought I'd be tired, but I wasn't.

Reggie rode up to my coach and stopped. She started to speak but stopped when she saw Armor.

"He came with the coach," I said. "I promised the previous owner I'd take care of him,"

"You'll go broke feeding him."

I smiled.

"Father wants a briefing on last night's events this evening before dinner."

"Of course."

She nodded, then rode on.

I looked at Armor, "I'm glad I have my own place now, otherwise I'd be sleeping with you." I tied Gray to the back of the command coach and went inside. I sat at the front working desk. I looked through all the drawers again, read through the notes, I learned nothing new.

Oaks stuck his head in the door, "We're about to pullout Captain."

I nodded, "I'm good in here for now, go ahead." Once we

were moving, I went to the curtain to see if I could still use the back room. I could not, the curtain would not part and the wall behind was solid. I found a fold-down bunk along the side I had not noticed before.

I went back to the desk and sat down. I took out one of the holding crystals and lay it on the floor. I reversed the spell, the equipment and clothes from the crystal appeared on the floor at my feet.

The clothes, and equipment that was not runed was of good quality. This one had a few coins in his pockets, his armor, weapons and his cloak were well kept. Something in the cloak caught my eye, there was an inner pocket sown into back of the cloak. Inside was a one-foot square of folded canvas.

I lay the canvas on the floor and started unfolding it. There were drawings on parchment on it. I recognized what it was and stopped. I would need more room to completely unfold it. It was a "Ground Sheet of Holding". I folded it back up and put it back in its pocket in back of the cloak. I'd wait until we stopped to open it. I put it all back in the holding crystal, and back in my pouch.

On our break they changed horses on the heavier wagons, since we had plenty of spares now. We made better time and could stop earlier in the day.

***

When we got to the caravan clearing. I sank a well for our water and made a livestock pond for all our new horses. When I returned to my coach; Oaks was standing at the rear looking. The back of the coach had a canvas-covered area that reminded me of an old stagecoach.

"Let's see what we have." I released the straps and the canvas unrolled onto the ground. It continued to unroll and then set itself up. It was an enclosed pavilion tent. Once it settled it turned the same color as its surroundings. Here, it was different shades of greens. I opened the front flaps, which were on the door side of the coach. Armor pushed passed and went inside. The outside of the tent looked to be about a twelve by twelve square, the inside was a lot bigger, and divided into multiple rooms. The front part had a table and chairs to seat eight, the back room was a sleeping area with a bed. These accommodations were not as nice as the ones inside the coach. Armor was lying on his bed by the front flap.

"That saves us a lot of work," Oaks said. I nodded. He left to set up the rest of our area. I looked at the table, in the woodgrain was a design like maps, and had the word "maps" by the design. Next to it was a design that looked like dinner ware and had the word "dining" beside them.

I shrugged and said, "maps." A large map of the area covered the table. The chairs went under the table out of sight. The pavilion illuminated by Mage light, and there were no shadows in the room.

I took the holding crystal I had out before and opened it on the table. I opened the cloak and took the groundsheet from the inside back pocket. I lay the groundsheet out and opened it. When it was completely unfolded, the parchments that had drawings on them became the objects depicted in the drawings. The drawing of a sleeping mat became a sleeping mat. Drawings of supplies, became supplies, etc.

The groundsheet was six feet wide, eight feet long. It held a sleeping mat, three day's rations including water and personal care items. This was their field pack. Everything was clean, serviceable, and good quality. Someone had invested a lot of time, and even more money to outfit these men.

I laid out the man's armor, and weapons on the sleeping mat. I folded a corner of the groundsheet. Everything turned into parchment drawings and lay flat. Then the whole groundsheet folded flat, weighing next to nothing. I slid the groundsheet back into the cloak's inside back pocket and set it aside.

I stepped back to the map table. I said "table" and the maps went back into the wood, and the chairs came back out. I moved all my personal gear into my new pavilion bedroom. There was a pitcher of water and cup beside my bed, the pitcher was full of cold water. There was another pitcher and a washbasin on the other wall for me to wash-up. Which I did. I also cleaned myself and my clothes magically.

***

I put on the soldier's cloak and went to the Royals area. When I got to their tent, two large chairs were set out like thrones. I stood outside the tent waiting. Before long Captain Motts showed up. We waited together in silence.

Half an hour later the King and Queen came out. The Captain and I bowed until they took their seats.

"Prince Aaron, give us your report on the events of last night, how did you discover the planned attack?"

"I had a dream, that I was in an ambush. I woke up and felt the enemy's presence." I relayed the events of the fight and meeting the Captain of the enemy mercenary company.

"And what did he say before he died?" The King asked.

"He said, they'll never stop coming after me. My enemies are from the South, North, and from the sea. But the one..." He started convulsing and his tongue burst into flames, his head melted like wax. Someone had put a spell on him to keep their secrets.

"So, they are after you?"

"So, he said, he said he was rich enough to retire, after he killed me. They had paid a lot of gold to hire his company to kill me."

"Did you find gold?" He sat up a little straighter.

"I did not, I did however, find this." I took off the cloak and took the ground sheet from the back pocket, I laid it out and opened it.

"Every member of his company was equipment like this. Runed armor, runed weapons, shielded bracelets, supplies, and magic groundsheet of holding. Someone spent a fortune hiring and equipping this company to attack and kill me. I got the impression that if you also died, it would not be a problem. But I was their primary target."

The King and Captain looked through the equipment on the groundsheet, and the groundsheet itself. "We heard no fighting; how did you kill all those men?"

"Quickly and quietly, Sire." I bowed.

He shook his head. "So, it would seem." He returned to his chair. "You are dismissed for tonight; we will think on these things."

"Yes, Sire, with your permission I would like us to hold in this position tomorrow, so we may issue our men the equipment I took from the enemy. We may need every advantage we can get."

"You would give away your fortune to arm soldiers in my army?"

"I can get more gold Sire; I cannot replace a man's life. If what I have saves one life, it is money well spent."

The Queen smiled.

The King nodded. "We shall rest here for the morrow, then move on the next day. Captain Motts, help Prince Aaron with the issuing of equipment."

"Yes, Sire." we bowed and left the Royal tent.

Once outside, "how do you want to do this?" Captain Motts asked.

"I was thinking, one squad at a time at my wagons, after breakfast."

He nodded, "thank you for this. Few, if any, would give away a fortune to arm an army, even their own."

"If I don't survive to spend it, what good is it?"

"There is that," he said smiling.

We separated; he went to his area. I on a hunch, went to my captured supply wagons. I searched through the first one, it was all food and cooking supplies. In the second one I found what I had hoped to find. There were more groundsheets of holding, some of these were different colors. I put them all in a single crystal and put it in my pouch. The rest of the supplies in the wagon was for the horses.

I went back to my coach, Oaks and Moss were there. "We are staying here tomorrow." I took out two crystals and put them on the ground and opened them. "Everyone will get this equipment in the morning." I showed them what it all was, and they put on their new runed armor, and the shield bracelets. Then I showed them the groundsheets of holding, that held all the other equipment.

Moss looked astonished, "You're giving us this?" he asked.

"I'm issuing soldiers, soldier's equipment. It does no one any good in my pocket." They both nodded. "I'll need you both to help in the morning. After breakfast, one squad at a time will come here to be issued the new equipment."

"Yes, Captain." They saluted.

I went into my pavilion and took off my armor. I felt more comfortable doing so now that I had my bracelets and circlet. I took out the crystal that held the groundsheets from the supply wagon and lay it on the floor. I opened the crystal, then opened one of the green ground sheets. It was a standard issue type for a soldier; I folded it closed.

I opened a blue color-coded groundsheet; these sheets were bigger than the green ones. This one held archer's equipment. Twenty bows, twenty quivers, arrows, strings, and wax. I left the ground sheet open.

I open the red color-coded groundsheet. It held runed spears. I picked one up to look at it and was surprised to find that it also magically extended into a Cavalry Lance. There was roughly a hundred of them on the groundsheet. I nodded, more equipment to be issued.

I took two of the spear-lances out to Oaks and Moss. They were suitably impressed. Back inside I put the groundsheets in three separate crystal and put them in my pouch.

CHAPTER 9

"Dining table," I said as I approached the table. I had not yet eaten, and I was hungry. The table became a dining table set for one. There was a pitcher of cold wine, and I poured myself a cup full. I sat down, and a plate of food appeared before me. It was a thick steak with home-fried potatoes, sautéed onions, and green vegetables. Just the way I liked it.

Armor came over and lay-down beside my chair, I cut the bone out of my steak and gave it to him. He was happy. "Hot tea." A cup of hot tea appeared. I had developed a taste for hot tea working with the Brits, and the Aussies.

I sat enjoying my tea letting my mind rest. I took the crystal containing the Mercenary Captain's equipment out and tossed it on the floor. I opened it and started looking through the gear. His armor was heavyweight, where mine was a medium weight. Basically, his armor had the same things mine had. I had added runes to mine to make them weigh less.

I got my scribing tools out and went to work. I would trade up, but I needed to add some things, like groin area protection for my femoral artery. I would also make everything lighter. His bracers, greaves and boots were better than mine, having better shielding. I added my runes to improve them.

Our helmets were much the same coming up from the collars. His had a full-face shield that slid down from the top like a fighter pilot's helmet. I added my runes to everything improving them where I could.

Our weapons were much the same quality, but I liked mine better. I'd store his. "Where is the weapons storage?" A light blinked on the wall over a sideboard. I went over and opened the top drawer. There was room, so I lay his weapons in there.

I opened the next drawer and found a prize. There lay a set

of runed Mithril daggers. They were pulsing with magic. "Dude, why didn't you use these?" I picked them up and fell in love with them. They danced in my hands. They were almost the length of my forearm. I took mine out of my arms and put them in the drawer. I practiced with the new ones, they folded into my arms like the others had. I left them in my arms, they were my new conceal carry daggers.

I went into my bedroom, "two armor stands." Two armor stands appeared along the wall. I hung the two sets of armor up on the stands.

The last item was his cloak. I read its runes. It would change colors like a chameleon, among other things. The cloak itself was armored, and would conceal, and mask. It also had inside pockets one on each side in the front and one in the back. All three had groundsheets.

The groundsheet from the front left pocket was his sleeping and personal gear and was a 6×8 sheet. The right pocket sheet was a field office. It had a small desk, chair and tent and was a 12×12 sheet. The back pocket held a 15×15 sheet and had chests of gold, jewels, gems and other supplies. He carried his fortune with him everywhere. Or did he? I folded all the sheets back up and put them back into my new cloak's pockets.

"Seal the front door." Red light showed over the front door. "Are there any other doors?" A green light shown from the bedroom. I went in there and moved the curtain aside. There was a second curtain which I moved aside. This door connected this pocket dimension to the one inside the coach. I now could go to the bathroom without going outside. Nice.

"Seal the front door to the coach." Red showed over the door curtain. I went back in the lower, not in the coach, pavilion. "Where is the gold vault?" A green light came on in the main room wall. I moved the curtain and inside was a vault with a few chests in it. I went back up into the coach room. "Where is the gold vault?" A green light showed on a wall which I opened. It also held a few gold chests. "So, you didn't put all your eggs in one basket. Seal vault doors." The lights over the doors turned red, then went out.

"Unseal this room's front door, and seal the side connecting door. The red light came on then went out. "Warn me when anyone is coming to the pavilion. If I'm asleep, wake me if anyone or anything enters either of the pavilions, not counting the dog, Armor. A green light flashed across the ceiling.

That was about all I could think of to do tonight, so I went to bed.

***

I woke at my normal time and got up. I needed to exercise I started to go outside but stopped. "I need an exercise area 15×15 put it over here on this wall." The pavilion wall slid away from me giving the area I asked for. "Raise the ceiling in this area to 12 feet." The ceiling raised.

I began exercising in my new exercise area. The floor was solid, and the area had plenty of ventilation from somewhere. Why rough-it when you can travel in style. I practiced with my new Mithril daggers. They were a dream to handle. They also interlocked with my staff.

I finished my work-out and was getting cleaned up, when a mellow male voice said, "Princess Regina approaches." It scared the crap out of me.

I took a deep breath and chuckled. "Thank you, allow her entrance."

"Allowed."

I would have to rethink how I interacted with my house. Which was a crazy thought. But not so crazy anymore.

I knew when Reggie entered, "Aaron, may I come in?"

"Come on in, I'll be out in a minute. Have you eaten?"

"No, have you?"

"Not yet," I said as I came out of my bedroom. I looked toward the table, it was set for two, with hot tea already waiting.

"Some hot tea to start?" I said pulling out her chair. Armor watched her as she walked by. She ignored him.

"Yes, thank you." She said sitting down.

I poured our tea, "two breakfasts please." Two breakfasts appeared at our places.

"Thank you," and she started eating. I did as well. As she ate, she looked around. "Nice place you have."

"It beats sleeping on the ground."

"The Royal pavilion is much like this, minus the food serving table."

"It helps when you can't cook." She nodded smiling. We finished eating, and I poured us more tea.

"I'm sorry I yelled at you yesterday. I shouldn't have done that. I was scared. When you came back, perfectly fine with a wagon train of spoils. It made me mad. I don't know why. Anyway, I'm sorry."

"I'm sorry I worried you, I'll try not to do it again. It was not something I planned, it just happened. On the upside I increased my wealth."

"And you are spending most of it this morning, according to father."

"More of an investment, really. We are, more than likely going to fight again. I'm investing in our survival. I can always make more money. Unless I'm dead, that would make it a little harder."

She laughed, "I can see that." She turned serious, "you really believe we will have to fight again?"

"I do, they have invested several fortunes to kill me and failed. They have too much invested to stop. And I believe this is all part of a larger plan. I think this is about an invasion and taking over at least three Kingdoms, maybe four. They have to kill me."

"Why you specifically?"

"I believe it's because I'm marrying you. I think part of their plan is for someone to marry you to make the takeover look legitimate to avoid an all-out war with your people."

She chewed on that thought for a while. "Who?"

"That part, I don't know. Who's the most powerful of the

surrounding kingdoms?"

"Your father's."

"Who is next?"

"They are about the same."

"From overseas then."

"That could be a long list."

"We have to have more information. But back to the main question, yes, we will be attacked. They have been ahead of us at every attack. They've had all the information, and advantage. We need to change the game and take away their advantage."

"How do we do that?"

"They know where we are coming from and going to. They'll be waiting along that route we either change the route or change the time. But first things first. Let's get you into some better armor." I took her by her hand and led her onto my bedroom. "Take your armor off and put that armor on." I pointed to my old armor.

She started changing; I left the room. I took the crystal holding the standard groundsheets out of my pouch. I lay it on the floor of my exercise area and opened it. Reggie would get a new issue of field gear, as would the King and Queen if they wanted one, I would offer.

I opened one groundsheet and checked the inventory. The standard seemed to be a sleeping mat with blankets, three days war rations with water, a runed sword, shield bracelets, and a runed cloak. The cloak having a back pocket to carry the ground sheet.

"Aaron, I need some help."

I went back into the bedroom. My armor had swallowed her. She had the breastplate on and was holding up the skirting. I smiled. I fixed the thought in my mind and touched the breastplate. It shrank to fit her; I did the same to the skirting. We got the bracers, and greaves on and fitted to her as well. I made sure the helmet worked and fit well, before I was satisfied.

"How does it feel?"

"Light, hardly any weight at all."

I nodded, "good, I added runes for that. Ok, next equipment issue. You may never need it, but better to have and not need, than to need and not have."

I showed her the groundsheet and how it worked. She had her own sword, and shield bracelets so did not need the issue those, "leave them in there. It won't change the weight, and you never know." She nodded. We folded the groundsheet and put it in the cloak's pocket. She put the cloak on, and it shrank to fit her. I took my extra bag of holding out and strapped it on her. I had emptied it; she'd have to fill it.

I stepped over to the weapons sideboard and took out my old daggers. "These are yours now." She took them and looked them over.

"Nice."

I flipped one of mine out and showed her how to hide them in her arms. We practiced a few times until she had the gist of it. "We'll practice more later. Let's go get the troops equipment issued."

We went outside, Captain Motts, Oaks, and Moss were there by the wagons. We walked over to them. They bowed, "Princess."

She nodded, "Good morning Captain, Troopers."

I took out the crystal with the spear-lance ground sheet and opened it, then opened the ground sheet. I picked one up and extended the spear to a lance. "We'll be issuing these as well, Captain." I tossed it to him. He caught it and worked with it at both lengths for a bit. He was smiling.

"Yes, we'll start training with these as soon as we issue them."

"Do we have any archers; I don't remember seeing any."

"Ten, they are on the scout teams."

"I have new archery equipment for them."

"I'll start the men through if you are ready."

I nodded, "let's get you issued first."

***

The men came through in groups of five. I would toss down a crystal and open it, as it was opening, I removed all coins, and jewels from the kits. Everyone got the standard ground sheet kit and a spear-lance. The archers got the archery equipment, which they sorely needed, in addition to the standard issue groundsheet.

As each group got their issue, they would come to attention, fist over their heart saluting me in the supposed old roman style. I returned their salute. Word had apparently gotten around, probably by Oaks and Moss, that I was financing the new equipment issue. This was no small thing for these men. To be outfitted was one thing, to be outfitted with magical equipment and weapons was unheard of. True to his word, the Captain had the men practicing with their new weapons.

The spear-lances that were left we put in the common equipment wagon. I took the large ground sheet and the standard ground sheet with me to see Cookie. Cookie saw me approaching, wiping his hands on his apron he came out to meet me.

"Captain?"

"Cookie, I know you and your men were busy, so I brought your equipment issue down to you." He got a confused look on his face.

"Captain, we don't get issued like the troopers do, we're just cooks."

"Cooks you may be, but if the enemy breaks through and the throat cutting starts, I believe you'd do your share of it." He nodded. "Everyone in this company is a trooper. Some are scouts, archers, cavalry, and some are cooks."

"So, you are not just cooks. You and your squad will get the same issue, less the spear-lance that every other trooper gets. In addition, you will get a large groundsheet of holding for extra supplies and you will take charge of the captured ration supply wagon."

He stood straighter, "Yes Captain."

I showed him how the large groundsheet worked, then issued him and his squad the standard trooper kit. This must have been the first time anyone had treated them like soldiers. I suspected change was coming to the mess area.

I turned to find Reggie watching me. "What?"

"Nothing." she said smiling.

I froze. I'm sure my eyes glazed over. I had an epiphany about the spear-lances.

"What's wrong?" She asked coming to me.

"I just had an epiphany."

"A what?"

"A vision, an idea. I need to look at a spear-lance."

We went to the weapons wagon and got a spear-lance. I read all the runes. What I was looking for was not there. I smiled. "Boys, you left money on the table." Reggie frowned at me. "I need to make an addition to these." I put them all in a crystal and headed for my pavilion. Reggie followed.

***

I took my scribing tool fixing what I wanted in my mind I wrote some additional runes along the shaft of the spear-lance." Ok, let's go test my addition." We went outside. "Oaks."

"Captain?"

"Bring your spear-lance over here." He came over with his spear-lance.

I want you to stab me with the butt of your weapon. I will hold my spear-lance like I'm about to thrust, but I'm not going to move. My shield should stop your attack. He nodded. We took our stance. I nodded. He thrust. Once the butt of his weapon got past my spear-lance point, its shield flared and stopped the attack.

"Oh, yeah." I said.

"I didn't see any of the others doing that during training. How do you do it?" Oaks asked

"I just adjusted this one, I'll have to do them all before they have shields."

I turned the spear-lance tip down and stuck it in the ground. I stood on one side, Oaks on the other. "Attack," He did. The shield that flared this time was three feet wide and five feet tall.

I nodded. "Perfect."

"You can do that to all of ours?"

"Yes, but it will take me a while to do them all. Trade me." He gave me his and took mine. I'll start working on the ones I have, then we'll trade them out. After the first ten, it only took me about five minutes to make the additions. I kept working, while Reggie traded the new ones for the old ones.

"This is the last one." Reggie said as she handed it to me. I nodded taking it. It was something like four AM when I finished. I lay my head on the table and went to sleep.

***

"Mother, No!" I stood up, wide awake, shields up, daggers out. The Queen was well away from me. Hands up in front of her, holding a blanket.

"Aaron!" Reggie called. I looked at her. "It's ok, we're safe. Mother was about to cover you with a blanket. She didn't know." She looked at the Queen, "He reacts violently when touched while he is sleeping."

I dropped my shields, and my daggers folded away. I bowed, "I'm sorry M'lady."

"No dear, I'm sorry, this is your house. I know now to call to you before touching you." she said smiling.

"Thank you, M'lady, that would be wise," I said smiling. "Is it time to move?"

"No, the King has decided to stay here another day. The camp was up most of the night with you. While you made improvements on the spear-lances, the men practiced. We all need a day of rest."

"You'll get no argument from me. Have you eaten?"

"We have not," Reggie said.

I looked down at the table, "breakfast for three, please." Three breakfast meals appeared on the table with hot tea. "Ladies breakfast is served."

They sat down and we started eating. "We have got to get one of these for our pavilion." The Queen Said. Reggie nodded.

I wondered why "the house" had not wakened me when the Queen come in. "Have you been here all night?"

They nodded, "we kept the spear-lances coming while you worked. By the way, that was an ingenious addition you made."

"Thank you." That answered that question, they were here all the time. I ate the rest of my meal in silence, half asleep.

Once we had finished, "I'm going to get some sleep." Reggie said, the Queen nodded.

"I think that is a great idea." Once they were gone, "seal the doors." The red light came on over the door, I went to my bedroom. Someone had slept in my bed. I didn't care, I crashed in. That someone smelled like Reggie. *"I bet she did that on purpose,"* was the last thought I had before sleep took me.

CHAPTER 10

I woke around mid-day, I exercised, cleaned up, and had lunch. I had fixed everyone else's armor and weapons; it was now time to check mine. I brought my new armor out. I left it on the stand, so I could see it. I read the runes on all the pieces. It seemed, what was for these people, a standard setup.

There was the material of the armor itself, then the runes, warding, and the shields. I walked around the stand looking at the armor for weakness. I already knew about the crotch weakness and would upgrade that. What was basically battery life, was short, and the re-charge rate slow. I'd upgrade that.

I needed some materials to do the upgrades. Gold I had, better steel, or mithril would be best. I had none of that, so I'd use the steel I had available. I needed sunstone quartz for the battery life and recharge. I wonder, "are there any unused sunstones in the vaults, or anywhere else in the pavilion?"

"There are not."

I took, what I now thought of as my vault groundsheet, out of my cloak and opened it. I opened each chest and lay my hand on top of the contents. I then knew what was in the chest without having to look through everything in it. I found a small bag of sunstones, there was enough there to do my upgrades. I'd add more later if I needed to.

I divided my chests into thirds. I teleported one third of the chests to the coach vault, another third into the pavilions vault, the last third remained on the vault groundsheet. I folded the vault groundsheet up and put it back in the cloak's back pocket.

I sat down at the table, "Hot tea please." It appeared on the table. Armor came and lay down beside my chair. "Steak, medium-rare." It appeared. I sat the plate down for Armor. It didn't set there long. I took out my notebook, and read what was there about runed, warded, and enchanted armor. I made some notes and plans for what I wanted. Once I had everything planned out, I started.

I teleported some steel swords in from the weapons wagon. I used the steel to upgrade the underlying armor material. I positioned the sunstones where I needed them and applied an interlocking spell on them. Strikes would be shared over the whole armor and not just in one place. I scribed the runes, wards and enchantments in gold, and upon completion, locked them all together under an enchantment.

I put on the upgraded armor and it fitted itself to me. I raised my helmet and lowered the face shield. I moved through some weapons drills. The armor fit like a second skin and was nearly weightless. I had built this armor to be twice as good as my old set. It still had the skirt, but I added leather armored pants. I was pleased at how it turned out. The armor and cloak could turn any color I wanted them to, but I left them black for now.

I went to the table, "maps," the table became a relief map. "Show present location," a small blue wooden horse appeared on the map. "Zoom out, show my old home and the Port City of Shornwick." The map zoomed out. "Show the King's trade road. Show towns, and villages at this view." Six appeared, with these names beside them.

I wondered out loud, "Why aren't any of the towns on the King's trade road?"

"Building a town on the King's trade road violates the treaty. No town or castle may dominate the King's trade road." The pavilion answered. I smiled and nodded.

"I take it you only speak when we are alone or when directed to?"

"Correct."

"How far are we from Shornwick?"

"12 day's travel, at present rate."

I looked over the map looking at the names and saw a small notation of "Abbey of St. Philip," I smiled. *"Patron Saint of Special*

Forces, fancy meeting you here."

"How far to the Abbey of St. Philip?"

"Two days." I nodded. A plan started to form in my mind.

I went outside in full armor and cloak, helmet down. I walked the perimeter and camp, Armor walked with me. Staying at my left knee as if on a "heel" command. Every trooper stood and saluted, hand over heart, as I passed. "Captain," nodding their head in a bow. I returned their salutes and kept walking. After I made my rounds, I returned to my pavilion.

I removed and hung my armor in my bedroom. I went back to the table to look at the map again. "The King, Queen, Princess and Captain Motts approach."

"Allow them entrance." The ceiling flashed green. "Tea for five please. leave the map in place." A tea service appeared on the end of the table.

The King entered followed by the Queen, Reggie, and the Captain. I bowed, "Sire, M'lady."

"Prince Aaron, you are rested?"

"I am, Sire. Thank you. May I offer you some tea?"

"Please," he said while looking at the map table.

I poured four cups of tea; they took theirs.

He pointed at the map, "What think you?"

I took a swallow of tea forming my response in my mind. I looked down at the map. "They will hit us again, sometime in the next week. Probably in this area." I pointed.

He looked. "Explain." They were all looking at me,

"We are 12 days from Shornwick, they have to hit us before we get any closer to reinforcements, and away from witnesses. They have invested and risked too much now, they have no choice but to attack or abandon their cause completely. I don't think they will abandon their cause. Someone wants me dead, and your kingdom too much to stop now. Your kingdom and Princess Regina are the prize. With me, her betrothed, dead someone could eliminate you, the Queen, marry her, and take the kingdom. For their plan to succeed we have to die."

"They know our route home. All they have to do is sit and

wait for us to come to them. If it were me, I'd have a second group following in behind us to catch us between two forces and end this. I believe the southern enemy is waiting here. The northern enemy is following behind us or waiting off to the side for us to pass. Then they'll close in behind us."

They were looking at the map as I spoke. The King nodded. "How would you counter their moves?"

"They build their plan on the fact that Princess Regina and I are not yet married and will not be until we reach Shornwick. They must kill me before then. If not, and they push their plans, it's all-out war. They would rather not fight a war, it's too expensive and takes too long. They want everything intact and in working order. We have to force them to change their plans and the battlefield."

"I propose we go to the Abbey of St. Philip where Princess Regina and I will marry. We'll send notices to all the kingdoms. At the same time, you must call up your army and prepare for their counter strike. If the Midwick enemy is in this area, as I believe, I will strike at their undefended home causing them to have to rush home."

"That would mean war."

"It's already war Sire, we are just going on the offensive."

"And where would your wife be while you attack Midwick?"

"At the Abbey of St. Philip with you and the rest of the company. Call up reinforcements to escort you home. I will return when I have caused enough chaos."

"Do you have an alternate plan?"

"Increase our speed to get further ahead of the Midwick enemy, then fight our way through the Volwick enemy."

"You make it sound so simple." The Queen said.

"Simple yes, easy no."

"How far to the Abbey of St. Philip?" Reggie asked.

"Two days." I answered.

They looked at the route to St. Philip's Abbey.

The King nodded, "Captain, we move at first light for the Abbey of St. Philip."

"Yes, Sire." He bowed and left.

***

I was up earlier than normal because I did not know what to expect closing the pavilion. I dressed in full armor and ate breakfast. Just to make sure, "We are about to close up and move." I said to the house.

"When you are ready say 'close pavilion'." The house replied, I nodded. I went outside, and closed the curtain, "close pavilion." It collapsed, folded and rolled itself back up on the rear of the coach. Oaks and Moss secured the straps.

"We're all set Captain."

I nodded, "did you eat?"

"Yes Sir, Cookie had us up early feeding us."

Gray was saddled with a spear-lance standing up in his saddle mounts. Out of habit I checked Gray and his saddle. Everything was good to go. We moved out before daylight. We travelled until noon, then stopped to change the draft horses. We ate war rations while we waited for the teams to be changed. As soon as they were through, we were on the move again.

Just afternoon, we turned off the King's trade road on to the road that would lead us straight to the Abbey. I cast a spell removing our tracks where we changed roads. I rode with Reggie; she was quiet. I left her to her thoughts. I had my own. I ran war game scenarios over in my mind, making sure I had missed nothing. We continued moving passed our normal stopping time using all the daylight available.

We stopped at a stream, so I didn't put in a well. I walked through the horse herd looking for injured animals I healed a few hooves, but overall, they were in good shape. After they were watered and our water barrels refilled, the thorn brush barricade went up.

My pavilion was already set up when I got through with the horses. I stripped out of my armor and washed myself. I dressed in fresh clothes and went to the table. "Hot tea please." I took my cup of tea and went over to the exercise area. "When I don't need to use this area for exercise make this a sitting area with a couch and chairs. Nice comfortable ones." A couch, three chairs, two and tables and a coffee table appeared. I sat down in a chair; it was comfortable.

"Princess Regina approaches."

"Allow entrance." the ceiling flashed green.

"May I come in?" she asked as she stepped inside.

"Always." I said. "Tea?"

"Yes, please." The tea service appeared on the coffee table. I poured her a cup and gave it to her.

"I'm sorry I wasn't very good company today."

I shrugged my shoulders, "You have a lot on your mind." She nodded.

"Are your mother and father coming for dinner?"

"No, just me."

"Then let's eat, I'm starved."

We moved over to the dining table, "steak, potatoes and green vegetables." I said, my plate appeared.

Reggie looked at mine, "Me too," she said smiling. Her plate appeared. We enjoyed a quiet dinner.

I walked her back to the Royal tent and sat by their fire with her for a bit, before saying good night.

***

We were up and on the road before sunup. The King wanted to get to the Abbey as soon as possible and was pushing a bit. We stopped before noon to change horse teams and eat our war rations. Before we started again a rear scout came galloping in. *That can't be good.* I rode forward to where the King was getting his report.

"At least one thousand cavalry moving fast. They will be here with-in the hour." The King nodded. I looked around at the terrain. We were stopped in an open area between stands of trees. We were on a slight hill, so we had the high ground, such as it was. Not the best terrain, but not the worst.

In for a penny... "M'lord I stepped down from my horse. We'll meet them here. They and their horses will be tired. You, the Queen, the Princess, and an escort will make for the Abbey. The rest of us will join you there." He stared at me; the only sound was the wind blowing across the grasses.

"Captain Motts, choose ten men for our escort, you will lead us to the Abbey." He didn't like it, but followed the orders. He called out the ten and prepared to leave.

Reggie jumped down from her horse and came to me. She kissed me, "Do not be late for my wedding," she looked around, and raised her voice, "Any of you." We all bowed.

"Yes, Princess." We stood, watching them leave. "Not married yet, and she's already telling me what to do." I said, everyone laughed.

"You ain't seen nothing yet," an old man called out. We laughed and mounted. I looked at the battleground and ran options through my mind. I turned to the 90 men I had with me. I saw Cookie in the bunch and nodded.

"We'll meet them here, at the edge of the trees, before they can widen their column. We will be dismounted waiting. They will see us and think they have an easy victory and charge us. That will be their undoing. Just before they hit us, we will plunge our lance shields into the ground. They will crash into our shield wall and those behind will crush the ones in front. We'll kill everyone left."

"Archers you will be on the flanks. As soon as they hit our shield wall, kill as many as you can. When I pull my lance, we all do. Then the real killing starts. Your shields, armor and weapons are better than theirs. Protect each other's left and right don't rush in alone. We'll move in together. This will be a fight to tell your grandchildren about. The day that 90 troops defeated over a thousand enemy cavalry. And you better not die, I'm not taking a beating for you not being at the wedding." A shout went up.

We took our position where the road exited the woods. The sergeants sorted the men out. I felt down into the earth through my feet. I sent my Mage Sense out into the forest on either side of the road. I put my magic to work. I thickened the forest so the enemy could not break out into the wood and flank us. I set sharpened spikes of limbs for those who tried. I firmed up the ground we were on but loosened the road's in front of us.

We didn't have long to wait; we heard the hoofbeats approaching. They rounded a slight bend in the road and saw us. A cheer went up from them, and they charged, lances down.

"Steady men, steady." They were coming hard, horses charging our dismounted line that was spread across the road. "Three... Two... One... Now!" We flipped our lances and plunged them into the ground. I pulled energy from the earth to reinforce the shields just in case. Time slowed for me. Looking along my lines, men held their lance-shields stuck in the ground, eyes closed. No doubt praying the shield wall would hold. Archers, arrows notched, waiting for the moment to draw and release.

It was a sight to behold. One second they were at a full gallop, the next at a dead stop. The crashing sound was deafening, the screaming of horses and men was terrible. It was worse than the worst car pile-up you can imagine. Our shield wall turned blood red, flared like fire, but held. Our archers went to work. losing arrows as soon as they had targets.

Their horses went mad with fear and started bucking and fighting. The harder they fought the worse it got. Using magic, I dropped trees behind the column and thickened the blockade so there was no escaping the ambush.

"We will pull these middle two lance shields and let the horses out one at a time." I shouted. "Make a lance shield wall here and here to funnel the horses out and away from us. Kill anyone trying to escape." They all nodded and built the shield wall funnel.

I stepped back preparing to use my magic. I nodded to the two troopers, and they pulled their lance-shields. Horses saw a clear path to freedom and fought to get to it, they trampled anyone in their way. I cast a calming spell in the funnel area for the horses to run through. They ran through our formation and out into the field behind us and merged with our horse herd.

The screams of wounded horses was a terrible sound. I took out my staff bow and began killing wounded animals. Then I began killing enemy troops. It was a slaughter. Only ten percent of their troops had Mage Shields, most of their armor was standard issue and did not hold against our attack. Especially against our upgraded weapons.

Horses were coming out, the dead and dying lay on top of one another. There was no fight left in this army. I cast a calming spell over all the horses left inside the ambush area. I amplified my voice, "yield and live, throw down your weapons and come forward." Weapons began to drop. A few hardcore warriors charged and died on our arrows. That broke the back of their spirit.

"Who is the ranking man left among you?"

One came forward, "I believe I am, Captain Monet, Third Lancers."

"Gather your men over there Captain, they may bring out water with them. Nothing else, I'm in no mood for leniency." They moved forward in a daze. Of the over one thousand troopers, three hundred were killed out-right. Another four hundred would die before day's end from their wounds. The rest were walking wounded. We lost no one.

"Is your King among the dead?"

The captain was in shock and spoke without thinking. "No, he is with the rest of the army on their way here. They sent us ahead to overtake you."

"How many men is he bringing?"

"Three thousand."

"See to your men Captain." He nodded and walked away.

Our men had recovered their spear-lances and were watching the prisoners. They gathered together all the horses. I didn't want prisoners; I didn't have the men to watch over them, and I didn't want to kill them.

I walked over to their captain, "Do your horses carry war rations for your men?"

He nodded, "they do."

"You and your men will go and get the war rations; you will unsaddle the horse. You may take one horse each. Only the horse, bridle, and rations. Return to your King, tell him to go home. Tell him that Princess Regina and I were married at The Abbey of St. Philip. Their gambit has failed. If he continues to press the fight, I will destroy him and his army. Questions?"

"No, I understand."

I nodded, "see to it Captain, I hope we never meet in combat again."

He nodded and got his men moving to do as instructed. My men watched them, but there was little need. They moved like zombies.

I walked along the road, looking at the dead. It was late afternoon, and if we stripped the battlefield in the usual manner, we would be here through the night. I found their banner; it was a boar's head. I took it off and turned it upside down and reattached it. I thrust the staff into the ground.

I took a saddle bag from a dead horse. I fixed in my mind what I wanted to do. I cast my spell. The dead, both human, and animal came out of their clothes and equipment. The forest took them back to the earth. I walked the road, putting equipment, clothes, and weapons into holding crystals. When I was finished, I had a saddlebag full of crystals.

I went back to where the men waited, one had the boar's head banner. The enemy troops were gone. Two scouts were following them for a while. We still had over four hundred captured horses. I put the saddles the enemy had stripped from their horses into crystals. I added them to the saddle bags with the rest of the crystals.

"To save time I have stripped the battlefield of all the spoils. You will all share equally with those who went with the King as escort." There was a lot of head nodding.

"Cookie?"

"Here Captain." he stepped forward out of the crowd.

"You will keep the spoils until we divide it." I handed him

the saddlebags.

"Yes, Captain."

"We have won a great victory here, and I thank God that we lost no one. Because the Princess would have killed me." Everyone burst out laughing.

"Mount-up, gather our horses, we have a wedding to attend." A cheer went up.

CHAPTER 11

I turned the company over to Captain Motts reporting all present, saluting him. He returned my salute and took charge of the men.

I went to the Royal pavilion to make my report. The King and Queen were seated in their throne-chairs.

I approached them and bowed laying the captured banner before them.

"We will hear your report."

"We met the enemy, numbering over a thousand on the road to St. Philip's Abbey. They were overconfident. They lost 700 men and left with a few over 300 wounded. The men performed exceptionally."

"And our losses?"

"None, Sire,"

He frowned, "You fought a force of over 1000 with 90 men, and lost none?"

"We were fortunate Sire, and the Princess did ordered all of us to be at the wedding and not to be late." The Queen laughed.

Reggie burst forth from their pavilion, she came running and launched herself on me. I caught her, "You better be glad you followed those orders too." She said as she stood beside me.

"What did you do with the 300 prisoners?" The King asked.

"I gave them each a horse and sent them back to their King with a warning. If he came further, I would destroy him and his army."

"You think he will heed your warning?"

I shrugged, "we have at least warned him, what happens next is on him."

***

The Princess and I walked the camp. She greeted each Trooper and thanked them for their service. The mood was light, Cookie had told the escort they were to share in the spoils. That soothed any ill feeling if there were any.

I had Cookie pour the saddle bags of crystals out on the ground; I opened all the crystals, and let the spoils spill out. We left it to Captain Motts and the sergeants to divide it all out.

"Did you talk to the priests?" I asked.

"Yes, they will be ready at noon tomorrow to perform the wedding."

I nodded, "Good, let's go have dinner."

***

I couldn't sleep so I went out for a walk. I levitated up and out of our camp. I looked over the Abbey. At some point in the past it had been a decent place but had fallen into disrepair, almost ruins. The priests were rebuilding it, but it would take them years to complete it.

I landed and walked the grounds. This St. Philip was supposed to have been a warrior Mage and devout man of God. He had quelled the unrest and kept the peace in these kingdoms during his lifetime. I stood in the middle of the shrine and buildings. Wondering if it had ever been finished to begin with.

I sent my Mage Sense out through the earth. I felt the buildings, the walls, and the crypts. They had not set the foundations properly, that was why everything had fallen into disrepair so quickly. I set myself to work with the earth and stone. I repaired, strengthened, and leveled the foundations. I repaired walls, stone works, and floors.

"What the heck, I'm here, and our SF owes him one." I smiled. I concentrated on the earth, and the surrounding structures. I raised unfinished buildings. I raised walls, restored crypts, I repaired or built all I could feel, roadways, walkways, and statues. I made the chapel a church and made it bigger. When I felt I was finished, I looked around, at all I had built, and rebuilt. I might have gotten a little carried away. I shrugged.

I went into the church. They would have to make or buy their own furniture. I felt a crypt beneath my feet. I looked down; I concentrated and dropped through the earth into the crypt. It needed repairing too. I repaired it to its original glory.

An apparition appeared. "Do you come to worship?"

I shook my head, "no." I smiled.

"To steal then?"

"No, I came to repair, the crypt was in bad shape I wanted to fix it."

It walked toward me," you are a Warrior Mage, as I was."

"Perhaps, I don't know all my abilities yet. I'm still young and growing into them."

"You came on a quest, to gain something?"

"No, no quest, just to repair things that were broken."

He studied me. "You are more than you seem. You are not just a Mage, or Warrior Mage. You defend the weak, protect those who can't protect themselves, a guardian and are vigilant of evil."

"That's a little dramatic, isn't it?"

He chuckled, "maybe, but true all the same."

"Maybe." I smiled.

"Your name, brother?"

"Aaron."

"Brother Aaron, I offer you a trade, your armor for my armor." A stone wall slid aside. There in a pile lay what had once been a suit of armor. He watched me.

"It's seen better days," I said.

"We've been down here a long time." We walked over to the pile. "You said you came to repair."

I chuckled," I did, didn't I." I could tell the armor had mithril steel backing." Can I use pieces of my armor to repair it?"

"No, it's a trade, all or nothing."

"What's the catch?"

"As you would say, no strings attached." I looked at him. "I said you were more than you seem."

I don't know why, impulse maybe, a challenge. I don't really know. "Ok, I'll trade."

"Place your armor on the floor beside mine. Then it is yours."

I took my armor off, placing it on the floor beside his old armor. It would take a lot of work to repair that old armor. I hoped the mithriI was worth it.

My shield bracelet armor and circlet flared. I was thrown across the room; I hit the floor and rolled up, daggers out. All I saw coming at me were teeth and claws. Time slowed for me as my runes kicked in. Its reptile skin was like armor, but my mithril daggers were cutting through. It screamed and attacked again; I was blocking most of its attacks, and my bracelet, and circlet shields were handling the rest. It still hurt to be bounced off the floor and walls.

I was pulling energy from the earth recharging. His powerful kick bounced me off the wall, I used the rebound to go low and hamstring him. That slowed him but didn't stop him. He closed with me, trying to overpower me close in. My shields were holding, but they were at almost a constant flare. I needed to end this.

I folded my right-hand dagger away. I stiffened my fingers straight and my shield-armor surrounded them. I punched up through his neck and into his skull grabbing his brain. The old Mage in me cast a spell. I took the beasts powers and knowledge. I staggered back against the wall, dropping the dead reptile-man.

"Well fought warrior. But I'd be careful using that spell, it's dangerous, and addictive."

My eyes focused, there was another apparition there. "Am I going to have to kill you too?"

He laughed, "no, I'm already dead. That was Tallick, a thief. He trapped himself in here long ago trying to loot my crypt."

I looked around the room the floor was covered with bones, armor, and weapons. "It seems I was not the first to fall for his tricks."

"He was very good at casting illusions and beguiling." I nodded,

"Yes he was. I don't suppose you want to trade armor either do you."

He smiled, "sorry no. My son inherited my armor when I died. The only thing down here is me. Tallick was a victim of his greed. However, there are some nice pieces lying around from unfortunates, you are welcome to them. The best pieces belonged to Tallick. Ironic that his armor, and his powers wound up being the prize." The apparition faded, "fair well Warrior Mage."

I cast a light spell and the whole crypt was lit. I looked around the crypt. Tallick had his armor and all the booty stacked in a corner. He had survived by eating all those who had come down here. He would hibernate until his next meal showed up.

I cast the spell putting everything in a crystal and put it in my pouch. I teleported back to my pavilion. I cast a spell to clean myself and my gear. I got undressed and went back to bed. "If I'm not up by eight o'clock, wake me." The ceiling flashed green.

***

I was up before eight and had breakfast. I got out the crystal with Tallick's armor and booty in it. I must give it to Tallick, his armor was better than mine. The metal used to make his was mithril, covered with reptile skin that was good armor in itself. There was also a shirt and pants of the same skin.

If he'd been wearing this when we fought the outcome might have been different. He also had shield bracelets, for wrist and ankle, they were better than mine. His circlet was also better, I traded up. His armor had more and larger sunstones. His bracers also had reptile skin gloves. Like my bracers his had shields, but with blade protrusions on the outside of the forearm. His greaves were taller and had shields, and blades on the sides and spikes on the heel and at the knee.

I read all the runes, some were in his language, which I could read. He could scribe runes also, which added to my knowledge. His helmet was like mine, as it came out of the collar.

His looked like a dragon's head and face. The whole thing was made of what he called "dragon glass." Which could be formed into whatever shape you wanted. It was perfectly clear from the inside. The outside was black, or whatever color you wanted.

I put it all on and it adjusted to fit me perfectly. His hooded cloak was made from the same reptile leather as the armor. It made no sound when it moved and weighed nothing. Now that I thought about it none of his items weighed anything and made no sound moving. The inside of the cloak had several pockets, including a large one in the back. I transferred everything over from my old cloak to my new one.

He had a mithril sword, but I didn't like the design. I put it in the weapons drawer. Everything else went back in a crystal, and in my pouch. I was now fully dressed in my new armor. My old set I put away.

It was almost time to go to the church, I might as well go over. If I'm late, I'm a dead man. I walked out, helmet down, and headed for the church.

***

The King and Captain Motts had the men lined up inside the church, two ranks on each side forming a corridor. The men had cleaned up as best they could. I cast my spell, as I passed down the corridor the men's armor turned shiny black with gold accents, red cloaks, and spear-lances of gold. Mine and the Captain's matched the men. The King not to be out done made his all gold.

When the priests were ready, the King went to bring Princess Regina in. The front doors opened, "Honor guard, Post." The Captain commanded. The trooper raised their spear-lances to form an arch for her to pass under.

Reggie's armor was all white, a bright white, and she wore a white veil. She was a beautiful sight to behold. As she and the King passed under the spear-lance arch, the troopers would come to attention and face the front of the church. It was nicely done.

When they arrived at the front, The King raised Reggie's veil and kissed her on the cheek. He passed her hand to me. We walked up the steps and knelt on the top step before the priest.

"Brothers and sisters, we are gathered here before God to bind these two in Holy Matrimony, where the two shall become one." The Priest said.

I zoned out after that; I had dodged this bullet a few times. I had been best man at some, and drunk at others. All I had to do was say "I do," have a ring, and I'm good to go. Oh, and not say anything my warped brain may think is funny. Brides have zero sense of humor. Like when Billy burped "I do" at his wedding. All the men laughed, for about two seconds, Bad idea. "I do," I said, right on cue. I didn't drop the ring either. I kissed the bride to cheers and tears.

We rolled up the sides of my pavilion and my table fed everyone a feast and served wine. "It was very sweet of you to repair the Abbey. I'm sure the priest appreciates it; I most certainly do." Reggie said.

"I didn't want your wedding to be in a rundown shack, you deserved better."

"Thank you." she kissed me. The Queen finally kicked everyone out at early evening, and we lowered the sides of our Pavilion.

"Seal the outside doors." I said. The ceiling flashed green." Pavilion, this is my wife Princess Regina, I grant her full access to all areas of the Pavilion."

"Full access granted, greeting Princess Regina, and welcome."

"Thank you." She said smiling. "You've been keeping secrets."

I nodded, "Thousands." I said smiling. "Let's get out of this armor." We took our armor off and hung it on the stands in the bedroom. I held my hand out taking hers, I led her through the door going into the coach Pavilion. Where the larger bedroom and the bath was. Pavilion had made the bath larger for us. We washed each other's backs and held each other the rest of the night.

***

I woke with a start, with someone's arm over me. "It's ok, Aaron, it's me. We're safe." I relaxed and folded her into my arms and went back to sleep. We didn't leave the pavilion until afternoon. Reggie wanted to move her things over to our pavilion.

"We have sent messengers with the news of the wedding. We have also sent for reinforcement from Port City. They'll be coming, but not by the King's trade road, we'll wait for them here." The King said.

I nodded, "tonight I'll see if the Midwick's King heeded my warning. If he did, I may not have to go north to raid."

"I hope not, but I'm not making any bets."

I shrugged, "just in case let's move everyone inside the Abbey's walls. I'll add more to the fortifications. If he gets here before our reinforcements, at least we won't be so exposed."

"Yes, let's do that."

I had made the Abbey's wall eight feet high and four feet thick. I doubled the walls to sixteen feet high and eight feet thick and added a better gate with a portcullis.

We moved the camp inside and manned the walls of Fort St. Philip's Abbey. I also added wells while I was making improvements. I was getting better at manipulating rock and was now beginning to be able to manipulate wood, and metal.

Our preparations were not in vain. Just before sundown the Midwick King and his army arrived. From our walls we watched as his vanguard came in fast, riding around the fort. Seeing it was a complete fortification, they set their forces to keep us under siege. Their King came forward under a white flag. "As you can see you are surrounded with no hope of escape. Surrender Prince Aaron."

"You are too late, they are wed." King Briska answered.

"That makes no difference, she'll be a widow by tomorrow night anyway. If we must take the fort, most of you will die."

I stepped forward, "you've made your threat," I said, "Now here is my promise. I sent you a warning that if you came south, I would destroy you and your army. You ignored my warning and came south. By sunrise tomorrow not one man in your army will be alive."

"Normally Kings are ransomed. You are not a King; you are an errand boy sent to do your master's bidding. You will die like everyone else out there. Your one, and only one chance is to turn and ride for home now."

His face turned red, "We shall see boy." He snatched his horses head around and galloped back to his army.

I turned and walked away. King Briska followed me. "What's your plan?"

I stopped, turning to him. "I'm going to kill them, before they kill us."

***

They didn't leave. I didn't really expect them to. He brought his army here; it would finish him as a ruler if he turned tail at a threat from a young Prince. Even if we did kill 700 of his men, he had to stay. I ate a small dinner and separated myself from everyone. I told them I needed to prepare myself for what I must do. Reggie wasn't too happy but said she understood.

"You had better not get killed." She kissed me then left me alone.

I watched the Midwick Army from the wall for a while. They didn't try to hide their numbers. They wanted us to see how many we faced. I studied their camp's lay-out and fixed positions in my mind. I left the wall and stood on the ground. I sent my Mage Sense out and found their King; he had also brought two mages with him. I would need to deal with them first.

I rested and meditated. Just before their guard changed,

I wrapped myself in my lizard cloak and levitated straight up 100 feet. I moved out over their camp. The two Mages and the King had spaced themselves out, to better protect the camp from Mage attacks, I guess. I sighted in on my first target he was, if not sleeping, at least laying on his bed. I could not see or feel any traps, but I would assume they were there. I needed to strike first, and lethally.

CHAPTER 12

I readied myself and fixed in my mind what I wanted to do. I remembered the saying, "no plan survives first contact with the enemy." I teleported right in on top of him. As soon as I hit him, he dragged me down into the earth. He was an elemental Earth Mage. I wrapped my legs around him and squeezed. He started to cast his spell, but I drove my knife- fingers through his eyes, into his brain. The old Mage in me cast his spell. I convulsed as I took the Earth Mage's powers and knowledge. Runes flashed and leapt from his body to mine, becoming part of me. I held on to the dead Mage until my mind cleared. I let go of him and the ground around him solidified.

The earth around me reacted like water. It was like swimming, but I could breathe down here. I looked up; it was like looking up from a swimming pool, while you were swimming underwater. I watched the tent above. Nothing happened, no one had heard anything, at least not enough to cause anyone to come investigate. I stayed where I was and gathered my thoughts. It would take some time to assimilate the Earth Mage's powers, and knowledge.

I stayed underground but went deeper. I didn't want to chance anyone feeling magic passing underfoot at an inopportune moment. I moved to where I was under the next Mage's tent. I considered my attack options. The Earth Mage's powers gave me other options that I considered.

I fixed my attack plan in my mind and sped up toward the sleeping Mage. I drove my knife-fingers through the back of his head as he lay in his bed. I cast my "powers capturing" spell and pulled him down into the earth. I convulsed again but not as bad. This Mage worked more with water and air elements, but mostly air. I held him until my mind cleared. When I let him go the earth solidified around him.

I waited to see if there was any reaction to my attack. There was not. *"Two down, one to go."* Because I had these two Mages' knowledge, I knew the King had set a trap in his pavilion. They expected me to go straight for the King. I searched the body of the Mage, taking everything and putting it in my pouch, I took the corpse and moved toward the King's pavilion. I centered myself under the pavilion and cast a levitation spell on the Mage's corpse. It raised up through the floor as soon as it was out of the ground lightning struck it from the four corners. Lightning continued striking the corpse.

The King came out of a concealed shadow box laughing. "Young fool, you thought to kill me?"

I struck, I drug him under and thrust my knife-fingers up through his chin, and into his brain. I cast the capturing spell and took his powers and his knowledge. He had a shocked, surprised look on his face. I convulsed as I absorbed his powers. I released his corpse, took his crown and put it on. *"The King is dead, long live the king."* I cast a guise spell to look and sound like the King. I raised up into the Pavilion leaving the dead King underground.

Guards were waiting outside, "guards!" They rushed in looking at me then the burned corpse in the floor. "Roll that up in a rug and get it out of here." They rolled the burned Mage's body up in the rug and left. I dropped into the earth and followed the squad of guards. I cast a beguiling spell on them, "kill the traitor before he kills you." They dropped the rug and attacked each other.

As soldiers ran up to the fight, I cast the spell again. The killing continued. I conjured a fog; the whole camp was now in a pea soup fog. Before long everyone was fighting each other, killing "the traitor".

I went back to the Earth Mage and stripped his corpse of everything. I searched his tent taking everything of value, putting it all in crystals and into my pouch. The fighting was still going on outside. I went under, and back to the King. I stripped his corpse and put everything in a crystal.

I came up through the floor of the pavilion; I looked around and realized the King had intentionally left the pavilion unsealed and unprotected as bait. Foolish.

"Seal the pavilion."

The ceiling flashed green, "sealed." she said.

I smiled. "Nice change of pace."

I knew because of the King memories, that he was suspicious of everyone, and greedy. Because of this quirk, I now had most of his Kingdom's gold in my new pavilion's vault. "It's nice to be rich."

I went to the table, "cold water." a glass appeared. I took it and enjoyed a few swallows. I walked to the throne and sat down. "Comfortable." I nodded.

I looked in the corner where the King's armor stood. He had left it there as bait. It was also part of his payment for invading south and killing me. I looked at with my Mage Sense. All mithrilium metal, large whole sun stone, and a mithril sword. All of which were covered in runes. His cloak was a fine cloak but not as strong as mine was.

I felt out across the camp. They were still killing each other.

I took the King's Armor, sword and cloak and lay them on the floor. I took off all my armor, weapons, and shield jewelry and lay it all on top of the pile. I took out the King's jewelry from a crystal and added it to the pile. After considering it, I added my mithril arm daggers, my staff, and my lizard skin clothes to the pile. The only thing I didn't add to the pile was the King's crown.

I knelt on the pile. I focused my mind on what I wanted. I drew extra strength and power from the earth. When my power was sufficient, I cast the spell. Combining the best of everything into one set of armor, weapons and jewelry shields.

I kept sustaining the power going into the spell until I felt it was complete. The pile was pulsating a purple glow. Then it calmed. The King's armor and sword were no longer there.

The only outward difference I could see in my armor was it had a purple hue to the black lizard skin. Inside it was all mithril.

My weapons and my staff were black mithril, with a purple hue. My jewelry; wrist bracelets, ankle bracelets, and circlet were thicker and wider. They were now black mithril, with that same purple hue.

I could feel the power and energy emanating from everything on the pile. "Thank you, Santa." I put on my new armor, weapons, and jewelry, it fit perfectly, and weighed nothing. My arm daggers went back in, as did my throwing knife and staff.

I didn't have time to look through the whole pavilion. This was new to the King, he didn't even know what all it had, or was capable of. It was almost time to wrap up this show. I stepped outside and waved my hand; the pavilion closed. It became swirling pages, then finally into a book that closed in my hand. I held the book to my right thigh; it sank into my body. *"I'm a little paranoid too."*

There were only a handful of enemy troops left. I took my staff bow out and finished them. *"Now for the theatrics."* I caused lightning to strike all over the camp which started a few fires. I let the thunder roll for a bit. I put my helmet up and face shield down. I covered myself in blood, then lifted the fog.

The sun was just rising when I walked out of the enemy camp. I carried the King's head held by its hair. I stopped and picked up an enemy's spear and plunged it into the ground. I put the King's head on it and walked toward the Abbey's gates.

I lowered my helmet so they could see it was me. "Open the gates." Was shouted down from the wall. The King and Reggie were waiting when I came through the gates. As was every trooper. I put on my best thousand-yard stare and walked toward the King. I handed him the crown, "I'll be in the church." and kept walking.

"Of course," The king said.

As I passed Reggie, "I'll be home later." She nodded

The Captain was next on my way, "Captain."

"Sir?"

"Have the men strip the emery camp of anything we can

use and share out the spoils."

"Yes Sir," He bowed.

The troopers had formed a corridor, as I passed, they saluted and bowed; I kept walking. As I reached the church doors, they opened and closed behind me. I made the blood evaporate leaving me clean. I walked toward the front and lay down on the floor feeling the earth refreshing and recharging me.

"That thunder and lightning show was a bit dramatic wasn't it?" I recognized St. Philip's voice and knew he was smiling.

I chuckled, "maybe a little, but everyone loves a show, or so I've heard."

"That's true, they do love a show, it breaks up their boring lives that are spent just trying to survive. What next?"

"Sleep."

"And then?"

"To Port City probably, unless I have to go kill the Volwick Army, and I'd really rather not."

"Rest well brother, I have the watch."

"You have the watch," I smiled and went to sleep.

***

"Woof," I opened one eye. Armor was laying there looking at me. I closed my eye ignoring him. "Woof."

"All right, I'm awake." I rolled over and sat up. I looked at Armor, "Did Reggie send you?" he looked away. "Traitor." I stood up, I didn't feel tired, or sore. I felt refreshed, the earth had recharged me.

I left the church and headed for my pavilion. There were few people inside the walls. Most everyone was out plundering the enemy's camp. It appeared that even the King was walking the battlefield. I glanced over; we had quite the horse herd.

Outside my pavilion stood two enemy guidons with the banner upside down, signifying their defeat. Odd they weren't in front of the King's pavilion.

Armor and I entered; Reggie was in the sitting area reading. She rose and came to me. "You are well, my husband?"

I nodded, "I'm fine I just needed to rest." I hugged her, and she relaxed. "I am hungry though."

"Let's get you out of your armor first." She helped me out of my armor and hung it on the rack.

We moved to the table and sat down. "Steak, eggs, hash browns, and hot tea." My plate appeared, and I set to it.

I saw she was watching me. "I didn't see any wounds, are you ok?"

I took a swallow a tea, "Yes, I'm fine, no wounds, my armor and shields did their job."

"They say you killed everyone." she watched me.

I nodded, "I gave them warnings, and a chance to leave. They ignored both. Word of this will spread. The next time I warn someone they may take me seriously."

"Word will definitely spread, it's already started. Father has decided to leave tomorrow and meet our reinforcements on the way. He also sent word to Midwick of their army's defeat and the death of their King."

I nodded chewing my steak. "Good, we should have a clear road to Port City."

"Why didn't you ransom their King?"

"I don't leave enemies like him alive behind me, who can hurt me. I would have had to kill him, eventually."

"You sound as if you have done this many times before and please don't say you read it in a book. You can be honest with me; we'll face whatever it is together."

I thought a moment, "I have memories of those who have done these things before. I've had these memories with me since I woke up from the serum. They don't control me; they give me experiences to draw upon to make decisions."

She nodded, "tell me if anything changes, I'm here if you need to talk."

"Ok, I will, but I'm ok. Really."

***

We left Fort St. Philip's Abbey at sunrise. Once we were clear, the priests closed the main gates. I hope they used their new home wisely. Someone might try to take it from them, then I'd have to come back.

We followed our normal travel routine, stopped at noon to change horses, eat then move on. Our reinforcements met us at midafternoon. They had brought four companies of cavalry. They joined us on the move, as we continued. We stopped as usual, in late afternoon, and set up our standard camp.

We dined with the Battalion Commander and his four troop Captains. "What is the situation in Port City?" King Briska asked.

"Much the same Sire, sea trade continues, but we've seen more cargo vessels who stay a few days longer than usual once they have sold and bought goods."

The King nodded, "spies looking us over."

The Commander nodded, "we keep a strong presence on the docks and wharfs. We watch them watching us. Crime is down. The southern border has it usual patrol encounters, nothing new there."

"Anything that stands out as odd?"

"Not to me, but I don't hear the daily reports from your staff."

"Excuse me Commander, did you see any Volwick scouts on your way here?" I asked.

"No M'lord, we didn't, they always stay to the south, they never come this far north."

"Thank you, Commander. We ride at first light." The King said. Everyone took that as a dismissal and departed.

The family stayed. "You have concerns, Aaron?" the King asked.

"Is your Commander a competent leader?"

"I don't know him personally, but I would assume so."

"I find it odd, the Volwick Army plays tag with our patrol all the time, so they must be watching us. But then allows a large force to leave Port City and doesn't follow to see where they are headed? And your Commander ignores that and assumes they always stay south. That seems odd to me, and odd makes me curious. I think I'll check our southern route to make sure our southern friends aren't planning any nasty surprises for us between here and home."

"Do you plan on attacking them?" Reggie asked.

"That depends on where they are, and what they are doing. I'm not going there to attack them, but I won't know until I get there. They may not even be there."

"But you don't believe that."

I shook my head, "I do not."

"All right, scout forward, see what we are facing." The King said.

Armor, who was laying at the front entrance growled. I looked at him; he was watching the door. "Speaking of odd." I walked to the entrance and stepped out. Oaks was walking towards me holding Moss by his collar. Moss was staggering drunk.

"Sorry to bother you Captain, but you said if I caught him again, to bring him to you straight away. Drunk on guard duty, Sir." He cut his eyes around.

I sent my Mage Sense out. There were a lot of the new troops gathered close to the King's Pavilion. That in itself was not unusual, but Oaks' actions were all wrong. I nodded, "I guess the threat of the lash wasn't enough. This will cost you ten Moss, wait here." I turned and stuck my head inside the pavilion. "We have enemy in the camp seal the pavilion, we'll take care of it." I left before anyone replied. I turned back to Oaks and Moss. "Bring him." I started walking back to my area, with them following.

"I take it we have trouble?"

"A butt load. Those new troops ain't ours, or they have turned coats. None of our boys know any of them, which is possible, but they volunteered to take all the duties so we could rest. No troopers do that, no matter what army you're in. The Captain sent us to warn you. Our men, in our red cloaks, are gathering in small pockets getting ready for the party to kick off."

I nodded looking around. "Pass the word, I will start a diversion on the road in ten minutes. Ignore what you hear, when it starts converge on the King's Pavilion, and protect the King."

"Yes, Sir," and continued their way.

I sank into the earth and moved to the Battalion Commander's tent. "We strike at first guard change," the Commander was briefing his Captains. "Two companies will attack as quietly as possible, one company held in reserve, and one company goes to the King's Pavilion."

"Yes Commander," They answered.

"If we do this right, we'll all be rich," They all laughed. "You have your orders." They saluted and left his tent.

I opened a cave around me. I thought through what I wanted to do. I rose to just beneath the Commander's tent. I reached up, grabbed him, and pulled him under. I took him straight down to the cave. He was screaming when I left him. I smiled; he could scream all he wanted no one would hear him down there.

I put the guise of the Commander on and rose into his tent. I cast an illusion spell of an army marching toward us and made it loud enough to be clearly heard. I stepped out of the tent looking toward the road, as was everyone else.

"Captain."

"Yes, Commander?"

"Our Army's Vanguard approaches, get the Battalion into formation."

"Yes Commander." He started shouting orders.

I went back into the tent and sank into the earth. I dropped the Commander's guise and moved to the King's pavilion. Our men were arriving. I emerged out of sight and walked to them.

"Captain Motts."

"Yes, sir?"

I've captured and secured their Commander. If they want to surrender, we'll let them. If not, well, they made their choice. We won't risk our men being nice about it.

He smiled. "Yes, Sir." He gave the orders, "battle formation, archers to the rear."

The men formed up spear-lances held ready. These men had not been battle tested, not really. Now they would be. Let them see how their armor, shields and weapons performed.

I stayed in the background. Rodrigo-San was also in the rear. I guess he wanted in on some action. When they were ready, I ended the illusion. The camp was dead silent. The only light was from the few scattered fires around camp.

I conjured a ball of light and threw it up. It levitated over the camp, giving us enough light to see the whole area.

Their battalion looked up at the light, and then around, in confusion.

I amplified my voice. "Your treachery has failed, your Commander taken prisoner. Surrender and be spared. Fight and you will all die."

CHAPTER 13

I'll say this for them, it didn't take long for them to decide.

"Attack!" Their Senior Captain shouted. They rushed us in mass, no coordinated effort. They thought to just bull right over us.

"Prepare lance-shields," Captain Motts ordered. When the charging troopers were with-in ten paces, "Shields." He ordered. The front rank plunged their lances into the ground forming our shield wall and drew their swords. "Archers, fire."

The enemy charged head-long onto our shield wall and were stopped cold. Their front rank was crushed by the ranks behind them and could not defend themselves. The killing began in earnest. It was a slaughter; they had no enchanted armor, shields, or weapons. They didn't realize how fast they were being killed. The rear thought they were winning and continued to push forward. There were no survivors. When it was done, a cheer went up for the victors. They were all now blooded warriors, and proud of themselves.

I stepped to the pavilion, "Inform the King the fighting is over, and we secure the camp." I stepped back and waited. A moment later the King stepped out in full armor. I bowed, "The men fought well, Sire."

"Losses?"

"None, Sire."

"Excuse me Sire, one." Captain Motts said. We looked at him. Rodrigo-San. A freak accident, an arrow ricocheted off a shield, and went through his throat.

He nodded, walking forward looking over the battleground. "Well done, men, very well done." Another cheer went up. He turned back to me, "The Commander?"

"I have him in a holding cell, before I question him. Do you wish to be there?"

"Do I need to be?" he asked looking steady at me.

I shook my head, "No Sire, I'll take care of it." He nodded and went back into his pavilion.

"Captain."

"Sir?"

"Strip the battlefield and divide the spoils."

"Yes, Sir."

I found Rodrigo-San. I raised a crypt for him, the King presided, and we lay him to rest with honors. *"I guess if you got to go, it's best if it's a surprise. Rest well my friend."*

✳✳✳

I stood in full armor face shield down watching the Commander. My night vision was far better than any electronic NVG's I had ever worn. He was sitting, head back against the wall. He seemed asleep. I waved my hand, and it sounded like a large snake hissing, and slithering around. He jumped to his feet moving along the wall away from the sound. One hand on the wall, the other held out toward the sound. I stopped the sound, and he stopped moving, listening for movement.

"Who paid you to turn traitor?"

He jumped. My voice sounded loud in the darkness. I tossed a ball of light up. I made it bright; he had to cover his eyes with his arms. My face shield compensated, so it looked normal to me.

"Who is your master?"

He held up his right hand. On his wrist he wore a warded bracelet. "You can't use your magic to make me talk."

"I guess we'll have to do it the old fashion way then." In one motion I drew my sword and cut off his hand. His hand and the bracelet fell to the floor. I flicked my finger, and the bracelet came to me. I dropped it in my pouch. I set the bloody stump of a wrist on fire cauterizing it. He dropped to his knees screaming, trying to put the fire out. He fell face forward into the dirt unconscious, I put the fire out.

I searched through my joined memories to see if there was a way to take memories that didn't need me to stick my hand into his brains. There was, it was extremely painful for them, unless they were unconscious. At this point, for this person, I really didn't care. I waited for him to wake.

"Are you ready to talk?" He said nothing cradling his burned stump. "Round two then." I levitated him bringing him to me. Of course, I had to give him a show. I held my glowing red hand up before his face. "Tell me what I want to know, or I will pull your brains out through your eyes." He started thrashing about. I cast my spell, "Tell me all I want to know." He started screaming and convulsing. After a few seconds he passed out, I took all the information he had. He was not a nice guy. I lay him on the ground. I sifted through the gained information while I waited for him to wake.

When he woke, he rolled over and puked until his stomach was empty. He held his head groaning.

"You and General Shakes have been naughty, Commander." He groaned, and dry-heaved. "Let's go talk to the King, shall we?" I grabbed his collar and took us up to his tent. I walked him out and toward the King's pavilion. There were now guards outside it I stopped, pointed at the ground, "sit." The Commander sat.

It was now mid-morning, so I was sure the King was up. I entered the Pavilion, and the King and Queen were there, at their table. I bowed, "Sire, M'lady."

"Come in, tea?" The King asked.

"Please." I came forward taking the offered seat. The Queen poured my cup and handed it to me. "Thank you."

"You have news?" The King asked.

I took a swallow at the tea nodding. "I have. The person behind this little mess is General Shakes."

"What?! Are you sure?"

I nodded, "there is no doubt. He has also subverted half of the commanders in your army, although I don't have all their names yet."

"Is the Commander still alive?"

"Oh yes, he's right outside."

"Guards." one of the guards came in.

"Yes, Sire."

"Bring the prisoner in."

He bowed, "Yes Sire."

They brought the Commander in. He stood before the King cradling his burned stump.

"Why?" The King asked. The Commander said nothing.

I levitated him off the floor. "Round three?" I asked.

"For gold. For riches, and power." He answered. I dropped him. He hit the floor, groaning holding his stump.

"Tell him the rest." I said

He looked at me, then the King. "General Stakes promised us riches and has been paying us double our pay for the last year. Your time is over, we decided since the Kingdom was going to fall anyway, we might as well profit from it. We'll be part of the new ruling class."

"Who else is involved?"

"I only knew of my four captains. Only the General Stakes knows everyone."

"Tell him where your pay was coming from." I said.

He laughed, "The Royal treasury, The General is carrying more troops on the rolls than actually exist."

"How many more?" The King asked leaning forward.

"At least six battalions, maybe more." The King leaned back. The King's eyes became hard. "You have been found guilty of treason and are sentenced to death. Do you have any last words?"

The Commander's shoulders slumped, "No."

The King looked at me and nodded. I flicked my wrist, and the Commander's neck snapped, he fell over dead. The guard took his body and left.

I poured myself more hot tea. "According to the Commander, Volwick's Army has pulled out, and are heading home. There are no other enemies between us and Port City."

"We just have to clean out a nest of vipers. This will be

messy."

"Maybe not too messy. I have the information on General Shakes. Let me go ahead of you and cut off the heads of the vipers, the bodies will wither and die."

"You're suggesting I stay here while you go ahead?"

I shook my head, "No, we head for Port City in the morning, you should be there, in what? The day after?" He nodded. "By then I'll have General Shakes, and his commanders is a dungeon. When you arrive, we'll finish cleaning house."

"How long will it take you to get there?"

"I'm not sure, six hours I'm guessing."

"You can fly that long at one time?"

I shrugged, "I don't know I've never tried. If you approve, I'll leave tonight, to give myself plenty of time to get there, and to do my part."

He sat thinking; I drank my tea, waiting. After a time, he shook his head. "I don't like it, but of the options we have, it's the least bad one."

The Queen set listening, "what of Reggie?"

"She stays with you, that way I can concentrate on what I have to do without worrying about her safety."

"She won't like it." The Queen said.

I nodded, "I don't like it, but I think it's our best option to end this with the least amount of bloodshed."

"Well, don't get killed, if you do, I'll never hear the end of it." The King said smiling.

I laughed, "I'll do my best."

"And you have to tell Reggie," He said. I stopped laughing, and he started.

***

Reggie was not happy, "father agreed to this idea?" I nodded. "Was the Queen there?"

I nodded, "yes."

She nodded, "when do you leave?"

"In a few hours. Everyone else leaves at sunrise."

"Promise me you will be in full armor at all times." I nodded. "All right, it sounds like you have thought this through. Let's eat and enjoy dinner before you go."

"A bath first." I said. She smiled and took my hand.

***

I had been levitating flying for an hour. I could tell I was using a lot of energy. I landed and sank into the earth. I could feel the earth recharging me as I rested. I started moving underground toward Port City and found I could recharge on the move.

I went deeper into the earth to swim or fly under rivers, and crags. I kept going faster and still able to recharge. I concentrated and flew faster. I reached Port City in three hours. I went under the castle and rested for a while. While I rested, I sent my Mage Sense out and learned the lay-out of the castle.

I went to the dungeon; it was empty. I concentrated on the wall and sealed off the door to the dungeon. I found the keys to the cells and made sure they were all locked. I put the keys inside a wall for safe keeping.

The General Stakes' quarters were here in the castle, I went up through the walls to his room. He was asleep. I cast a deep sleeping spell on him and took him down to one of the cells in the dungeon. I lay him on the floor and cast the information taking spell. I stayed with it, taking everything, I thought I might need. He and his group had been busy. I now knew who all his people were and where all the gold and supplies he had stolen were.

I also found out who the General was working for. Well the person, not the Kingdom. He was a Master Merchant named Nee-Carr. He represented an overseas nation that had promised to make General Shakes the Governor of the Kingdom. Giving them a toehold to expand into the North and South Kingdoms, Of course the Other kingdoms didn't know about that part of the deal.

I went back to his quarters and put his adjutant in a deep sleep. He was his second in command of this little operation. I took his information. It was much the same as the generals, but the adjutant had been skimming, fattening his purse. *"It's hard to get good help these days. The dungeon is going to get crowded."*

I started down the list. There were ten Battalion Commanders, fifty Captains, various officers in procurement, supply and finance. Some of those had sergeants working for them. I had to expand the dungeon.

By the time I was finished, I had 116 prisoners in the dungeon. I left them all sleeping. It had taken me most of the day to gather them all. I had to wait until they were alone before I took them. I wanted this to be a complete secret, or at least a complete surprise.

I went down under the castle and opened a cavern. I made it big enough to open my pavilion book, as I now thought of it. I pulled the pavilion book out of my leg," Open." The book jumped out of my hand and opened.

I went inside, "Welcome Your Highness." she said.

I smiled, "Not yet, Captain will do for now."

"Yes, Captain."

"Seal the doors." The ceiling flashed green. I was underground in a cavern I made, but some habits you don't want to get out of. I sat down at the table. "Beef stew, hot buttered rolls, cherry pie, and cold sweet tea." I loved these tables.

After dinner I looked around to see what the previous owner, the king, had left me. I looked through his wardrobe; he was a bit of a clotheshorse. On the upside I now had plenty of clothes, shoes, and boots to wear. And since he had been a King, they were all made of the finest materials.

He also liked to indulge himself. His bathroom was more of a small heated pool, and steam room. Don't get me wrong I used and enjoyed it. After my bath I went to the sitting area. "Are there any books?"

"Yes, in the library on the second floor."

"What?"

"Yes, in the library on the second floor?" I thought a moment,

"How many floors are there?"

"At the present, there are only two."

"Where are the stairs?" A green light came on over a curtain, I opened the curtain to a staircase and followed them up. Sure enough, there was a library. Larger than the one back at home. Well, Aaron's home. There was a large table as well as a sitting area.

"It's nice to be King."

***

After resting a while, I went back to the offices, and homes of the leaders who had kept records of what they had done and were doing. I gathered all the records to give to the King, as evidence. Next, I recovered the gold, gems, and jewels they had stored in various vaults, and chest. I teleported the valuables to the Royal treasury. The King would be happy about that.

I had saved Nee-Carr for last. He was on a cargo ship in the harbor. Which I suspected was not a cargo ship at all, at least not only a cargo ship. I travelled underground when I got to the harbor; I opened an underground cavern to serve as a temp holding cell. I went up through the water to the cargo ship. I stopped below the ship looking up at it. It was strange hovering here underwater breathing like standing on dry land.

I sent out my Mage Sense and looked the ship over. It was heavily warded, but only from the top there was nothing stopping me from coming up from underneath. I went up into the wood of the ship. It was strange, as long as I stayed "in the wood", no matter how thick, I was completely hidden.

I searched the ship from inside the wood. It was a spy ship. It carried cargo to maintain its cover. I found Nee-Carr in his quarters. He was asleep. I cast the deep sleep spell, but nothing happened. I looked closer he was wearing warded jewelry.

"Ok, we do it the hard way." I reached up and grabbed him and pulled him under. He struggled, but I was able to take him down and drop him in the cavern. I punched him in the temple, knocking him out. I used his hand to take off the warded bracelet. I put it in my pouch, to study later.

I cast the deep sleep spell, then the info spell. He was in fact a military spy for Kingdom of Dunwich, one of this kingdom's biggest trading partners. Their King was getting greedy. There were also two other ships in port right now awaiting the attack orders. They would attack when the rest of the fleet arrived. All their crews were active duty Navy. It was going to be a long night.

I went back up to the ship, to crew berthing and cast the beguiling spell. "The traitors are trying to kill you. Kill them all." It was like a match to gas. In less than an hour no one was left alive on the spy ship. I told the ship's wood to get the bodies and blood off the ship. The bodies, and blood sank into the wood to be expelled into the harbor. Fish needed to eat too.

I went under to the next ship. This ship was different there were men in cages, or more like jail cells throughout the ship. I went to the captain's quarters, put him under, and took his info. The ship's cargo was, for lack of a better word, gladiator mercenaries. They fought for their freedom. Once the attack started, they would be loosed to cause havoc and chaos. If they survived, they would be freed... Supposedly... They were all Navy, or former Navy under a death penalty. I might be able to work with this.

I broke the captain's neck and left him where he lay. I did the same to the rest of the crew that were not mercenaries. I went down into the hold and got a keg of rum. I opened the main cell door and went into the holding area. With a wave at my hand I unlocked all the cell door.

"All right men bring your cups get your ration of rum." They came out and lined up. They were watching me and looking around for the rest of the crew. I waited until they all had filled their cups.

"I have a proposition for you. Hear me out before you do or say anything. I want you to fight for me. Not just for your freedom, but for gold. Dunwich wanted you to fight and die. I want you to fight and live. I've taken this ship. I want you to man it and sail her out to find Dunwich ships and take them. We'll split the spoils; I'll buy the captured ship from you. I'll resupply you and out you go again."

"Once we sail out what do we need you for?"

"You don't. You could do all those things on your own. But, if you do them for me, you'll have a safe port to resupply and a place to sell all your captured booty. And, it will all be legal. You'll be sailing for the crown, you're not pirates."

"You'll be the captain?"

I shook my head, "No, that will be one of you. You've fought together, know each other. I'm not a sailor, I'd be in the way."

"You said we'll be free, after we take how many ships?"

"None, if you agree you're free right now. If you need resupply, we'll do that, if not you'll leave tomorrow. I'll tell you what, you think about it. I've got to go take another ship over there and make them the same offer. I'll be back for your answer," I teleported down to the cavern. "That'll give them something to think about." I smiled.

The other ship turned out to be a supply ship for the incoming fleet and was crewed by active duty Navy. Well, as I said, fish must eat too. I now owned Two ships... that the King would probably take, unless I didn't tell him. *I have to make a living too.*" I laughed.

I teleported all the gold from the third ship to the pavilion cavern. I teleported to the spy ship and teleported half of all the gold, gems, and jewels to the pavilion cavern.

I teleported back to the deck of the merc-ship and walked down to see the mercs. "So, what have you decided?"

A man stepped forward, "We'll take your deal, my name is Wilks, the men have chosen me as their Captain. We don't need resupplying We can leave now, if you're agreeable."

"I'm agreeable Captain Wilks. Good hunting." I shook his

hand.

"And your name Sir Mage?"

"Prince Aaron, Princess Regina's husband and Consort. I've left the gold on board for you to resupply in foreign ports when needed."

He bowed "Thank you, M'lord."

They sailed with-in the hour.

I teleported down to my pavilion, put my spoils in my vault, and went to bed.

CHAPTER 14

I woke early, worked out, had breakfast, and started writing reports on all the prisoners. I didn't want to have to sit and recite everything I knew about them. The good news was I just laid my hand on my notebooks page and it transcribed everything.

Most everyone only took a page, the General took three. Master Merchant Nee-Carr took three pages as well. I fudged a little on the amount of gold recovered and the two additional ships I took. That was a need to know line item, and he didn't need to know. With that complete, I closed my pavilion and travelled under to meet the King's Company.

I emerged well ahead of them and waited beside the road. Reggie had told them to expect me and Gray was saddled and ready for me.

We talked as we rode. "Any trouble?" The King asked.

"None worth mentioning Sire, I did have to expand your dungeon. We had more guests than anticipated." I said smiling.

"They won't be staying long, I think."

"We also have a foreign spy from Dunwich. He is the one buying off your General."

"Dunwich? You're sure?"

"Yes, Sire. I have it all documented." I handed him the briefing book I made. "He was on his spy ship in the harbor. We now own it and its cargo. Master Merchant Nee-Carr awaits your pleasure as well."

The King took the book and thumbed through it. "You recovered the gold from the treasury?"

I nodded," The totals are on the last page, well as close as I could tell on short notice anyway." He flipped to the last pages.

"I will skin him alive, then hang him. How many had he

139

turned?"

"116, all are in the dungeon."

"I'm not even going to ask. On another subject, the spoils you took, specifically the arms, armor, and horses. The Crown will buy them from you. I will levy a fifty percent tax against the amount. You will receive the difference. The coach and pavilion are yours with my thanks for your service. What of the special arms, and equipment you issued the company?"

"The equipment remains with the company to be used by the troops of the company from now on. We would probably have survived, but it would have been ugly. They are now the elite of your army."

He nodded, "Our Army Captain."

I nodded, "Our Army, Sire."

"Go see your wife before I have to hear about it." He said smiling. I laughed and dropped back beside Reggie.

"About time you got back." She said smiling. "You were successful?"

"I was. All the conspirators are in the King's dungeon, and gold recovered."

"How many were there?"

"116, and most were officers."

She stared at me. "116."

I nodded.

"That's not good. I thought maybe ten or twenty at the most. But a 116. Lord have mercy."

I gave Reggie the high points on the way in to pass the time. She had a quick mind and asked good questions.

"Father needs to call up the army and expand our Army right away."

"That would be a good first step. I have a few other ideas I'll suggest to him when this dust settles."

***

The King had sent riders ahead so by the time we arrived

the castle staff was ready to receive us. I had Oaks park my coach in the inner courtyard. I had a feeling I was going to need it. I had not taken the time to look around the castle much. Now that I took the time, how could I say this nicely, it needed work, or TLC.

"I ask that you have patience." Reggie said, "We don't have a wing, or an apartment. We have my room for the time being."

"I have an idea, let's take over the General and his adjutant's quarters. They have other accommodations and will no longer need them. Or, we could stay in our pavilion until things settle."

She nodded, "I honestly like the pavilion idea. I'll let mother know. Stay close I have a feeling father will call on you soon."

Soon turned out to be the next morning. We all ate breakfast together. "I read through your report last night. Very thorough." I said nothing. "As soon as we finish eating, we'll hold a closed court and get this business over with. I don't want a scandal or to cause a panic."

When the King and Queen were seated and ready. "Bring up the General." I looked through the floor and concentrated on the General. I teleported him up before the King. I stood to the side but between him and the King.

"Sire, I must protest!"

"Be silent, or I'll have you gutted where you stand." I guess he believed him, he stayed quiet. His trial was the reading of my report, the General listened. The more that was read the more his shoulders slumped.

"We have found you guilty of treason and conspiring to overthrow the Crown. I sentence you to death, and I don't care if you have any last words." The King cast his spell and broke the General's neck.

The rest of the trials were a copy of the first. I brought them up, the King read the report of their activities and they would be executed.

The last to come before the King was Master Merchant Nee-Carr. I teleported him into the throne room. As soon as he was there, he started an incantation. I threw a knife pinning his foot to the floor. That broke his concentration. I punched him in the temple dropping him to his knees.

"Next time I won't be so nice." I said getting him to his feet.

"Well, Sir Spy, you have been busy."

"I have done nothing I am a peaceful merchant."

The King began reading but stopped halfway through.

"I have information to trade maybe we could come to an agreement."

"Oh? what kind of information?"

"The names of those who are working against you."

The King read of the list of names who had been tried and executed. He continued reading the report on Nee-Carr.

Nee-Carr looked at me, "my compliments, well done." I gave a slight bow of my head.

"Why?" the King asked.

Nee-Carr shrugged, "because Kings are greedy."

The King busted out laughing, "I can't argue with that."

"I follow orders, my King says do thus, I do thus."

"Duty, I can understand," the King said, "You will be my guest until I decide what to do with you."

He bowed, "You are most kind, Sire."

A servant came in. "Show our guest to his room. Make sure he has what he needs."

"Yes, Sire."

"Before you go," I said. I healed his foot. "We can't have you tracking blood all over the place."

He tried his foot. "Thank you." I nodded. He followed the servant out.

When we were alone, "what are you going to do with him?" The King asked, smiling,

I chuckled, "I hadn't really thought about it. I'll have to get back to you on that. Any preferences?"

"None, you decide." I nodded.

"Come, let's go have some tea." the King said. I followed him and the Queen back to their sitting room. Reggie was already there. I took the offered seat, and servants brought us tea.

Reggie poured our tea. "So," the King started, "We have the threat of invasion from the South-east, the North, and the East, overseas. Your father, who always bears watching, holds the North West." He watched me as he spoke. I nodded. "You will someday be advisor to the Queen. If that were now what would your advice be?"

I took a swallow of my tea gathering my thoughts. "The first thing I would do would be to consolidate my army. We've gotten rid of the rot in our leadership, which means some units lack leadership. We need to correct that..." I almost said ASAP.

"Go on."

"Next call up half of your militia and make sure they are trained, armed and ready to fight. Which could be at any moment. Once they are trained, start rotating the trained units with the other half of the untrained ones. Block off our harbor, so we control entry to it. Raise our Navy, to start with, by issuing 'Letters of Marque' to armed merchant ships." I was expecting the question, so I waited sipping my tea.

"What is a 'Letter of Marque'?"

"It is when the Crown gives permission to a kingdom's merchant ships to capture enemy cargo ships. The Crown gets half the spoils, the capturing ship the other half. The Crown buys the captured ship at a reduced price, recrew it, and sends it out to do the same again."

"So, it's legalized piracy."

"In a nutshell, yes. But when you have little or nothing, you do what you must. And since we have closed our harbor, we must start patrolling our coast looking for where they may land their army, should they press the war."

"What about Midwick, and Volwick?"

"I don't think we will have to worry about Midwick. Unless I miss my guess, my father is already making a move against them. Volwick we keep an eye on."

"Anything else?"

I thought a moment, I already knew what I wanted to say, but I wanted them to think I had considered things, which I had.

"Repair and expand the castle or built a new one."

The King laughed, "You repaired St. Philip's Abbey?"

I nodded, "partially."

"I approve of your thinking, a well thought out plan. I have promoted a colonel to General and given him the task of reorganizing the army. Letters are being prepared to call up the militia. You may restrict harbor entry and issue the 'Letters of Marque'. I want to hear more of this plan to expand, or build a new castle, but not now. Give me a few days."

"Of course, Sire." I took that as my dismissal. Reggie stayed behind. Once I was out of the room, I stepped "inside" the wall and went back to eavesdrop, or spy to be honest. I hadn't known these people very long and did not know what their mind set was. Everyone has self-interest, I didn't know how deep it went.

"Where are his loyalties?" the King asked Reggie.

"He is not like his father and brother. He is not blind to their actions."

"He may still have motivations of his own. Where does he come up with these things? Letters of Marque?"

"He reads a lot, History, Armies, tactics, whatever he finds."

"He must. I'm just having trouble trusting him completely. He does not ask for anything."

"So, your complaint is, he does not ask for money. He basically gives you all the spoils he fought for, and that's why you don't trust him? What would you do if he pitched a fit about the Crown taking half of his spoils in a tax? Do you tax the other Royals, and courtiers at that rate?"

"That's different, these were spoils, they were free to him."

"They cost him blood. I think he will be friendly if you let him, but he will only be pushed so far until he reacts. And when he reacts, it is with violence. And as far as I know, no one has survived it. Treat him fairly and he will do the same." She got up and left.

"She is right," the Queen said. "It has gone beyond testing his motives. If you are pushing him for a reason, I understand. But I seem to remember a story his little brother told about him having teeth." The King said nothing, only nodded.

***

I went underground and down to the harbor. I came up in an alley out of sight. I walked the wharfs looking at the state of repair until I found the Harbor Master's office. There was one old man in the office, he looked up as I entered.

He stood, "How can I help you M'lord?"

"You are the Harbor Master?"

"I am."

"My Name is Prince Aaron, I'm Princess Regina's husband."

He bowed "welcome M'lord."

"Thank you, I come seeking knowledge. The King has set me a task, and I need your help to do it correctly."

"How may I serve?"

"Let's take a walk." He came from around his desk and followed me outside.

I talked as we walked, "let's play a 'what if' game. What if, let's say by magic you could have new wharfs, new buildings, a new harbor gateway where would you put them? Where would be the best place to put all of it?"

He nodded, "Oh, I understand. Well, let's see. Since we are wishing, I'd make all these wooden wharfs stone with piers jutting out into the harbor for the ships to tie off to."

"What about the depth of the harbor?"

"Oh, she's plenty deep all the way around."

"Let's say I wanted to restrict entrance to the harbor and, in case of attack, close it off completely?"

He looked to the harbor mouth. "The harbor mouth is pretty wide. On the right-side is the beginning of rocks and a reef, but it doesn't extend into the mouth. That would take a lot of building. I guess if we could have or do anything, you could put rock on both sides of the mouth and build out across the mouth as much as you wanted. But the water is fifty feet deep there."

"Any crazy currents to worry about?"

"Not really, she's pretty peaceful."

"What is your greatest need on the waterfront?"

"Storage space, warehousing. It's always a fight for storage space for cargo coming and going."

"I don't know about here, and I not accusing anyone. But what about smuggling? I'm talking about the dangerous things not an extra roll of silk here and there."

"It's that way in every port, the only way to slow it is to wall off the wharf from the city. That would slow it, but not stop it."

I nodded. I waved my hand, and a masa rose from the ground. It had a 3D model of the harbor area on it. He looked at it smiling.

"If I understand you, what we are talking about is something like this." I waved my hand and the model changed showing the proposed changes. We had talked about. I had walled off the wharfs, added warehouses, added stone wharfs with piers out into the harbor. I added rocks and reefs at the mouth with forts on either side and a great stone chain stretched between the forts. There was also a city gate that separated the wharf from the city, it was a small fort.

He studied the model, looking at it from different angles. "Can you add more warehouses down on the beach end? Extend the rocks and reef further down to protect that end?"

I made the changes; he looked it over again. "The wharf needs to be wider to handle the heavier traffic to the warehouses." I made the changes. "I'm not a military expert, but I'd make the forts bigger and armed to the teeth."

I chuckled, "sound advice. Any reason the other side of the harbor is bare?"

"Not that I know of, the harbors good over there. They just built on this side first and never have done anything over there."

"Thank you, Harbor Master. I appreciate your help."

He bowed and went on his way. I had all the information I needed. Now I just needed to make it happen.

***

Reggie and I ate alone in our coach pavilion. "Do anything interesting this afternoon?"

I smiled," Nope, not a thing."

"Don't make me choke you." We laughed.

"I was down at the harbor seeing what it would take to protect it. I figured while I was at it, I'd improve the wharf."

"Really? what did you find?"

"The Harbor Master and I had a good meeting, and he helped me with some good ideas." I raised the harbor model from the table, so she could see it.

"That looks wonderful. When do you plan on starting?"

"Tonight. We need the harbor secured as soon as possible."

She nodded. "I agree. Is there anything I can do to help?"

"I'm not sure. Where do your talents lie?"

"So far I can manipulate fire."

"Oh good, you can burn the wharf down and I'll rebuild them." She screamed and jumped on me. I was going to be late getting started on the wharfs.

***

I waited until two AM to start my urban renewal program. I went underground to the harbor. First, I added the rocks and reefs outside the harbor. I raised bedrock up under the harbor's building foundations. With the model in mind, I went to work. I replaced the wooden wharfs with wide stone ones. I added the piers, the warehouses, and walled off the wharf area from the city. I added the city gate fort.

I raised two forts, one on each side of the harbor mouth. I built them to jut out into the harbor mouth narrowing it. I suspended a huge stone chain between the two forts. I enchanted the chain, so it didn't weigh so much. I made the forts a good size and put reefs around them to protect them. I would arm them later.

It had not taken me long to raise the stone buildings. I was tired and rested in the earth. I put on the guise of a fisherman and went up to the wharf. The new buildings did cause a stir. I started a conversation, with no one in particular.

"It was the Prince that did this."

"What Prince?" One of the crowd asked.

"The new one that married Princess Regina. Prince Aaron. He said the King wanted to help the people and protect the harbor so, Prince Aaron fixed everything." That was all it took. Gossip took over from there. I went to breakfast.

"How did it turn out?" Reggie asked

"Good. You may want to send word to the city watch to man the new city gate at the wharf. And send a like message to the army to man the new forts at the harbor mouth. I spent a lot of energy, so I need to rest."

She nodded. "I'll take care of it." She kissed me on the head as she left.

CHAPTER 15

"It's called a ballista or bolt thrower," I explained. I had made mine like a giant crossbow verses the tension type. "You hook this, to this rope." I demonstrated. "You then crank this to draw it back until it locks in place, like so. You take the pull rope off the bolt rope like this. Then you lay the bolt in the grooves right here. You aim at your target, by turning the base, and raising it up or down. When you are ready, you pull this lever to release or fire the bolt." I made sure everyone was clear. "You must give commands, so it kills no one on the team. It would sound something like this."

"Weapon ready to fire: All clear to fire: Fire." I had made practice bolts for them to train on. The real ones would be metal tipped. I made four ballista per fort. The men began training on them as soon as I showed them what to do.

"And these bolts will go through the side of a ship?"

"Yep. We can even set some of the bolts on fire before we shoot them and set fire to the ships."

I spent some time warding the forts against magical attacks. It probably wouldn't stop everything, but it would help.

I went to see the Harbor Master," Amazing M'lord, truly amazing. I never expected to see anything like this in my lifetime."

"It turned out rather nice. Tell me, who handles the collection of fees from the warehouse rental?"

"I have been."

"Fine, that first warehouse is mine. The rest you may rent."

"Of course, M'lord,"

"I'll bring my manager by so you can meet him." he bowed.

I travelled under to the castle. I found Nee-Carr in the library. "Good place to spend time."

"It's peaceful." he answered.

"Tell me, your cover as a Master Merchant, are you really a Master Merchant?"

"I am, if I were not, the real ones would know it, and I could not carry out my missions. Besides my King made me earn my money, which he taxed,"

"Yes, I've heard kings are greedy." We smiled. "Do you have a family? Wife? Children?"

"I do not, they would have been in danger. I decided not to give anyone leverage to use against me."

"So, no real reason to go back to Dunwich?"

He shrugged. "Not really."

I nodded. "The King has tasked me of deciding what to do with you. I can't send you home. I can't release you, not yet anyway. How would you like to work for me?"

"As a spy?"

"As a merchant, here in our port."

"You would trust me?"

I chuckled, "let's be real. I can put a bracelet on you that will tell me if you work against my or the kingdoms interests. You work for me as a merchant, I'll finance you. You make us rich."

"I am known, and if anyone from my country sees me…"

"I'll give you a guise ring that will change your appearance. You will be free within the city. Someday after all this is over, you can leave, but who knows you may enjoy working for me."

"At what percentages?"

"fifty-fifty after expenses, which would include the King's taxes." We laughed.

"Why?"

"We are both new here, we have no friends, only enemies, I need to make money, you need a job."

"That simple?"

"I'm a simple man."

He laughed, "not on your worst day."

"It would be better than watching the world go by from this library's window, would it not?"

He looked around, "True. When do we start?"

"I'll see you in a day or two, I have to make the jewelry." I left him reading.

The guise ring I already had, I adjusted it so it would show only one guise. The loyalty bracelet took a while to get right. I didn't want it burning his hand off just because he said, "I hate my job."

***

"You caused quite the stir in the harbor," Reggie said. "It seems the King had you build a new harbor for the good of the people."

"Well, if that's what they say, it must be true."

"At any rate father is happy for the good will from the people."

"It helps to keep the people on our side."

"What are you up to today?"

"Surveying the castle to see what needs repairing."

"I'll be working with father. See you at dinner."

She kissed me and was gone. I went up through the castle to the library. Nee-Carr was there and alone. I went out onto the hallway and came in through the door. "Good morning."

"Good morning," he said standing.

I held up the guise ring. "It only does one guise. Hold the thought of how you want to look in your mind as you put it on. That will be the look you get from this ring." He nodded. I gave him the ring.

He closed his eyes in concentration and put the ring on. The color of his hair and eyes changed. He now had a close-trimmed beard. "Well?"

"Looks good, not too much of a change, but good." I handed him the loyalty bracelet. He looked at it. "If you act against me, or the Kingdom it will burn into your skin and I will know you have betrayed me." He nodded, took a deep breath and fastened the bracelet around his left wrist. It sank under his skin out of sight. He felt his wrist, then shrugged.

"I have a request."

"And that would be?"

"I would like to get my clothes and personal items from my old ship."

I thought a moment, "if someone were to look through those things would they know they had belonged to you?"

"Not specifically, they are all common enough items."

"Ok, are you ready to go?"

"Yes."

I teleported us to his cabin on the ship. He sagged a moment, then was ok.

"Lay everything you want to take on the bunk." He nodded, when he was through, I cast my spell putting everything in a crystal. I gave it to him. "When you are ready, step on, and break the crystal." He put the crystal in his pocket.

We walked to the Harbor Master's office where I introduced my Master Merchant Dov-ess. Then to our warehouse. I made a second-story apartment for him to live in, and a basement with a vault for our money. I gave him a purse of gold for him to use to furnish his apartment and for personal expenses.

I concentrated and teleported a chest of gold into the vault below. I took him down and showed him the vault and the gold. "That should be enough to get you started."

He opened it and looked. "It will do," he said smiling.

I took him out to my captured cargo ship. "You may recognize her." He nodded. "Your first task is to set up a business charter. Sell the cargo. Hire a captain and crew."

"You'll need to find a special captain and crew?"

"What kind of special?" I explained about Letters of Marque.

"We will also need fifty fighters to go on the ship to take Dunwich ships." I watched this reaction.

He thought a bit, "they will be a shady bunch."

"To say the least, one step away from pirates."

"Not even a whole step. Ok, I can accept that."

"I, or should I say we, already have a ship out on a cruise to take other ships. I'll try to be here when they come in." He nodded. "Can you think of anything else you need right now?"

"Not at the moment, but I'll let you know,"

"Good, go make us rich."

***

I surveyed the castle. The first thing I did was to raise bedrock up under the foundations. There were several weak places, and the bedrock solved those problems. I raised the places that had settled but stopped there. I wanted to see what the King had to say about my building things. I wanted to see if he would become demanding.

A week had passed before the question came up. "What did you do with Nee-Carr?" The King asked during one of our meetings.

"He tried to escape; he didn't make it."

He nodded, "have you looked into the castle repairs?"

"I have, and I raised bedrock up under the weak places in the foundations before it got any worse. I did nothing else until we talked. I didn't want to overstep, I'm sure you have some things you'd like to see done."

"I have some things I'd like changed, but I'd like to see some of your ideas."

I raised a masa up from the floor. I made the model look like Bourtange Fort in the Netherlands. It was a pentagon design with arrowheads at each point of the pentagon. I made lower walls on the perimeters and high walls inside. The Castle proper was in the center pentagon. The base of the pentagon was in the harbor. Moats completely encircled the complex.

The King, Queen, and Reggie got up and looked at the model.

"How big is it?" The King asked.

"As big as you want it, but this model looks like this by the harbor." I shrunk the model down and included the harbor, and the city so they would have an idea of its size.

"That is a city in itself."

"It could be or scaled down to just the bare minimum."

"How long would it take you to raise such a structure?" the Queen asked.

"I'm not sure, I've done nothing this big. This would help protect our harbor and the land side."

"And what would you do with this castle?" The King asked.

I shrugged, "turn it over to the army, or the city, or remove it altogether. If you remove it, turn it into an open-air market, are a few thoughts."

"Interesting ideas, we will think on them."

I bowed, "Yes, Sire." I took that as my dismissal and left.

We talked as we ate dinner in our pavilion. "Father liked your ideas but is concerned at how the people will view it, they may see this as him wasting money."

"I can see that. If he didn't like that, he surely wouldn't like my whole plan."

"What would that be?"

The city and harbor model rose from the table. It was all completely enclosed with-in a wall. The harbor forts became part of the harbor mouth forts.

Reggie looked at it, "I like it. Maybe someday."

"I'II keep it in mind." I said smiling.

***

I took a midmorning stroll through the city heading toward the harbor. I looked at businesses along the way, the people seemed prosperous.

I went to see Dov-ees. Our warehouse had a lot of goods in it.

"Good morning M'lord."

"Good morning, how are things?"

"Doing well, I found our captain and crew for our ship. She will sail in a few days." I looked at the pier where she was docked.

She had a crew working on her getting her ready to sail.

"Good, on another subject, Are you familiar with 'money changers'?"

"I am, some ports and cities have them, some more than others."

"Have you ever done anything like that?"

He nodded, "to some extent all merchants do, not all gold coins weigh the same."

"I want to open a money changer office. One that will also issue letters of credit, and make loans against assets, and back some ventures."

"Branching out, are we?"

"Yes, I need to put my money to work."

"Where do you want to do this?"

"Any reason we could not do it here?"

"No, just build me another office, fund it, and I'll do the rest."

"Show me what you want and where you want it." I added an office to one side of the warehouse with its own entrance. I teleported another chest of gold down with the vaults and we were in business. We noticed some excitement along the wharf and went outside to see what was happening.

Two ships were docking both were worse for wear, "that would be our first armed merchantman returning with spoils it seems." We walked out on the pier and met them.

"Captain Wilks, do you have wounded that need attending?"

"We do M'lord." I levitated aboard the ship.

"Take me to them." He nodded and took me below. "Show me the worst first." Most of the men had wounds of some kind, but seven were in bad shape and not expected to live. I started with the one gasping for breath at death's door. He had a sucking chest wound. I healed the wound sealing the lung and teleported the blood from his lung. He started to breathe normally and fell asleep.

I moved down the line, healing all the wounded. Most were

cuts and stabs. One was a head wound which I was not sure I could help, but I did what I could and put him in a deep sleep. The crew watched me as I worked. They had never seen a Mage healing. They were not worth the effort, when hurt they either lived or died on their own.

"They should be ok now, they just need some rest and food."

"Thank you M'lord." Everyone bowed as I passed them heading back up topside.

"Captain Wilks, this is Master Merchant Dov-ees. You will work with him. He will see to all your needs. He'll buy your cargo and resupply your ship. Are there wounded on the other ship?"

"Minor only, we kept the worst on our ship. The other ship's cargo is a good haul."

"Good, I'll buy your half of the ship as agreed, to be shared out with the crew. Dov-ees will have carpenters here tomorrow to start repairs, on both." Dov-ees nodded. "Do you need anything else?"

"No M'lord, thank you for healing my men,"

"They're my men too, Captain. I can buy more things. Life is irreplaceable."

I left Dov-ees there to work with Captain Wilks. Everyone bowed as I left. I heard one telling another, "I hear his men call him Captain even though he's a Prince. He takes care of his own."

"Aye, you can see that."

I needed to arm our ships better. Either with ballistas and crossbows or cannons. Maybe start with crossbows and work my way up. I'd have to introduce gun powder before cannons. Maybe explosive tip bolts for the ballistas.

***

I used my notebook to draw a basic crossbow, well, a refined basic crossbow, and bolts. I listed all the specifications needed. I found out there were three established armorers in the city, and one new one just getting started. I went to the new one.

His shop was in a low-rent end of the tradesmen's street. There were a few items on display, some old that were probably traded or sold by someone needing money.

"Good day Sir, how may I help you?"

"I need a few things," I picked up a sword, a knife, 2 staffs and a bow. I lay them on his counter, "what's your price?" He glanced at what I had.

"Three silvers." he said,

I nodded, "a fair price." I paid him. I lay my hand on the items and fixed in my mind what I wanted. Then conjured a crossbow.

He stepped back looking at me then down at the crossbow. He stepped closer studying it. "May I?"

"Please." I said pointing at it.

He picked it up and examined it. Nodding his head. "May we shoot it?"

"Let's," I said smiling. He gathered the three bolts, and we went to the rear of his shop; He had a short range there. Before anything, he fitted the bolt and saw how it all worked together.

"If I'm correct, you use the stirrup on the front for your foot, then pull the string back to lock, then lock the arrow in the guide?"

I nodded, "exactly. But they are called bolts, not arrows."

He nodded, "bolts." He put his foot in the stirrup, cocked it and loaded the bolt. I showed him how to shoulder and aim. He aimed and fired. The bolt went through his target and into the wall behind.

"It went through it."

I nodded, "they are deceivingly powerful."

"Do you want to sell it?"

I chuckled, "No, I want you to make some for me."

"But you can make them."

"Yes, but that would put you out of a job wouldn't it."

His eyebrows went up. "Yes, it would."

I took out my drawing and lay it on his work bench. "That one is for your pattern. This is all the information you should need to make them."

He looked over the drawing. "How many do you want?"

"Ten, to start, once I see the ten, I'll order more."

"How many more?"

"At least two hundred."

His mouth fell open. He handed the drawing back to me. "M'lord, I am a small shop only recently in business. You should take this to one of the bigger shops. They will make them faster than I could."

"You would send me to a competitor, so I could get them faster, even though you would lose money?"

"I could make them, no problem. It's the time it would take me to do it. I would fail you. I will not do that."

I nodded. I took out a large purse of gold and sat it on his workbench. "Hire the people you need, if you need to rent a bigger shop do it. You will be making my crossbows for me. My name is Prince Aaron, and we will do more business together."

He jumped up and bowed, "Yes M'lord. I will start right away making your crossbows."

"If you need anything, send word to the castle,"

"Yes, M'lord." I couldn't help but smile, he was in a daze when I left.

I had not considered the pettiness of medieval military contracts. Three days later I was summoned by the King. When I arrived, there was quite the crowd in the throne room.

"This ought to be fun."

I approached the throne and bowed. The King, the Queen, and Reggie were there. "Sire."

"Prince Aaron, Master Armor Smith has brought a complaint before us. He claims you have broken an agreement we have made with him."

I looked at the Smith, he had a "cat that ate the canary" grin on his face. I didn't like him already.

"I'm sorry Sire I will explain what happened to Master Smith, there is no need to waste your time on this matter."

"No, you should explain it to the King now." Smith said.

I turned toward him. "If you interrupt me again, I will tear your tongue out of your head. But since you insist on having this conversation in public, by all means let's have it. The crown did not engage an armor to make weapons, I did. Me. With my money. Not the treasury's money, mine. I chose who I wanted to make my weapon based on skill and integrity. Not based on the gold gift you bribed everyone with to get the contracts, so you could charge the Crown twice the value for inferior products."

I raised my hand, his sword leapt to meet it. I caught it and looked it over. "Would you say this is some of your best work?" before he answered, I drew my sword and struck them together. Mine, of course, cut his in two, "I'm not very impressed with your work." I dropped the other half of his sword.

"If you ever come before me again with a bribe, or to try to bully me into changing a contract, I'll seize your business, and properties. I'll have you thrown in the dungeon, and tortured until I tire of your screams, then feed what's left to the pigs. Is that clear enough for you, Master Smith?"

"Aaron." Reggie soft voice broke through my anger. I had not realized how mad I had become. A halo of blue fire surrounded me, and my sword. My armor's spikes were out, the only thing that was not up was my helmet. Without moving my head, I saw everyone had backed as far away from me as possible.

"Aaron?"

I looked at her, "I think he gets the point dear." The halo around me went dark, the spikes on my armor folded away, and I sheathed my sword.

I bowed to the King, "Forgive me Your Highness, my Queen." They nodded, I stepped to the side facing the crowd. I kept my stone face on.

"Was there anything else you wished to discuss Master Smith?" the King asked.

The Smith was ghost white and visibly shaken. "No, Your Highness."

"Present your accounting book to the Royal auditors in two days. We want to insure we have paid you for your work."

He bowed. "Yes sire," and backed out. I don't think that went the way he had planned.

The King stood, "That is all for today." Everyone bowed as the Royals left the room. Reggie held her hand out for me. I took it and followed.

We sat down to lunch. "Had you ever met Master Smith before today?"

"I had not, Sire."

"You didn't seem to like him."

"I don't like his kind. They buy their way into and out of everything. They are bullies who think they are better than everyone else."

"So, you have met him." The King said smiling. "What is this weapon you are having made?" I took a copy of the drawing from my pouch and handed it to him.

"A crossbow."

CHAPTER 16

I armed my three ships with ballistas, now they truly were armed merchantmen. I put a large ballista on the main deck, one medium one on the foredeck and two smaller ones on each midship side. They had both been repaired, restocked and crewed. They were all out hunting.

Word was spreading about the Letters of Marque, and some captains were approaching us with questions. No takers yet, but when they saw others getting rich from taking spoils, greed would do the rest.

I passed by a church that looked a little unkept. I went under and raised bedrock under her and repaired her foundation and adjusted her stance. She looked better now, and I felt better for helping.

I had become a known person, and someone not to be trifled with. I was being called Captain at the wharfs, and Prince Aaron in the markets, and the city. The common people were not afraid to be around me or to interact with me. I always paid for whatever I got, fruit, pasties, or a meal. I accepted nothing for free. I addressed the common peoples as equals, and they loved it.

"Miss. Ruby, are those apple tarts ready?"

"You know they are, M'lord."

"If my wife asks, you don't know anything."

"If she asks, you are on your own."

Everyone in the bakery laughed. I left eating one.

Master Armor Young sent word my first ten crossbows were ready. I went to see them. He had them all laid out for inspection. His new employees watching.

I walked by picking up one at random and inspected it. They had done an excellent job. I test fired it. It worked beautifully, as I knew it would.

"Well done, Master Armor. What is your price per crossbow?"

"Ten silvers."

I knew he was low balling it. "I'll pay you twelve silvers per crossbow." and paid him.

"But M'lord you're already paid for these."

"No, that was to finance you getting set up to make them, not the price of them," I gave him another large purse of gold, "keep good accounts. I need 200 more crossbows and 2000 bolts, if you need more money to buy materials let me know. Send them to the Castle in batches of ten crossbows, and 100 bolts."

He bowed, "Yes M'lord."

I took the crossbow with me to the castle armorer. I showed him how to use it and told him to start training the troops on their use. More would be delivered. He liked the new weapon and said he would.

***

I received a message that one of my ship was in port and wanted to see me. I teleported down to the pier where they usually docked. The captain was waiting by the ship.

"M'lord," he bowed.

"Captain." I nodded.

"They have taken your other two ships, M'lord. They caught us in an ambush; I was on the outside and was able to break away."

"When and where did this happen?"

"This morning, at Storm Island. We were after two cargo ships; they made a run for it. We chased them, looking back on it, they were leading us. When we rounded Storm Island, their fleet was waiting."

"How many in their fleet?"

"Ten or twelve that I saw."

"How far to Storm Island?"

"20 miles east off the coast. It's a place ships that are caught out can ride out a storm. It's an old volcano crater harbor, with fresh water."

"You did well bringing me the news."

I walked in between two buildings out of sight and sank into the earth. I flew under heading east to Storm Island. We had only seen small ships passing our harbor since we had raised the forts. Storm Island may be their staging area.

I found Storm Island; it was indeed the mouth of an extinct volcano. The west side of the volcano was on the southeast end of the island. There were twelve Dunwich ships in the harbor plus my two. I came up through the bottom of Captain Wilks' ship. They had a hand full of guard watching Captain Wilks and his crew who were locked in the hold. I emerged up behind each guard and stabbed them up through the back of their skull. They never made a sound.

I brought a keg of rum up and opened the door to the hold. "This is becoming a habit with you lot." I said smiling. They laughed breaking the tension. They got out their cups and had a taste.

"We've got bigger troubles M'lord. I heard them talking. This is a supply fleet; the troop fleet has already landed south of Port City. They are joining forces with the Volwick Army to attack Port City."

"How long ago?"

"Couldn't say, they were here to refill fresh water before going on."

"So, it couldn't be too long otherwise they wouldn't be here." I thought a moment. "Wait here I'll be back."

I went to my other ship and freed them and told them to wait below until I returned. I didn't waste time I went through each ship like the Angel of Death, breaking necks and moving to the next one. I did the same with the crew that was on the beach.

I cast a spell, and the bodies slid down through the ship leaving the clothes and equipment behind. The same happened on the beach. I held Captain Wilks' ship back, but sent my other one to Port City to tell them we were coming in with a captured fleet.

When Captain Wilks was ready to sail, I cast a spell commanding the captured ships to raise anchors. I cast another spell for the water to push the ships along behind us following each other. As we left Storm Island, we had twelve Dunwich ships following in our wake.

We timed it so we would arrive at Port City after sunrise. As we approached the harbor forts, I teleported to them to let them know all was well. I had the captured ships dock at the piers and tie up. To be honest, it was kind of a freaky sight watching an empty ship do that.

Dov-ees was waiting for us. "Unload and inventory the ships cargos. Move everything into our warehouse. Strip the ships of everything but do nothing else to them yet. Keep all the intel papers separate, I'll look through those, you don't have to," He nodded. "I must go see the King."

I teleported to the coach Pavilion, Reggie was not there I walked over to the castle proper and started toward the dining room. Something was wrong there was no activity. No servants walking about, no sound of conversation. The first body I found was in the hall outside the great room. She was blue and had foam around her mouth.

My military training kicked in, I put my helmet up and closed my face shield to filter my air, just in case. There was a trail of bodies leading to the dining room. I entered the dining room it was obvious everyone there was dead. I did a quick check; Reggie was not among them.

I cursed myself for a fool and checked my ring for her location. I ran down the hall to where the ring said she was. I found her; she had crawled from the dining room coughing up blood. She was still alive, barely. I teleported the blood and mucus from her lungs and healed them.

She began to breathe easier. I teleported us to the harbor and into the water, washing us off. I didn't know what poison they had used, but if there was a chance that water would wash it off, I'd take it.

She come to coughing and fighting. "I got you, I got you." I held on to her. She stopped fighting when she heard me.

She grabbed me, "mother and father?!"

I shook my head. "No!" She screamed. I held her. While she wept. I teleported us back to our pavilion. She dropped into unconsciousness, so I put her to bed.

I teleported to the castle gate guard post, "Captain."

"Yes M'lord?"

"Close the gates, lock the castle down. Someone has assassinated the King and Queen. No one in or out except for a runner to the Army fort, put all forces on full alert. Have the Red Cloaks report to me at the castle entrance now."

He started shouting orders. I put my face shield down and teleported back to the dining room. I looked over the room, trying to determine what had happened. No one was sitting at their places. They had all choked to death. Food and dishes were overturned on the table.

I looked for the things that were out of place, a flash burn mark was on the floor, and the wall in one place. There was a small broken clear glass beaker jar. There was also blood on the wall by the burn mark.

I cast a detection spell, whatever had done this was gone now.

I went to the castle entrance. The Red Cloak were gathering, "Captain."

"Sir?"

"Someone has assassinated the King and Queen. Princess Regina still lives. Search every inch of the castle and grounds. Gather everyone here in the courtyard, alive preferably."

"Yes Sir." He saluted. He broke everyone down into groups of threes and began searching. I questioned everyone on duty. No one saw anything unusual, or out of the ordinary.

I went underground and searched secret passages and escape routes. Nothing. If this was a prelude to war, or coup, I was going to ruin someone's day. I went out one thousand yards from the city and raised a wall fifty feet high, and thirty feet thick of solid rock. It looked like the Great Wall of China.

I kept raising it until it completely enclosed the city, including the harbor. It had no gates, and no stairs going up to the top of the wall, I'd add that later. There would be no escape, unless they swam, as I had raised the chain closing the harbor.

The Red Cloaks had gathered everyone in the courtyard. Everyone was accounted for; they were either in this group or dead in the castle. I cast a truth spell and questioned everyone. None of these were responsible for the deaths. Now there was only Reggie.

I set the servants to preparing the bodies for burial. I also sent for the priests. The death bells began tolling, and news spread through the city.

I went to wait for Reggie to wake up. Armor was on the bed with her. Hopefully she could tell us who had done this.

***

Reggie walked out of the bedroom at midmorning. She looked at me, "did you get him?"

"Did I get who?"

"Arms Master Smith."

"He did this?"

She nodded, "he broke a jar of something that became a mist, everyone started choking. I tried to kill him by burning him alive but only got part of him before the mist got to me. He shouted, 'we'll see who gets fed to the pigs,' as he ran."

"Your fire probably saved your life. It killed most of what was trying to kill you. He's not going anywhere I put up a wall around the city with no gates. I'll go find Master Smith. Should I bring him back, or just kill him?"

"Bring him back, first he'll stand trial, then you can feed him to the pigs."

I went outside. Oaks was there. "Bring me the magistrate."

He saluted, "yes Sire." I guess I was King now. Not what

I wanted, but I had the job now. I waited until the magistrate arrived.

I took him inside to see Regina. "Magistrate issue an arrest order for Arms Master Smith. For the murder of the King and Queen and 15 of their staff. The Princess has positively identified him as the murderer." He looked at her and she nodded.

He bowed, "At once, my Queen, Sire." and left.

"I'll be back." I said. Reggie nodded.

I went underground and flew to Master Smiths house. I found him hiding in his hidden basement. He was in bad shape. Reggie had cooked half of him to a crisp. I healed him enough that he would not die from his wounds.

I waited for the magistrate to arrive, then cast my beguiling spell. "The building is on fire; you have to get out!" He moved as fast as he was able up the stairs and out into the arms of the magistrate and the city watch. They delivered him to the castle dungeon to await his trial. When they searched him, they found a guise ring. He had made himself look like one of our guards. That was how he got in and out with no one giving him a second look.

**

The King and Queen were entombed under the Church where the previous Kings and Queens had been. After three days of mourning, they held our Coronation. We were now Queen Regina, and King Aaron.

Arms Master Smith saved us the trouble of a trial. He killed himself by bashing his own skull in against the dungeon wall. I still fed him to the pigs, just not alive. The Crown confiscated his business, properties and assets. I let his family keep their home, and the money they had in a vault in the basement.

At night I would hold Reggie while she wept. I let her take as long as she needed to grieve. I would take care of everything until she was ready to take over.

I lowered the chains across the harbor mouth, so ships could begin moving once more. I went to see Dov-ees, "You still have contacts in the cities we trade with?"

"I do."

"I need to know what is going on, in those cities. What the markets are doing, the mood of the people, what the militaries are doing."

He stared at me.

"I'm not asking you to spy on your former country, I'm asking what our neighbors are doing. How it will affect us. I also want you to contact the best mercenary naval force you can. I want to hire them to train our Navy."

He nodded, "what do you want done to the cargo we took off of the ships you captured?"

"What was the cargo?"

"Mostly food, some weapons, and equipment."

"Keep the food, unless it's perishable. Send the weapons and equipment to the Army."

"When will you be opening the wall?"

"Tomorrow, I think. I'll put in a main gate to start and get the army to man it, and the walls. Our standing army just got bigger. Have you gathered the papers from the ships yet?"

"I have, they are in a chest in the basement along with the gold we recovered."

"Add the gold to our operating funds, I'll take the papers."

***

Before I made a gate, I needed to know what the Dunwich forces were doing. I went underground and followed the coast south. I found where they had come ashore, there were no ships there now. They had moved inland from the coast, so I followed.

They had made camp a few times moving further inland more south than east. They had stayed at one camp for a few days then moved straight south. I guess they had seen our wall and had to change plans.

I followed them south and found them camped outside of Volwick's capital. That was all I needed to see for now. I had a lot of work to do to make our main gate. It would take me a while to get back. The earth blurred by me, and I was under the wall where I had been thinking of putting the main gate. "I wish you had done that sooner." I never thought to question my memories whether "fast travelling" like in a video game was possible here.

I added a main gate on the west side of the City's wall. I gave it plenty of support and a portcullis. I made a small fort as part of the wall there that could house a company of guards. I added ramps to the wall every three hundred yards with guard stations. I raised bedrock up to support the wall so it could not be undermined.

I raised a stone road from the main gate to the fort, then to the main street of the city. I continued to the harbor, connecting it to the wharf. I put in a drainage system that emptied into the sea south of the harbor.

I went to the army fort. "Colonel."

"Sire." He bowed.

"The Dunwich Army has landed. They have moved south and joined Volwick. I have added a main gate to the west wall and ramps along the inside for you to man. There is a gate garrison that will hold a company of troops. You will man that at all times. The gate will be closed at sundown and opened at sunrise. You will keep the whole army on duty for the time being. What do you need from me to carry out your orders?"

"A proper fort with barracks would help."

"How many do you want to house?"

"At least a thousand, but how big of a standing army do you plan to keep?"

"I will build two forts to house and train five thousand at a time. 2500 on the south wall and 2500 on the north wall. We will also build a new castle. Your main headquarters will be there."

He bowed, "Yes Sire."

"You and your men are being paid?"

"We are Sire,"

"Good. It will take me some time to complete the buildings and forts. In the meantime, man the walls and the main gate. We may open other gates close to the North and South forts, but that remains to be seen. Let me know if you need anything else."

"Yes, Sire." He bowed.

CHAPTER 17

I would do my work at night improving the city, the wall, the harbor, and the new castle, I would rest in the earth, which restored my strength quickly. When I raised the castle, I set the base in the harbor and gave Navy ships a place to dock. I made quite a large complex so everything in government could be close by. Farmers started farming the thousand-yard buffer zone between the city and the wall. I added more wells all over the city, and a sewer system.

I raised the two forts and gave them plenty of room for a security zone, and training areas for their horses. They started running patrols outside the walls to the North, South and West. Every evening over dinner Reggie and I would talk of the day's events and what improvements I had made. It was a week after our coronation before she started showing signs of interest again.

"Is the new castle complete?"

"It is, I've got it all closed until you are ready to move into it."

"Tomorrow we will start the move, and I will start acting like the Queen." I made the move a little easier by put the things in each room in a crystal. It still took us a week to get everything moved over to the new castle.

Once it was finished Reggie gave me a drawing, a lay-out actually, of a park. "I want you to sink the old castle into the ground, bury it. In its place I want a park built like this, for people to enjoy and remember mother and father."

I nodded," I'll take care of it." At sunset the castle sank into the earth, by sunrise a park sat in its place. It had a central fountain with a sculpture of the King and Queen. The city came out to see it, and memory park was born. Reggie loved it.

I found her standing on the high terrace of our Royal apartments. Amour was with her, as he now almost always was. "You have done wonders for the City and the Kingdom, thank you."

"Anything for you my Queen, my love."

"I want to do more for our people."

"What did you have in mind?"

"That is what I want you to tell me. What does your memories say about it?"

I thought a few minutes. "A few things come to mind. Schools: the education level of our people is low. We could open schools, and make it mandatory for children to attend, but offer it to everyone. Run and taught by professional educators. Hospitals and doctors: run by real doctors, that would help the overall health of our people. Military Service: everyone must serve two years in the military. When they reach an age, they will be trained and serve in the army or navy for at least two years."

"When you say everyone, do you mean men and women?"

I nodded, "everyone, men and women, rich and poor, highborn and low born. Everyone."

She nodded thinking, "start with the hospitals, once they see the good, we'll open schools. Then we'll give them the bad news about military service." She said smiling.

I chuckled, "good idea."

"I'm not sure if we will have trouble with the healer's guild or not."

"We won't, if we have any, I will abolish the guild and put them in prison. If they think they are in charge, they're confused, and I'll un-confuse them."

She chuckled, "You can't kill anyone."

"I won't have too, after the first few, everyone else will catch on that it's not wise to test me."

"Some people are slow to change."

"Some people are greedy and don't want to lose the power and wealth. I'll show restraint if they let me."

***

The seas had been quiet; we took no ships, and no one tried to take ours. Dov-ees had kept our ships going on cargo runs, so we were making money. There was a new ship in port, it didn't seem to be a cargo ship. At least not only a cargo ship.

My curiosity got the better of me and I teleported over to the wharf. It looked like a military ship but had no kingdom banners or flags. I hoped it was the mercenaries I was looking for.

I went to the warehouse and checked with Dov-ees. He was talking to some people, when he saw me, he came out.

"King Aaron, may I present Captain Roker. He's the Mercenary's Naval Training Officer."

"Captain." I greeted him.

He bowed, "Your Highness. I understand you wish to hire us to train some ship's crews for your Navy."

"If you are of the quality I'm looking for yes, I have ship's crews, what I need is a Navy. Trained officers, and men who can defend our ships and trade routes. I need an Officer Corps that will then be able to train more. This could be a long-term contract."

We discussed their experience and what they could do for us. I agreed to pay them to train one crew, then we would see if we both wanted to do more.

I turned to Dov-ees, "while they are training our Navy, outfit six more ships and get them working."

Dov-ees nodded, "Yes, Sire,"

***

I went to the Healing Guild house; it wasn't large, but it was nice. I walked in and a clerk greeted me. "Good morning Your Highness, are you expected?"

"No, I just dropped by to talk to the Master Healer."

"I'll see if he is available to see you."

"Stop." He stopped. "He is available to see his King right this second. If he is not, I'll come visit him and you in my dungeon."

He bowed, "Of course Sire, please come this way."

"Thank you." I followed him; he opened the door.

"I'm not available this morning," the Master Healer said.

"His Majesty, King Aaron." the clerk announced.

The Master Healer stood, as did his two guests.

"Master Healer, thank you for seeing me."

"Of course, Sire. How may we serve?"

"The Crown has been making a lot of improvements to the city, and I thought we could help each other."

"How so Sire?"

I'll build you a new larger guild house, and in exchange you will see the sick and hurt of the city.

"Who will pay us to see these people."

"The Crown will pay a set fee for seeing them. The rest will be your payment for the new complex."

"It will be very expensive to see everyone. You do not understand the complexities at the healing profession."

"Really? How many bones in the human body?"

I don't see what that has to do with anything.

"206. How many internal organs in the human body, and what are their functions?"

"I still don't see what that has to do with how much we charge for our healing."

"Ok, how about this, what would you charge for seeing someone with a cold?"

"Well, that's difficult to say, there could be several reasons for the cold."

"That was not my question. No matter how they got it, they have it. What would you charge them and what would you give them?"

"A silver, and a very complex salve."

I shook my head; "you mean crush eucalyptus leaves to open their sinuses. Tell them to drink water and eat watered soup. And in a week or ten days they'd be better. For that you'd charge a silver?"

Once they saw I would not be baffled with bull, we came to an agreement. I wouldn't put them in prison for fraud, I'd build them a building. And they would see all the sick and hurt at a set fair price. I would supply the accounting clerks. I raised a very nice hospital for them; they were at least happy about that.

It took me a week to get the hospital, and healers working close to like I wanted. Next, I went to the church. In this time and place, the priests were the most educated. I'd have to tread a little lighter here.

I went to the church and was met by the head priest. "Correct me if I'm wrong Father, but aren't all priests tutors, and educators?"

"Not all, but most can fulfill that duty."

"Good, then I need your advice. I want to start a school. Not just for the well to do, but for everyone, I'll build a schoolhouse, if you and your priests will teach them. The Crown will pay you to teach."

"What subjects would you want taught?"

"I want a well-rounded education. The Bible of course, math, reading, and writing to start. If any show promise and an aptitude for learning further, then we'll cross that bridge when we get there. One of my problem is, I don't know how many people we are talking about, so I don't know how big to build the school. We would also feed them breakfast and lunch."

He stared at me. "You're serious?"

"Completely."

"My Lord above. I don't know exactly how many would come, but free breakfast and lunch will get most of them. If you'll give me a week, I'll have a better idea of the numbers we are talking about."

I nodded, "Sounds good, I'll see you in a week."

The numbers they came up with were between 200- 300 children. I decided to build a stadium style seating classroom to hold 300 each. I started with 2 classrooms but could add more. I built a mess hall style kitchen and lunchroom to feed everyone.

Of course, we had to staff and supply everything.

They announced a new school system in church, so everyone figured it must be a good thing. Beside the Crown would feed the children two meals a day. That sold the idea. By the end of the second month, we had over 200 students attending. It was all costing a lot. Being King was expensive.

The rich were fussing about their high-born children being educated with "throw aways." I told them they were welcome to build their own school, hire their own teachers and feed their own children. They decided it would be a good education after all.

Reggie was dealing with the day-to-day government stuff, but we'd talk about things at night over dinner. She was happy with the way the school, and the hospital were progressing. To tell the truth, so was I.

***

"Breakfast?" Reggie asked

"Of course."

"What are your plans for today?"

"I thought I would look at how our Navy's training is progressing. We may need to hire more trainers, if we have enough recruits to man more ships. We may have to recruit more by offering a bonus to sign on."

"We need to talk about the treasury. More is going out than is coming in."

"Ok, tonight?"

"Yes, it can wait that long."

I had my usual bacon, eggs and potatoes. The hot tea was good, but... *"I wonder if I should start looking for coffee beans?"*

The Major-domo approached and bowed. "Excuse me, Your Highness. The Head Priest has requested an audience. He insists it is of great importance."

"Has he ever done this before?" I asked

"No Sire, he has not."

"Then let's go see what is so important."

Since it was a formal request, we went to the Throne Room, and took our seats on the Thrones. It was no big deal to me, but Reggie insisted it was important to maintain the dignity of the office.

The Head Priest and his hooded entourage came in and bowed. "Good morning Father, what great import brings you to see us?" Reggie asked.

He stepped aside and two people came forward from the back of the group. I used my Mage Sight to ensure they were not armed.

When they were beside the Head Priest, they removed their hoods.

"Catherine?" Reggie asked

Catherine, if that was her name knelt, "Yes cousin, I ask sanctuary for myself and my son Prince Roman."

The Young Prince had not knelt. He stepped forward toward me, his mother made a grab for him but missed, "Please." she said and covered her mouth tears running down her face.

Reggie waved her off, and she stopped.

He stood before me unafraid. "King Aaron, my father says King's speak plainly to one another." He was very serious this boy of, maybe eight or ten years.

I nodded, "They do, when both sides agree."

He nodded. "Then I would speak plainly to you King Aaron."

"Then we shall speak plainly Prince Roman."

"My Father, King William, has been betrayed and is now imprisoned in his own dungeon. The army he thought was his ally, has turned against him and seized the throne. My mother and I barely escaped with our lives. We seek sanctuary. And I also seek your help in freeing my father and retaking his throne."

I nodded, I looked at his mother. She was scared, I'm sure more for her son than for herself.

"Were you aware that your father was allied with this army against me, and that small skirmishes had already taken place?"

He frowned. "I was not. I was not aware of all the dealings with the Dunwich Army. Only that they had broken their agreement and turned on us."

"Yes, it seems when you are King someone is always trying to take what is yours."

"Was it you who was the aggressor, and my father defending his lands, or he the aggressor?" His mother sagged to the floor.

"This young man is bold, I like him."

"As far as I know, neither of us openly went after the other. As sometimes happens, it may have been a misunderstanding. But in this case, I suspect we have a common enemy from the outside. One who would like to see us at war, weakening the both of us."

"So they may defeat us both." He finished. His mind was running, looking at all the angles and implications.

I nodded, "just so."

"If it was a misunderstanding, we must clarify. We, as far as I know, are not seeking to invade Port City."

"And we, were not seeking to invade Volwick. We have more than enough to do taking care of our people and keeping an eye on Dunwich."

"In that case we are at peace?"

"We are until we are attacked."

"Then will you join us in fighting a common enemy, freeing my father, and reclaiming his throne?"

"And when your father is free, will he honor our agreement?"

He stood taller, "He will, I have given my word, He will honor it."

I nodded, "then we will join you, against our common enemy, freeing your father and reclaiming his throne."

"Will you accept my signing a peace treaty in my father's stead?"

"I need no paper to bind what you have given your word of honor on." I stepped down and we clasp wrists as warriors do.

"May our peace last down to our grandchildren."

He nodded, "and beyond."

Reggie came down and went to Queen Catherine.

"Thank you, Father for bringing them to us," I said.

He bowed, "thank you Sire for the wisdom you have shown."

"Will you stay for breakfast?"

"Another time perhaps, I must get back to the school."

I nodded. He bowed and left.

"Let's go eat and plan our enemy's demise."

***

Queen Catherine told us what had happened, as much as she knew. The Dunwich troops had started out staying outside the walls. Then they started taking part in patrols, then guard duty, then castle watch. Then it was too late, they were inside the castle. The King stayed behind fighting, she and Prince Roman got away through the escape tunnels. We were the only place she could run to.

I looked at them with my Mage Sight. I could not see any runes, or runed jewelry.

"Were you able to escape with any weapons, armor?"

"No. they attacked at night we only had time to grab our clothes."

"What is your talent?" I asked her.

"Fire, and Roman has not manifested yet."

I took a set of shield bracelets out of my pouch and handed them to Reggie. She passed them to Catherine. "These are shield bracelets they are runed against weapons and magic. Once you put them on, they will protect you even when you don't expect an attack."

Catherine put them on, and Reggie showed her how they worked. I gave Roman a set, and he put them on. I teleported two daggers up from my armory. I gave one to each of them.

"You can never be too careful."

Roman nodded, sliding his behind his belt. Before he had time to think I tried to punch him in the chest. His shields flared and stopped my punch.

"See, even when you aren't ready your shields are."

He was smiling, "Thank you, these are wonderful."

CHAPTER 18

"Sergeant Oaks."

"Sir."

"This is Prince Roman, while he is in uniform, he is Lieutenant Roman, take him to the Red Cloak Armory and have a kit issued to him, less the spear-lance."

"Yes Captain, this way Lieutenant." Roman followed him.

"Captain Motts, I'm going to recon the Volwick's castle. I'll be back in an hour. Assemble the Red Cloaks. We'll be going for a visit after I get back."

"Yes, Sire."

I went under and fast travelled to the Volwick castle. I flew under the Dunwich camp. Most of the troops were still there. They had not occupied the city or the castle. They did however control the access points. The main gate was closed, which was good for me. I moved around the castle and the walls. There were no large troop concentrations. The house guards and troops were nowhere in the area.

I circled back under the camp I was sure they had sent at least one Mage. I found him eating in a tent, not a pavilion. Just as he was about to put a spoon full of food in his mouth, I struck. I pulled him under and punched my hand into his brain and took his powers and knowledge. I searched his body, stripping him of everything.

I now knew there were two more Mages with the army. They were in the city at a brothel. I'd have to go find them. *Why don't any of the local Mages challenge these guys?* It took me a while, but I found them. I could tell right away that one was an Earth Mage. I'd hit him from above. It had worked before I hoped it worked again.

Once he was alone, I went up above the building and

dropped down with no magic. At the last moment I teleported in, punching into his brain, cast the spell and took him under. I held him tight as his body thrashed. This time was like before, runes from his body transferred to me along with his power, and knowledge. I found the last one and took him too. I stayed under for a while absorbing and assimilating what I had taken from the Mages. The earth restored my strength and helped me center myself. I stripped their bodies of everything.

I went back to the Dunwich camp and found their commander. He was asleep; I put him under deeper and took his knowledge. I also took their war chests of gold, and gems. *"Even a King has to make a living."* I smiled.

I flew to the castle and went down to the dungeon and found King William. There was only one guard. I pulled him under and ended him quickly. The King had been wounded but not bad. I sealed off the dungeon to keep him safe. I sealed the castle proper and killed every Dunwich guard I found, leaving them laying where they fell. Once I cleared the castle. I sealed the main gate and personnel gates.

I teleported back to my great room. The Red Cloaks where there and ready. Prince Roman was there kitted out in Red like the rest of us. I motioned for Oaks and Moss; they followed me to Prince Roman.

"Lieutenant Roman, these are my guardsmen. Sergeant Oaks, and Corporal Moss, tonight they will be your guardsmen." Oaks and Moss bowed.

"Men." Roman said.

"They are old soldiers for a reason. I listen to their advice; it would be wise for you to do the same."

He nodded.

I looked pointedly at Oaks and Moss. They nodded. I nodded in return. The young prince needed to be blooded, not dead.

I turned to the Red Cloaks, "We will go into a secured throne room. Once there Lieutenant Roman will lead us to the dungeon and free his father their King, we'll return him to the throne room. We'll clear the castle from there. Slow and easy. No rush. Cover each other. Everyone comes home,"

"Everyone comes home." They repeated, even Prince Roman.

I opened the portal. "First squad." They moved through to ensure the room was secured. They gave us a thumbs-up. Then the Prince and I stepped through, I thought his mother would faint. Reggie was with her holding her hand. The rest of the Red Cloaks were through and I closed the portal.

I unsealed the doors. "Fourth squad clear the floors above. Third squad clear the floor below. Don't leave the castle proper. Once clear, fourth squad return here, third squad, hold at the main doors."

"Yes Captain." and they moved out.

"Lieutenant Roman."

"Yes, Captain."

"Take second squad and clear the dungeon and free your father, then return here."

"Yes Captain." Roman said.

"Second squad," the sergeant said, "On the Lieutenant." They headed toward the dungeon.

I used my Mage Sight and saw there was no one in their path. I unsealed the dungeon door.

Fourth squad had cleared the upper floors and returned. "Go to the main floor, join with third and wait." They moved out carefully and quietly.

Lieutenant Roman returned with his father. King William stopped when he saw me. "Pressing your advantage?"

"No, this was Lieutenant Roman's idea, he came to me, and offered an alliance against our common enemy, I agreed. Here we are." The King looked at his son.

"And now?" He asked looking back at me.

"That would be up to you. We have cleared your castle, freed you. What are you going to do next?"

"My wife?"

"Safe with her cousin, Queen Regina. We granted them

Sanctuary."

"Their army?"

"Outside the walls. They don't know we are here. But once we start clearing the walls, they'll know. Where is your army?"

"Sent home. It was that, or see the city burned to the ground by the occupation force."

"Can I have them?" I asked

He frowned, "Who?"

"The occupation forces. Or do you want 5000 prisoners?"

He laughed, "sure you can have them, but you have to bury them."

I nodded smiling, "wait here, I'll be back."

I teleported to the commander's tent. I broke his neck and cast the spell that let his body slip into the earth leaving everything else behind. I put on his guise.

"Guard." I called. One came in saluting. "Pass the word, I want all Company Captains to report to me now and start breaking the camp for movement."

"Yes Commander," he saluted and left. Once the Captains reported, "we are moving toward Port City. Break the camp for movement, recall the men from the walls." I unsealed the personnel gate. "Once that is done. We will send corporals and below forward with the supplies and wagons. The rest of us will wait here. We will go into the city for one last party." I said and laughed. They all joined me laughing. They left to carry out their orders.

I called up a light fog. As they worked, I thickened the fog over the next hour. When the main force was ready, I cast a spell for them not to stop until they reached Port City. When they had moved out, I made the fog thicker. I cast an illusion of wine barrels and had them gather round. There were roughly 500 officers and sergeants left. I cast an illusion of their commander standing before them then sank into the earth.

I cast the beguiling spell, "There are traitors in the camp, kill them quietly then find the others. Kill them all." The fighting started slowly at first but picked up quickly. It was a bloody mess, 500 men hacking each other to death.

These men I could not use, they had been indoctrinated in the Dunwich way of war. The ones I sent north I thought I could save. If not, I'd get rid of them. When the fighting was over, I finished the last few. I sank the bodies into the earth and put all the spoils in a crystal. I sent the horses to join other horses, heading north.

I went underground and up into the castle. I found the King had been bandaged and was eating. I came out of the wall in a hallway out of sight. I joined him at the table. "You may recall your army now. The Dunwich army has been taken care of.

He stared at me." Already?"

"There were only 5000."

He chuckled, shaking his head, "ok."

"We will be leaving now."

He nodded, "my son gave his word, the alliance stands." We clasped wrist.

"He will make a good King, he has a quick mind, and courage."

"Yes, he does," King William said smiling.

"Captain Motts, form up the men we leave as soon as you are ready." He nodded and began giving orders. "Lieutenant Roman."

"Yes, Captain."

"You will return with us to escort your mother, the Queen, home."

"Yes, Captain."

I looked around and saw that the Royal colors were black and gold. I touched Roman's cloak, and it turned Black, with gold trim. He stood taller.

"We're ready Captain," Captain Motts said.

I nodded and opened a portal to our great room. "Lieutenant Roman, lead us through."

"Yes, Captain."

He turned and marched, leading the men through the Portal.

***

When the Dunwich troops arrived, I had a camp ready for them with food waiting. I was in the guise of their commander and had them eat, then set up tents. That night I beguiled pockets of men.

"The king has sold us to Port City. He said he would send ships for the horses because they were worth more than the troops were. He sent ships for the officers and sergeants, but not us. King Aaron takes care of his troops, we'll be taken care of. We'll become Port City troops. We'll be fed and paid like the regular troops."

Like all rumors, this one took off like a wildfire. By morning it was all over camp. After breakfast I went up on the wall overlooking their camp and amplified my voice. "Men, by now I'm sure you have heard that you have been abandoned by the Dunwich King. I am sorry to say but they were more worried about getting the horses back than you men. I told him he deserved neither, so I've kept you both."

"Here is my offer. You stay with me and become part of my army, you will be fed, clothed and paid, just like my standing army. We will treat you no different from any other troops. You won't have to beg and hope someone will remember to take you home after you're done your duty, you are already here. I will not ask you to invade other lands, only defend this one."

"Any who do not wish to stay and have the money to buy passage on a ship are free to do so. If you stay, you work. Because if you don't work, you don't eat." I let that sink in. "If you would stay with us, and I hope you will, take a knee." I knew none of them had money for passage. They all took a knee.

I turned them over to our army for integration. I raised another fort on the west wall for the additional troops. We paid the new men one month's pay in advance, so they had money, and felt like they were a part of us. Soldiers were soldiers and fell in on their new lives like any other day. Sergeants still yelled at them, just different ones. As long as they were fed, and paid, we'd have little trouble.

I flattened the land around port city and pushed the forest back a mile in every direction. The Crown then opened the new lands for farming on shares, there was no shortage of takers. Now that we had the Dunwich troops taken care of I added gates in the wall on the north and south sides, including gate forts.

Caravans were once again starting to move on the King's trade road. We had started to patrol it again to ensure caravan safety, and freedom of travel. Dov-ees was investing in caravans and our business was doing well.

"You were right," Dov-ees said. "Your father moved against Midwick and has temporarily made your brother, the Crown Prince, the governor.

"That sounds like dear old dad. I doubt Cain will be there long. They will appoint a permanent governor and make it part of their kingdom."

He nodded, "That is the rumor, yes."

"How is the training of our Navy going?"

"Very good, they now have a second ship manned, and working together."

"They say you have taken in the invasion troops from Dunwich after they were abandoned."

"Well, if that's what they say it must be true," I said smiling. "Besides, I didn't want to kill them if I didn't have to. They got a home, I got 4500 trained or kinda trained, troops. It was a win-win. On another subject, get our next two ships ready to go to work."

He nodded, "I'll get right on it."

***

We still caught each other up on the day's events over dinner. "We need to put people to work," Reggie said.

"What do you have in mind?"

"I don't know, normally I'd say a building project, but

you've taken care of that, putting us ahead by at least 20 years."

"Streets and roads. We can have them lay paving stones on all the streets in the city. I'll do the main street to give them an example, they do all the other streets."

"I like that idea; I hate muddy streets."

I laughed, "You rarely leave the castle."

"Well when I do, I don't like mud," she said smiling.

"We'll start right away." I laughed.

"I would also like the King's trade road paved throughout our lands."

"That is a lot of paving and would take them years to complete."

"True, but if we needed it finished faster, you could complete some of it."

I nodded. "I could. I'll get some contracts started. What about using prison labor for out on the roads? Make them work for their food and shelter like everyone else. No free rides, especially in prison. I'll make some bracelets that will keep them from being a problem."

"I bet that cuts down on crime too."

"I imagine it will."

We awarded the contract for paving stones to be delivered to the city. And one to stack piles of large paving stones close the dirt road into the city from the King's trade road. I made compliance bracelets that made the prisoners work hard and cause no trouble. It became the new policy that all prisoners wore the new bracelets upon sentencing. Not unexpectedly, crime went down.

City streets and the trade road were being paved, people were employed, and taxes were coming in. Unfortunately, money was still going out faster than it was coming in. I added some of my gold to the treasury but that was a short-term fix. We needed a long-term fix.

Our farms were producing, but that took time. We awarded some timber leases so we could harvest some of that, but again that took time. Then I remembered reading somewhere that there was gold and silver in all dirt. It was just more concentrated in some places. It also said silver was 75 percent more common than gold. What I needed to do was figure out a way to harvest that gold and silver.

After trying a few things what worked best for my gold and silver traps was a wood plank where I had inscribed runes on calling for raw gold to gather around a coin. I made a silver coin for silver. I took them down into the earth 100 feet and activated them. I left them there to see if my idea worked.

I went back the next day to check on them. It had worked. There was one pound of gold around the gold coin and almost three pounds of silver around the silver coin. I made ten more traps, both silver and gold and placed them a mile apart well away from the city. I started checking them once a week and was getting good results.

I built an additional vault under my bedroom and started putting my harvest there. I started making gold and silver coins of the correct weight. The gold coins had Reggie's father's face on it, and the silver coins had her mother's face on it. I started giving some to Dov-ees to use in the money changing business. That put them into circulation quietly.

I made sure the treasury was always well financed. The rest I spread around in my various vaults. To maintain proper records of accounts, I had to give the silver, and gold to the clerks. I told them it was to go into the general fund to pay Kingdom debt.

***

I received word that two of my ships had just returned to port and had been in a battle. I teleported to the pier where they had tied up.

"Anyone need healing?"

"Yes Captain, they are below." I went straight to them. There were only a few seriously wounded, which I healed. Then moved to the others. They had lost several men before they could reach port. They had been attacked by Dunwich ships and were able to fight their way clear, but it had been a close thing. They had made it home with our cargo but the price in men had been high. I paid the families of the dead men 1000 golds for their service to me. A small fortune in this place and time.

I needed to come up with better offensive and defensive weapons for our ships. I already knew I could put shields on the ships and the crew if I wanted, I was thinking more about offensive weapons. At the very least I needed something like exploding bolts for the ballistas. I just needed to figure out the best way to do it.

CHAPTER 19

It had taken me several tries, but I finally got it right. The bolt would launch and strike the target that would break the barrier between the positive spell and the negative spell which caused a catastrophic reaction. An explosion. Depending on the size of the warhead on the bolt, and the spells determined the size of the explosion.

I sized the big ballistas to take bolts from a 105mm to a 155mm sized artillery shell. The medium ballistas were my .50 cal. The 50 cal was like a grenade going off. The standard crossbows were just arrows or bolts. For improved targeting I put a crystal for the man to sight through. When it turned red, he was on target and could fire, and never miss. The range was now about 1000 yards.

As soon as I had perfected the weapons, I updated all the ballistas in service starting with the harbor forts. I then updated all the ships in port and would do the others as they rotated through. I also added runes to the ships to keep the hulls clean and watertight. I added ballistas to the city's gates. But locked them so they could only fire outside the walls. One can never be too careful.

***

"A Harvest Ball?"

"Yes, a Harvest Ball. It's a celebration of our harvest."

I gave her 'the look', "I know what it is, I'm just not sure I want to go."

"It's not for you it's for the people, nobles, and commoners alike. A travelling fair comes every year, and we have a Ball for the Nobles here in the castle."

"I think I'd rather go to the fair with the commoners."

"We shall do both. You won't have to do anything; I'll plan it all. You'll have to dance with me though."

"That I can do. Speaking of nobles, do they all live here in the city?"

"Yes." she looked at me strangely.

"None live on estates outside the city, or do they own any estates outside the city?"

"No, there are no estates outside the city. All lands belong to the Crown. All the nobles are merchants, and business owners."

"I have a proposal. We give lands to the third sons of nobles, to start estates out in the countryside. They would maintain the lands hire farmers to farm the land, who they would tax. We would in turn tax them. They would also have to maintain several fighting men to secure the area and keep the peace. They would get to build their fortunes, we put more land into production, and gain tax revenue or rental."

"They would not pay for the land?"

"That is an option, but mostly it's a reward for supporting, and fighting for us, the Crown. We may even give some estates to fighting men, for their service."

"How would we decide who gets this land?"

"Who are our most loyal supporters, who have third sons? If they don't have a third son, but want an estate, we'll sell them one."

"How far away from the city would these be?"

"I don't know, let's say 20 miles, and the estate would be 1000 acres. At least 200 of which would be cleared farmland. As an added incentive I'd raise a small, armed, walled hold. Like a walled in estate house. I'd also raise five farmsteads for their tenant farmers. They would not have to build anything right away. We can also put manned forts out on the borders for security, say 100 troops. They would also patrol our borders."

"I like the idea; it would make our lands more productive and take pressure off the city resources. Let's look at some maps and decide where we would put the estates."

We planned estates to be 20 miles from the city and 20 miles between estates. The first ones would be the first 20-mile ring out from the city. The first ring had five estates in it. The crown would buy supplies and equipment for the first year to get the estate up and running. After that we expected them to be self-sustaining, and taxable.

I let Reggie decide who would get the estates and all the rules, and regulation involved. She took to it like the proverbial duck to water.

The first fort I raised was to the North on the king's trade road. I put it five miles inside our border. I walled it, with six, .50 cal ballistas, a well, and stables for 100 horses. I had the men and supplies leave for there before I built it. Once they were six hours away, I raised the fort, and they moved right in when they arrived. We did the same on the West trade road. I left the southern route alone for now, but we still patrolled as they did.

When we put together a standard walled estate house, it was to support 30 people. Ten family members, ten staff, and ten troops. Farmers lived in their own houses on the farms. Once the first five were given away it become a status symbol. All the wealthy wanted one, and they paid through the nose to get one.

Not all could afford the price of the 1000-acre estates, so we sold a few 500-acre estates. Two bought 2000-acre estates. I guess keeping up with the Joneses applied here too. When we were done, we had three rings of estates around the city.

Our Navy was coming along nicely, we now had four manned and trained Navy ships. They were now out patrolling our shipping lanes. They travelled in pairs for now. We had two more ships and crews in training. I didn't think this calm would last.

***

The fall festival fair lasted 3 days, with the Ball on the last night. The fair was a big event for these people whose everyday life was spent just trying to survive. Reggie and I put in an appearance. We tried the foods, some games. But mostly we were just there to be among the people. The people seemed to enjoy seeing us there, being just regular people.

The Ball was different. All the peacocks showed up, everyone was trying to outdo the others. Daughters were being introduced to a prospective husband. We enjoyed the dancing, and Reggie enjoyed being around the other ladies. I had very little in common with these snobbish men, but I was courteous to them.

There was the usual political talk, alliances being made between houses. This or that noble trying to curry favor. Some dropping hints, rather crudely, that they would be interested in receiving an estate. The only thing that saved the evening was dancing with Reggie. She moved so smoothly. She was a wonder to watch.

"Challenge!" The music stopped, and the crowd separated from one of the peacocks.

"What are you challenging?" I asked.

"In days of old, any Mage could challenge for the throne and the right to rule. Ensuring the strongest Mages ruled."

"So, you are challenging my Queen for her throne, and as her champion, I will meet you. As you have challenged, I will choose the weapon. I choose magic and steel, to the death."

He chuckled, "you don't understand, it's not to the death, it's to total exhaustion."

"No, you don't understand. You have challenged my Queen, to get to her you will have to go through me, and I can assure you, it will be to the death."

This he did not expect and stood open mouthed staring at me.

"Perhaps you and your supporters would like to withdraw your challenge and reconsider."

He swallowed, "I cannot. I have challenged, to withdraw without trying would be cowardice."

"It is not cowardice to realize that if you fight at this time you would lose, but to withdraw to fight another day is a tactical decision of a wise leader. I think you have the potential to become a wise leader."

No one made a sound. He kept his eyes on me. "Then I have made a grave tactical error. You have both wisdom and strength on your side, and I had lost before I started. I withdraw the challenge." He bowed.

"Well said my friend." I bowed in return.

The Queen began to applaud, "Bravo, well said." Everyone joined in to applaud him. He had gone from looking the fool, to being the envy of everyone there.

"Music," the Queen shouted, and we danced the rest of the night away.

✻✻✻

I was just waking up, "what do you think of Briska for a boy's name?" Reggie asked.

I realized immediately what she meant. "Uh-huh, and if they said I'm the father, I'm not." She smacked me, palm flat right in the pocket of my back. "Ow," I yelled. Armor jumped up on the bed growling and put the whole calf of my leg in his mouth.

"That's right, get him boy chew daddy's leg off." He was growling and pulling me.

"Let go of me you traitor, and if you chew my leg off, who will run with Briska."

"I can run with him, keep chewing boy."

"I surrender, Briska is a wonderful name. Now call your traitorous dog off me."

She was laughing, "come here boy, come to mama. That's a good boy, you got that mean old daddy didn't you." she was hugging him.

I had never seen a 250-pound war dog act like a ten-pound toy poodle. I haven't laughed that hard in a long time.

"So, who's pregnant?"

"Get him, boy!"

I took off running with Armor, and Reggie right behind me.

***

"I want you to attend court today. I know you don't like it, but your brother has sent an envoy. I think you should be there."

"Any sign of what he might have to say?"

"None."

"I'm sure it not good news whatever it is."

Court opened with a few complaints to be heard, and some disagreements to be settled, finally the Crown Prince's envoy was brought forward.

He stood there looking at us. He did not bow or offer respect. This was starting off bad. "I'm going to go out on a limb here and assume you can speak."

"I can."

"And, you have a message for us?"

"Your brother, Crown Prince Cain, commands you to send him ten thousand golds. You are now part of the united Northern Kingdoms."

I nodded, "anything else?"

"Yes, he says if you don't send it, he will bring his army down here and take it, and more,"

"Ok,"

"Good, you will load the gold on wagons and provide my escort."

"I'm sorry, you misunderstood the answer. I meant, ok, we won't send the gold. Ok, send your army to take it."

"You fool."

I dropped him through the floor to his chin.

"Wait!"

"You mean you are still alive? I thought I had taken your head off. I guess I'll have to do it the hard way." I got up and drew my sword walking toward him.

"No, wait, wait!"

"Do you think if I send my brother your head, he will get my message?" I acted like I was thinking. "Probably not, he's not very smart, and neither are you." I raised him up, so he stood before us, he still did not bow or show respect. I slashed my sword and took off the front half of his right foot. I put flame to it, cauterizing it. I returned to my throne and waited for him to stop screaming.

"For the rest of your life you will remember that disrespect and arrogance have a price. And if you leave the Queen's presence without showing proper respect, I'll risk my brother not understanding what your severed head means."

He stood shakily, "Yes, Your Highness." He said bowing.

"Tell your Crown Prince that he will get nothing from us. We are our own Kingdom, if he brings his army south, we will destroy it to the last man. You may take your foot and go."

He bowed, "Your Highness, Majesty." He picked up the severed part of his foot and limped out.

"That could have gone better." Reggie said.

"Too much you think?" I smiled.

She shook her head, "I can't take you anywhere." That was the end of court for the day. We rose and left the throne room.

"So, what do you think?" Reggie ask as we shared lunch.

"Worst case they'll be back in four months with an army, six at the outside."

"You have a plan for us to avoid the worst case?"

"I will give him other things to think about instead of us. He'll be too busy to send anyone down here; he may need them elsewhere."

"Good, I don't want to have to send our people to war because of a spoiled brat," She said. I laughed.

***

I went underground and fast travelled to the northernmost place I had been. I flew underground the rest of the way to Midwick. I flew under the city looking it over. It seemed depressed. I went to the castle; it needed repairs. I checked the treasury, and as I suspected it was almost empty. I bet our father was behind that.

The first thing I did was dry up the wells inside the castle and castle walls. Then undermined the corner of the wall away from everyone and collapsed it. When it fell it took out a nice chunk of the two joining walls with it. That should keep his mind off us for a few minutes.

I went deep underground and opened a cavern. I opened my pavilion; she greeted me as I entered. "Welcome home Captain."

"Thank you." I walked to the table. "Hot tea please and open the map table." my hot tea appeared as did a map of the city. Expand the map to show the kingdom to the north, Klemstovel. I looked at the map as I drank my tea. "Is that the closest kingdom to us?"

"No, Norsewick, your father's kingdom, is closer by twenty miles." Interesting that she knew it was my father's kingdom. "Show me all fortifications between here and Klemstovel." The map showed two, one of theirs at the border, and one of Midwick's ten miles closer to us. I bathed and went to bed I needed to rest for a while.

***

I went around the city to the inns, and bars listening to talk among the people. I sat underground listening, these were not a happy people. Taxes had been raised, and new taxes invented. Food was short, and Cain paid for nothing he took. He felt he was entitled to whatever he wanted.

I might as well stir the pot a little. There were a few men drinking off to the side. I cast my beguiling spell. "The Crown Prince is emptying the treasury and sending it all to his father."

"Is that true?" one asked.

"I heard the same thing," another said.

"My cousin works in the castle, he says it's true. That's why he's always raising taxes he's bleeding us dry."

"Well, I for one have paid enough. I'll not pay anymore."
They all nodded.

I repeated this at every Inn and bar in the city. Then I went
to the troop's barracks. I cast the spell. "I hear they don't have
money to pay us, and if they don't I'm not risking my life for free.
I'm out of here."

I found the wash women and cast the spell. "I hear that
the Crown Prince has gotten some ladies with child and will not
recognize them, or that he is the father. He's an evil man that
one." That was enough for one day let's see what happens now.
I went back to my pavilion had a meal, a hot bath, and a good
night's sleep.

It took a few days, but all the merchants were now
demanding payment at the time of purchase. They accepted no
notes. The barracks rumor mill was running rampant. Things
were going missing, and discipline was suffering.

It also seems the Crown Prince was lacking
companionship. None of the nobles wanted their daughters
around him. A statue in the graveyard gave me an idea. I went
out to the cattle herd and found the drovers, beguiled them, and
sent them home. I made horses and riders out of dirt, wood and
stone. I cast an enchantment on these "trojan" horses and had
them herd the cattle north to Klemstovel. If they were chased,
they were to ride into the river and go back to earth. If they made
it to Klemstovel, leave them at the first fort they come to. Once
that was complete go into the forest and go back to earth.

Of course, the drovers reported the cattle stolen by a large
group of Raiders. They had tracked them to the border but went
no further.

I went to the money changers and beguiled them. "The
Crown Prince is going to confiscate your money." They were
gone the next morning. I let the pot simmer for a few days. I
spent the time reading in my library and rethinking all my plans.
I had a lot of irons in the fire.

I went to the north fort and beguiled them. "The fort is

on fire, a large force is coming, take everyone and ride to the main castle and warn them." The fort was empty in less than 30 minutes. I raised horse and riders and had them ride around the fort then over the border to Klemstovel. Leaving tracks of an invading force, I set fire to the fort and burned it to ruins.

The Crown Prince called up the army, but no one wanted to come. They had heard they would not be paid. Beatings were given proving to the men they had been right, there was no money to pay them. Cain started cross-border raids to get his cattle back, and to push back patrols coming across his border.

In less than a month I had given him more problems than he could deal with in a year. Then the envoy he had sent to me returned to give his report. I sat in on that. Cain sat silent listening to the report and my answer. He was gritting his teeth the whole time. He finally snapped, "Get out," and started throwing fire balls at everything. My work here was done... for now.

I closed my pavilion and cavern and went home.

CHAPTER 20

I now had to operate under the assumption, that it was not "if" someone was going to attack us but when. I guess it was the fact that we were young, in body, that made them think we would not fight. Someone would try us sooner or later. When they did, it would be with more than threats like Cain had done.

We needed better communications. I introduced semaphore to the military and set-up semaphore stations to each fort. I also put in an emergency bell in case the fort was about to fall. If they rang the bell at the fort, a bell would ring in the castle and I would know it. I could then teleport there to assess the situation and solve the problem.

"Do you know of any way to increase farm production?"

"I might, what's the problem?"

"Let's take a ride."

I think Reggie just wanted an excuse to go for a ride. I enjoyed it too, so we rode out to the farms to look at whatever she had in mind. As we rode past fields men were working the land. We rode out across the fields; men were turning the land by using shovels and crude wooden plows.

We stopped, and I got down to talk to the farmers, they all bowed. I could tell they were nervous. Why would Royalty be stopping? That usually meant trouble.

"Good Morning." I called to them.

"Good morning, Sire." They replied.

"We've come to check on the land, have we had enough rain?" If you want to get a farmer talking, ask him about the rainfall.

"Oh, aye M'lord, we've had a good bit so far. That's why we're out turning the land now."

"And we rotate crops fields and pastures from year to year."

"Right you are M'lord. Keeps the ground from being overworked."

"I am told that in another land they mix animal manure and water, then spread that over a field to help replace what crops take out of the ground. Have you ever heard of this?" I had been in Europe and smelled the honey wagons, and I knew it would work.

They all looked at each other shaking their heads. I nodded. "He swears by it. I'd like to test it. I'll pay you for the use of one field this year. We'll fertilize it, as he calls it, and plant. No matter the crop production, I'll pay as if it made the best crop. If it makes a good crop, we'll know it works."

They were all for making a guaranteed return on crops. We rode around a few other farms enjoying the day riding. After we returned to the castle, I visited the barrel maker and ordered two large tanker wagons. They already made them to haul water, so they know what I wanted. I paid for both in advance and told them I needed them as soon as possible.

My next stop was to the blacksmith's shop. "Master Smith, Good day to you."

"And to you M'lord, how may we serve?"

I took out my notebook. I lay my hand on it, and it copied the info and specs for an iron plow. I laid it out for him to see. "I'd like you to build an iron plow. We'll build one to test, when we are happy with how it works, we'll build more."

He looked at the drawings asking a few questions. He nodded, "We can do this easily enough M'lord."

"Good," I lay three golds on his table, "that is to get you started, I'll need it as soon as you can get it done."

He bowed, "Yes Sire."

Everyone in the kingdom knew we paid for everything, and most in advance, everyone was eager to do business with the Crown.

My head was full of ideas today, I went to a glassmaker's shop. He showed me around his shop. "Very nice work Master." I took a piece of raw glass in my hands and using magic formed a concave lens, I handed it to him, and picked up another piece and made a smaller convex lens. "can you make those?"

He looked at them nodding. "I think so sire, but I would need to experiment on a few to begin with."

I handed him two golds. "Please do so. Send word when you are satisfied with your work." I made two more lenses, for myself and took them with me. A few doors down was a tinker's shop.

"Good Day, M'lord, how may I serve?"

I handed him the drawing of what I wanted. Which was basically a tube to mount my two lenses in, to make a telescope. "I want these two lenses mounted inside the tube." I handed him the lenses.

He nodded, "Come back in a few days M'lord, and I'll have it ready." I paid him and let him get to work. As I started to leave his shop, I spotted something I had not seen here yet. A metal nibbed ink pen with a wooden handle. I picked it up. And looked at it was nice work. "I'd like to buy this."

"A gift for the business you will bring me when others see you shopping here." I rarely did that, it smelled like a bribe.

"I actually have an idea, and we can both make money."

"How so M'lord?"

I held the pen in my hand and concentrated. I formed a basic fountain pen, with a glass vial inside the wooden barrel. I put an enchantment on it to draw ink from an inkwell when it ran out. When I was done, I handed it back to him. I showed him all the parts and explained it to him; he was grinning from ear to ear. As an afterthought I placed another enchantment on the other end. When you touched the back end of the pen to the ink you had just written, it would remove the ink. But you had to make the correction before the ink dried. Once dry it was fixed to the paper. When he saw that, he could hardly contain himself.

"We will be rich."

I nodded, "even Kings have to make a living."

He busted out laughing, "You'd be the first I ever heard of that look at it that way." We laughed. I left the fountain pen with him to copy. I gave him four golds to finance our venture.

***

I was still harvesting my gold and silver traps. And was placing more out further afield. I was still getting a good return, some more than others. Out of curiosity I flew under to the mountains on our western border. I wondered what mineral deposits I might find there. I flew under the mountain range, finding gold, silver, quartz, coal and sulfur. I set my traps for the gold and silver.

I looked more closely at the coal. I knew they had surface coal mines in some parts of the world that made the coal mining easier. I concentrated on the coal vein and moved it all up to just under the surface on our side of the mountains. I'd hire someone to mine it for us, or... "*I wonder...*"

It had been easy to move the coal vein from its place around the mountain to one place. I wonder if I could move it closer to Port City. I concentrated. I didn't force it to move; I asked it to follow me as I flew along. I started slowly, and it followed me. Slowly at first, but it was moving. It felt like I imagine it would feel like flying in a headwind. Halfway home I had to stop and rest.

While I was resting, I looked around for some good-sized hills. We were outside the estate rings we had given and sold. I found what I was looking for a few miles further south. I made that the new home of my coal.

I hired a mining company to mine my coal on a 60/40 split after expenses. With the warning if he cheated the Crown, I'd put them in chains and have them mine it for free. I put up 100 golds to start the operation. They accepted my offer and took the contract. I sent our worst, and violent criminals to the coal mines to work. We hired unemployed citizens to replace them on the road work crews.

***

"Dear." Reggie said at dinner. I looked up at her. I knew by now when a conversation started with "Dear", something was about to happen.

"Yes?"

"I was looking over the treasury accounts today and noticed quite a few entries where you had made deposits."

There wasn't a question in there, so I waited. She looked at me waiting.

She blinked first. "Were the deposits taxes on something or someone?"

I took a swallow of my tea thinking. "Kind of."

She stared at me, "kind of?" I nodded; she couldn't stand it. My Grandmother, Mary, had been a bit nosey. When anyone started asking a lot of questions, we'd ask if their "Mary gene" was kicking in. "Where is the gold coming from?"

"I'm stealing it, of course." I held my face straight.

She stared at me. "Is that one of your tactical misdirections?"

I had to laugh, "I'm mining gold and silver from the land. I put half in the treasury and half in my personal vault."

"You have a personal vault?" her eyebrow raised.

"Did I say my, I meant our personal vault."

"May I see, our, personal vault?"

"Sure, when would you like to see it?"

"Now would be good."

"As in right now?" I was yanking her chain.

"I will punch you in the throat." She said smiling.

I laughed, "come on." We got up from the table. I led her to our bedroom. I closed the door behind us. "Put your hand here on this stone." She did, and the vault door opened. We walked inside and she looked around at the chests that lined the walls. She walked along opening them. She stopped after the first few.

"They are all full of gold and silver?" I nodded. "No wonder our treasury is doing so well, I was worried we might run short and have to raise taxes." She looked around the room, then back at me. "You are a good King, and husband." She came to me hugging me. "Now I can go shopping," she said laughing. I laughed with her.

***

The blacksmith had finished the iron plow, and we tested it. It worked well, but he wanted to make one change. "Make your change, but I want ten more made. As soon as people see what this will do, they'll be sold."

He nodded, "I believe it, I worked a farm, I wish we had had one of these."

Our "honey wagon" was the next thing we put into service. We fertilized our test field and let it set for a week then we turned the soil with our new iron plow. We'd have to wait and see what the harvest would be like. I knew it would be good, all things being equal.

My glassmaker was not satisfied with his efforts so far. He was having trouble getting the concave, and convex right in the lenses. But he was making progress.

The tinker had my telescope ready. It looked nice and worked perfectly. He also had five fountain pens ready. I enchanted them and filled them with ink. "Take two to the best jeweler you know. Have them encase one in ornamental gold and one in silver." I gave him two golds.

"I know just the man. When his customers see these, we'll have to hire more workers."

"Why wait I'll fund 100 pens, let's get started."

"I'll hire them tomorrow." I set a small purse of gold on his worktable, nodding.

***

Winter had been quiet, relatively speaking. There had been some cross-border run-ins with the north, but only a chase or two. No bloodshed. My inventions, though not technically mine, were doing well. The Blacksmith had sold all the iron plows he had, and they ordered 20 more. The glass maker had finally got his technique down and was producing lenses for my telescopes.

The fountain pens were selling as fast as the tinker could make them, both the ordinary ones, and the fancy ones. It made me nervous that everything was going so well.

I went to the General of our army. "I want you to draw up plans to counter an invasion. Think of where and how you would hit us, then counter it. I will do the same. Then we'll compare notes and see if we have missed anything."

"Have you heard of an invasion?"

"No, and that makes me wonder what they are doing. I'm sure they are doing something. Open this up to your officers. Make it a training exercise. Make them think tactics. We'll talk in a week."

When we reconvened the next week, I was impressed. They had multiple maps detailing multiple strategies. There were deployment orders supply lines, and troop movements. They had already shifted some of their patrols to better cover areas of concern.

After their briefing, "Well done gentlemen, very well done. Carry on." I felt a little better after that, but I still made my own patrols flying under to areas that we might have missed.

Prince Roman, and 50 troops arrived for a visit. They were all quartered at the castle. After dinner, "father wanted me to inform you we have had a visit from the Dunwich."

"Oh? And how did that go?"

"The representative appeared surprised, shocked, and mad. Surprised his men had turned on us, shocked we had defeated them, and mad that we had done so with no survivors. Father threw him out of the Kingdom, with a message not to return."

"That won't set well at home, but no matter."

"I would also like to discuss using your harbor for trade. We would like to bring in cargo and rent warehousing."

"Of course, we would welcome the business."

"I am also interested in buying the new iron plow your smiths are making. On the way here I saw some at work, they were impressive."

"They are making a difference in our production. We'd be

happy to sell you some. I'm not sure how many are available, but we can make more." I knew eventually other smiths elsewhere would make them. We might as well make money and friends at the same time.

He seemed a little apprehensive. "Was there anything else you wanted to discuss?"

He thought a moment, considering his words. "I do not wish to pry, but we've noticed a lot of small forts going up around your kingdom."

"The estates? We have opened lands to nobles as a reward or to be bought. So we may put more land under production. The estates, or small forts as you say, are incentives to get them to live on the land. It worked better than expected, and our crop production has increased substantially."

"And they willingly left the city?"

"They paid through the nose to buy the land to leave the city. It became a status symbol. If you don't own an estate, you are not an up-and-coming noble."

He laughed, "father will love this."

Prince Roman spent a week with us touring farms and estates. He ordered ten iron plows and paid in advance for them. I gifted him and his father with a telescope each, and a gold pen each. *"That will cause our sales to go up."* I smiled.

***

Something was nagging at my subconscious, and I couldn't sleep. I got up and worked out until I was soaked with sweat. I took a hot bath and lay soaking for a while. A thought finally percolated up.

"How would they get ashore?" My eyes popped open. If Dunwich was going to land another force here how they would get ashore. I had sowed reef all along our coast. They would have to go north. *"I'm an idiot."* If anyone would bring in Dunwich it would be Cain, and/or my father. Pay them to fight keeping their troops fresh in reserve. That would cost a fortune, but he had emptied the Midwick's treasury.

I got out of the tub and got dressed, at the map table, "show me the coastline north of Port City for 100 miles." The map came up. "Mark locations where ships could beach to unload cargo or troops." Nothing came up. Did that mean there were none or did the map not know? "Mark locations where long boats, could beach to unload cargo or troops." It highlighted two locations.

"Zoom in on the southern location." Nothing there and although there was a beach, getting off the beach would be problematic with the cliffs. "Show the northern location." This location had a beach, and easy access inland. That would be the place if there was a force coming in. I'd have to take a trip to find out.

If they are there how is Cain paying for them, gold? If I were them, I'd want all or a good portion of the money up front. Which means war chests of gold, and if someone was to intercept that gold shipment, no gold, no army. Better yet no gold, mad army on your doorstep looking to be paid.

CHAPTER 21

It could be worse, there could be twenty-thousand troop here. But the ten thousand that were here was bad enough. Fortunately, they moved like pond water. The loading and unloading was taking time. Moving ten thousand troops and their supplies ashore in longboats, was frustratingly tiresome. Tempers were short and getting worse. I added to the frustration by breaking the keel of one longboat as it was beaching. That was one less boat to use in unloading.

I moved around under the camp. Morale was low because of all the losses they had suffered in both ships and men. They had only been here a few days but the support that had been promised to them had not been forthcoming. There had been no fresh supplies, and the promised gold payment had not arrived.

I cast a beguiling suggesting they stop unloading until the gold arrived. The commander must have liked the idea because he stopped operation on the spot. The few men my brother had here to coordinate left to take the news that the unloading had stopped until the promised gold payment arrived. I followed along to watch the show.

Cain was in the stables when the messenger arrived. "Sire, they have stopped unloading the ships until their payment arrives. They said not one more troop will be landed until they are paid." I thought Cain's head would explode. But he had sense enough to get away from the horses before he started stomping and throwing fire around. *That man has anger issues.* I smiled.

"I told them their payment was on the way and would be here sometime today. Bring me my horse, I'll go and get things started again." He mounted, and they rode out. I headed out the other direction looking for the payment wagon. Even though it was late in the day, it shouldn't be too hard to find.

I found the two treasury wagons at dusk. The wagons were slow moving because of their weight. I went forward to the next wooded area and called up 100 golem cavalrymen, like the ones I used at the border ruse; I levitated over the wagons with my bow ready. As soon as they were in the kill box, I sprung the ambush. I froze the wagon with the ground stopping it. We attacked; the golem hit from both sides. The troops fought the golem as hard as they could, but steel does nothing to dirt and rock. I started at the front putting arrows through troops as I came to them. As soon as my arrow made its kill, it appeared back on my bowstring.

When the last troop fell, I had the golem form up around the wagons like an escort. I cast a spell on the horses and had them follow; I took the reins of the lead wagon, and the horses pulling the second wagon would follow mine. We moved out leaving the fallen troops where they lay. We took the first turnoff heading north to Klemstovel. Cain would strike first and think later. "Maybe I should leave them the gold for all the trouble I'm causing you... Nah..." I laughed.

I pushed the horse teams pulling the wagons for a few hours, then changed them out with golem horses. Then we moved again. I was making better speed now; golem horses don't get tired. We travelled all night until well before dawn. I sent all the live horses to graze out of sight in a field that had a stream. We moved on another mile, stopping in a wooded area. Opening the wagons, I put all their contents, and there was quite a bit, into crystals. I cut the golem horse teams loose and sent all the golem galloping toward the capital, but to go back to earth before sunrise. I sank into the earth and took a nap.

The vibrations of galloping horses woke me. They pulled up, stopping at the wagons. Men checked the wagons, "Empty Sire." The soldier called out.

"Find them, I don't care if we have to go to their Capital, find them!" They headed out chasing the golem tracks. Their horses were about done in. Cain must have brought every troop he had. Even at that, he only had about 400. This could turn ugly for him. Invading a neighboring Kingdom with only 400 men. They were already at odds. Not the smartest thing for him to do. *"Bless his arrogant heart."* I smiled.

"Well, I've come this far I might as well pour some gas on the fire." I flew under, racing ahead to Klemstovel's capital, some twenty miles ahead. I went up into the castle; the King was reclining in his bed. I cast the beguiling spell. "The Crown Prince from Midwick has invaded. If you capture him, you can ransom him for a fortune."

He jumped up and started shouting for his guards. I thought I had messed something up, until he started issuing orders for his army. That should keep them busy for a while. I fast travelled back to the beach where the Dunwich forces were landing. They hadn't unloaded anymore troops. When their commander was alone, I cast the spell. "They have no gold; they have lied to get us here. Load our troops back on the ships and let's go home. Let the King decide how to punish them."

"Quartermaster!"

"Yes Sir," a man said coming to him.

"Reload the ships, we are leaving, the quicker the better."

"Yes Sir." He saluted and started issuing orders.

***

I choked on my hot tea. Wiping my mouth and nose, "what did you say?"

"Twins, sire, The Queen has given you twins. The first, a son. The second a daughter." The midwife said smiling.

"They are all ok?"

She nodded, "Yes Sire, they are all fine. She is just tired. You may come in now."

I went in to see them. I used my Mage Sight to look at them. The babies were perfect and healthy, and I could see a Mage spark in them. Reggie looked tired but beautiful. I healed her and restored her strength.

She smiled, "That's better, thank you." Now I know why

first-time fathers act the way they do.

Although Reggie had help with Briska, and Margaret, there was no full-time nanny. We would raise our children, not strangers. Reggie was a great mother, and the twins were calm always having each other as company. I'm sure that would change in the future. I stayed home for a time helping with the twins when the women would let me. They all wanted to hold them, and the babies loved the attention.

I rescinded the Letters of Marque. We now had six ships in our navy, and eight ships in our merchant fleet. They could still take ships if attacked, we just didn't actively hunt them anymore... Supposedly.

Our Army Officer's Corps, and our army was improving, and we had enacted a mandatory service for all citizens. I dialed it down; it was like the national guard. One weekend a month, Two weeks a year.

Our farms were doing well, and honey wagons became the norm. Every farm owned an iron plow, and I had commissioned a wheeled cultivator. It was still in the testing phase.

Our coal mine was now in full operation and was shipping coal to Port City and to Volwick. Our relations with the Volwick continued to improve. They were renting a warehouse and were doing a lot of business. They had even bought two ships of their own. Prince Roman came to visit every few months and stayed with us a week. He was always looking for new innovations.

"May I ask about your magic?"

"Sure," I answered.

"You use it quite a bit, more than others, I mean."

"I suppose."

"Is your magic getting stronger?"

I nodded. "Magic is like a muscle, the more you exercise it the stronger it gets."

"Did your father teach you?"

"No, definitely not. He thought, that if he taught anyone, that one day they would take his throne."

"But isn't that what's supposed to happen, the King trains

his son to replace him someday?"

Yes, but I think it was the 'someday' he worried about. And in my family, it was a valid concern. No one trusts anyone. Which is why I'm glad I am here. We do things differently here. I want my heirs to be ready to take over when it's time."

"If your father did not teach you, where did you learn all your magic?"

"Books, trial and error mostly." I side stepped the rest of the story.

"May I read some of your books?"

"Sure, come on I'll take you to the library in the castle." Not all my books were there, but it would get him started. After that I could usually find him in the library. That started me thinking about teaching magic. How did one go about it? I checked my notebook and as usual found what I was looking for. There were a few examples of how to teach magic. Of course, you had to be a "Mage" in the first place. I guess there is a "Mage Gene". Anyway, the thing is there were ways to teach magic other than trial and error.

It is common knowledge that if you teach a subject; you get better at that subject, or task. So, I started helping Roman with his magic. The first thing I taught him was to levitate. Then had him practice while meditating. Each time he visited I would either help him with something he was having trouble with or teach him something new.

I also started teaching Reggie. She advanced faster because we were so close. I could do direct contact teaching. The thing was, you had to totally trust the other person because you opened yourself to them and were vulnerable. They were inside your defense's. Reggie was always inside my defense's, so I had no problem opening to her. Well, to some extent. Some things I kept shut off subconsciously.

I looked in my notebook for references on how the notebook was made. It was simple but not easy. Fortunately, I also found a place where I could make a blank copy of mine without all the trouble of creating a completely new one. I made two copies. One for Reggie and one for Roman.

In the notebook I would give Roman, I added some basic spells, and explanations. Things that a beginning Mage needed to learn, and a foundation for further learning. I also added The Map pages, these would help him in the future.

In Reggie's I put in much more, not everything that was in mine, she would start asking questions. Questions I was not ready to answer, not yet, if ever. Her notebook also included the map section.

Once I had made theirs, I realized I had not updated mine in quite a while. I had absorbed more knowledge, so I needed to update it. There were also books in the Royal library I needed to add to my collection. Now that I thought about it, there were books in my pavilion library I needed to read and add to it. There were also other libraries I needed to search, but that would have to wait.

I made time and updated my notebook. Everyone thought I was studying in the library, which suited me fine. The Major-domo brought me hot tea while I was taking a break.

"Sire, Nobleman Stevens has asked for a private word."

"Did he say what it was about?"

"He did not Sire. This the first time as far as I know he has ever asked to speak to the Crown, and he is the oldest living person in the Kingdom."

"Show him in." He at least had my curiosity up.

He bowed, "Yes Sire."

An older man approached, followed by a younger man," Sire, May I present Nobleman Stevens."

"Well met Nobleman."

Both men bowed. "Sire, thank you for seeing me." The Major-domo left. The young man stayed.

I looked at them with Mage Sight. Both were Mages, and both were unarmed. "I thought you wanted a private word Nobleman."

He bowed, "forgive me sire, but as it pertains to his life, I ask your indulgence."

"Very well, have a seat," They sat, and more tea was brought in and served. We waited until we were alone once more.

"So, Nobleman what's on your mind?"

"I have been watching you since your arrival, Sire. You have done more for the Kingdom than the combine Kings I have served, and I'm 103." He looked good for 103 even by modern standards. "You have helped everyone, regardless of their station in life. Built or improved literally everything in the Kingdom. It is with high hopes that I've come before you today."

"Now that you have pumped enough sunshine up my skirt," I said smiling. "What can I do for you?"

He chuckled, then turned serious again. "I want to adopt this man as my son, and heir."

I looked at the younger man. "Ok, what's the problem?"

"He is illegitimate."

"Ok, I still don't see a problem. If he's your son, even if he is not, and you want to adopt him, that's your business."

"There will be some who will want to have him killed."

I frowned, "Why?"

"He is illegitimate, and a Mage." They watched me closely.

My frowned deepened. "What am I missing?"

"It is not publicized, but for many years, I should say many generations, they killed illegitimate Mage. The nobles felt it a threat to their rule. If commoners could be Mages, next they would want to be equals. I personally think it started with the wives who wanted to protect their legitimate children. They wanted to protect their inheritance, and status. That is what it was in my case. My wife was adamant about me not acknowledging him. Though she gave me no heir. He was an embarrassment to her."

I shook my head, "stupid people." I looked at the son. "Your name?"

"Spencer, Sire."

"Your talent, Spencer?"

"Healing, Sire."

I look back at the father, "which is why you've lived to 103."
He nodded.

"I'm guessing that there are more people who know about your talent. You've healed them, and in gratitude they've kept your secret." They both nodded. "So, what has caused you to come forward now, what has changed to force your hand?"

"You, Sire. We felt you were our best hope of making Spencer my legal heir."

"And you were willing to bet his life on my benevolence?" They nodded.

I thought a moment. "This can't be the first time this has happened. Has any noble ever adopted, or recognized a mundane illegitimate?"

"I think there have been a few, Sire, but I can't be sure."

"So, if he was a mundane, what would be required for him to be recognized as your heir?"

"The Crown's blessing."

"You have it. Why not do it that way from the start?"

"I wish to help more people with my talent, not hide it." Spencer said.

I nodded, "I can see that. Ok, here is what we can do. You have my blessing. You need to go to a healer who will train you in the areas you are lacking. Do you know a healer who will work with you?"

"I've been working with one for years. He is getting old, and I do most of the work now."

"Good, get him to sign-off on your 'Masters' papers. No more problems, if one comes up, point them to me."

They nodded smiling. "Thank you, Sire."

"On another subject, I'm going to make some statements. You will not answer, just listen." They nodded.

"You can't be the only illegitimate Mage out there. If I were one and knew that if I was ever found out I might be killed, they'd never find me. Hypothetically we have some Mages out there that are wasting their talents, or using them, probably outside the law to survive."

"I'd like to get these Mages into a productive life, serving the Kingdom. I would pay them for their services. You may have heard of some of these people. Let them know I'm offering to make a place for them. I will not come looking for them. They must come to me. I'd meet with them anywhere they wish. We could all benefit from this." They nodded.

"Sergeant Major." I raised my voice. The Major- domo, who was a retired Sergeant Major, came back into the library sitting area.

"Sire?"

"Have papers drawn up showing the adoption of Spencer to Nobleman Stevens, as his legal heir."

"Yes, Sire."

They took that as their dismissal, "thank you, Sire." They bowed and left.

I looked in my notebook for "Mage Guild" and there was only a short reference to one Mage School many years ago, and yes far, far, away. I smiled.

Over dinner, "Have you ever heard of a Mage Guild or a Mage School?"

"No," Reggie answered." Magic is usually taught by parents or relatives. sometimes, tutors. But I've never heard of a school, and definitely not a guild. All Mages are nobles. It would be beneath them to belong to a guild."

"*Oh well, no Hogwarts.*" I smiled. "You are probably right; they have trouble agreeing on what time to eat." I said. I'll have to think on this. I wonder if anyone else realized that the "Mage Gene" was already out there.

"I have a gift for you." I said.

"Oh? What have you done?" she smiled.

"Nothing...that I'm going to admit too. Beside I didn't get caught." I handed her the notebook I made for her. It looked fancier than mine.

"Ooow, pretty."

"It's an enchanted notebook." I showed her how to us it. She fell in love with it immediately. I did good.

CHAPTER 22

I had always heard of the "terrible twos" but I had never seen it. Now I know why they call it the terrible twos. The twin's favorite word is "no". It was like watching a ping pong game between them, bouncing "No" back and forth. So, I choked one out, the other one started acting better... Ok, no I didn't, But I wanted to choke both little buggers. I sure love those little scamps, and so does Armor. Who is their horse, apparently.

We spend a lot of time reading to them and teaching them to count and say their ABC's. They are two quick learners, and smart. Do all parents say that about their children? Probably. But in their case, it's true, I smiled. Reggie is a great mom and keeps their minds challenged. She finds new things to occupy their minds and to teach them.

Having children made me more aware of other children. I talked to the Head Priest, and we built and financed an orphanage. They also went into the school. The school was doing well and was widely accepted. Especially since the Crown fed their kids two meals a day for free.

Half the streets in the city were now paved, and they would finish the main road heading to the trade road by the end of the year. More and more people had found other work. I guess road work was too much labor for them.

Our "National Guard" was doing well. They didn't like it. But they got used to it, and it gave them a little extra money. Some had crossed over to become full-time army. Conversely, some full-timers, became part-time guard.

Volwick had adopted most of our programs, though not on the same scale. Overall their Kingdom was doing better. I believed Roman was responsible for a lot of it. I had given him the notebook; he was speechless; I made sure he knew how to hide it in his body. He was continuing to improve as a Mage, and as a leader.

He had learned to levitate and was doing well at that. He had started "flying" some but stayed close to the ground for now. I had him start levitating objects and moving them around himself. He was up to two objects consistently.

"Can you teach me to build roads and buildings?"

"I'm not sure, we'll try, but your talent so far has been with fire, mostly. That may just mean you will have to work harder." I pointed at a rock. "Use your Mage Sense to see and feel that rock." He looked at it, I could tell he was concentrating. "Can you feel inside of it?"

"A little it feels like sand, but harder."

I nodded. "Yes, now without breaking it make it flat, don't try to 'Stomp' it flat, but do it easily."

I could see it working and it was slowly heading in the right direction. Sweat was breaking out on his face. "Stop. You are trying too hard to force it. Rest for a while and try again. It's just going to take practice like everything else we do."

***

I walked to the harbor, looking at things as I walked. Everyone greeted me, some bowing, some calling out from their work. I replied in kind.

I found Dov-ees hard at work as always, the smell from the kitchen upstairs was wonderful. "Admit it, you married her for her cooking didn't you."

"Of course, why else." we laughed.

"What news from the north?"

"It seems your brother, the Crown Prince, was captured while raiding Klemstovel. Your father had to agree to the marriage of your sister to gain his release."

I started laughing. "Something tells me they will regret that deal."

He smiled, "Perhaps, it was either marriage, or bankrupt

Norsewick."

"Yeah, and children are cheaper. Is the Crown Prince back in charge of Midwick?"

"No, your father installed a governor, and the Crown Prince is back at court. I have noticed more caravans coming from the north. They seem to be more interested in what's going on in Port City than in trade."

"I'm not surprised. He's always had his eyes on Shornwick, and especially Port City. Having me marry into it was icing on the cake. Sooner or later he'll try us. As soon as he sees a weakness, he'll try to exploit it. Keep your ears open."

***

I stopped by the school, more and more people of all ages had started attending. I would have to add to the mess hall, kitchen, and probably the classrooms. It would be worth the investment.

"Good afternoon Sire."

"Father, how are you today?"

"Fine M'lord. You have found everything satisfactory?"

"I have, you and the other priests are doing fine work."

"Thank you Sire. Do you have time for tea and to discuss some things?"

"I do." We went to his office and sat. Tea was brought in and served.

"A friend of Spencer wants to speak to you. He would like to meet with you, but he has a fear of people in power." I used my Mage Sight to see if there was anyone else with us. There was not, but to my surprise I saw the priest was a Mage.

"I understand. What can I do to help?"

"Would you swear before God that you are not seeking to hurt him?"

"I would, but you and I both know that if I were truly after him, me swearing to God would not stop an evil man. I'll make this easier for us. I want to educate and make him a productive member of the Kingdom as a Mage. His first step would be to get a basic education. If this person must work to support his family, or himself, I will pay him to go to school. Once he completes that, we'll talk about the next step. If he, or they, want to meet at any point let me know."

"I believe that would be acceptable. He works to support a family. Sire, your offer of paying for him to go to school is most generous."

I handed him a small purse. "Let me know when you need more. Tell him the same offer goes for any others that may find their way to your door."

"I will Sire."

"And what if we have one, or some who already have a basic education?"

I sat back. "Then we need to figure out how to continue their education in both, mundane and magic. I would need your council in that."

He nodded, "I'll see what I can come up with."

***

My chat with the Father started me thinking. Further education, military and civilian. And another need kept circling around in my head. Spies. I went back to see Dov-ees.

"Back so soon?"

"Something's come up."

"What's wrong?"

"Our talk and other talks I've had today, has shown me a weakness. I want you to train some people for me."

"Those, kind of people?" I nodded, "To what end?"

"Information. Other kingdoms are spying on us, I think we are falling behind. Information is power, we need to know what they are planning. I don't need assassins; I need information gatherers. I don't need to know how to take over a Kingdom, I have more than enough right here. I just don't want anyone taking what we have."

He nodded thinking, "As it happens, I agree with you. We are falling behind in that area. Do you have anyone for me to train?"

"Not at the moment, I'll leave that up to you. You know what type of person who works best."

He nodded, "I'll get started. I'll use some of what I already have in place as part of our merchant network, and I'll add to that."

"Good, let me know it you need anything. I'll need monthly in-depth updates. More if something important breaks."

"Of course." He bowed.

***

I fast travelled to Storm Island. There were no ships here now. I placed a rune on the sea floor at the mouth of the small bay. Now any time a ship came in I would know about it. I levitated higher on the Volcano cliff and made a small ledge. Now I could open a portal to look and see who was here without having to make the trip. I didn't want to do away with the place; it served everyone. Now it would provide intel on ship movements.

I started letting my paranoia show me weakness. I drew runes on the twins backs then let them sink under their skin. Now we always knew where they were and could teleport to them or them to us if needed. I set more wards around the castle and the city. I set wards under the castle in case someone with Earth Magic came to visit. When our ships were in port, I added more wards to them. I put a cloaking ward on all ballistas. Unless you were on the ship, they could not be seen. I added wards to the wall and gates and cloaked all ballistas. No need to advertise.

I made wagon based ballistas as our army's artillery arm. These I cloaked to look like supply wagons. I added .50 cal ballistas wagons to protect the artillery ballistas and other vulnerable assets and headquarters. I made sure all ballistas had plenty of ammo.

When our ships went out with their cloaked ballistas, they started getting attacked. The enemy thought they were no longer a threat. We now owned more ships, and the crews were happy with their share of the spoils. The Crown bought the ships and paid the prize money to the captain and crew.

We expanded our Army Signal Corps by adding Morse Code to their training. I figured out a way to make a wireless telegraph using sunstones. I made matched sunstone pairs and made a telegraph key to send messages. We could now communicate 24/7 no matter the weather with all our outposts. We set up a communication center in the military HQ at the castle.

I made another set of sunstone telegraph (SST) keys that, like the ground sheet, could be folded up and hid anywhere. If it was about to be taken just tear the paper in half. It would turn to dust. These I gave to Dov-ees for our trade network. All those messages went through him. It took time getting them in place, but once we did, we were getting close to real time intel. For our spies I made an SST that went under the skin of the middle finger and thumb. They could send and receive messages from anywhere, anytime. These too went through Dov-ees.

It took a while, but we could finally open a trading house in Dunwich. We concentrated on trade and ship fleet movement, especially troop ship movements. Unknown to anyone I had sent a small sunstone with the Dunwich traders. When they signaled they had arrived, I made plans for a visit.

Over dinner we caught each other up on our day. "We've just gotten word that the Dunwich trading house is up and running."

She nodded, "That will help us keep an eye on them."

"It will and will bring in some of those spices you like." She nodded smiling." I'll be leaving in the morning; I want to see firsthand what the monster looks like."

"How long will you be gone?"

"I'm not sure, a few days, no more than a week."

"Don't start any trouble."

"Me?" She just gave me "the look", shaking her head. I

laughed.

We shared an early breakfast before I left. I teleported to the sunstone's location but landed underground out of sight. I recovered my sunstone for future use. I needed to rest a bit. It had been a long-distance teleport and drained my Mage power. I rested in the earth for a little while and recharged.

When I was rested, I put on an illusion of the local dress. I toured the market, sampling the food, and looking at their wares. I looked at their horses and cattle. I was thinking of buying studs and bulls to improve our herds.

"Do you see anything you like M'lord?"

I smiled "I see a lot I like; you have some good stock here."

"What are you interested in?"

"I'm looking for two studs and two bulls to introduce some new bloodlines."

"What are you breeding for?"

"The horses for stamina, and bulls for weight."

He nodded, "I think I may have what you are looking for," and lead me to another area.

They were some beautiful horses. I rode them; they were marvelous animals. I bought two studs, and two huge bulls. Paying for them, "I'll pick them up later."

He bowed. "They will be ready when you are M'lord."

***

Once everyone in the castle had gone to bed, I went to their library. I sealed the door and started looking through the books. I found some I wanted to copy. I lay those on top of my notebook. The notebook made exact copies of them. I unsealed the door and left.

I searched the castle for the military offices. When I found the office, I was impressed with their reach. This was the first world map I had seen; it was not the landmasses of my world. I held my notebook on every map and note in the room. I now had troop locations, and movement. Ship locations, and movements, deployments and fort locations. It reminded me of England at the height of their empire.

They didn't have people on every landmass, but it was a lot. There were six major landmasses and many smaller ones. Islands were scattered everywhere, there was no way of knowing how accurate this map was, but it was a starting place.

I went under the castle and looked at their treasury. They were not strapped for cash. It looked like one of their main exports were troops. I wonder if they were operating like England, expanding their empire.

The port here was a major one, and there were ships of all sizes here to trade. Judging by the flags they were from many countries. This would be a good place for our business. We can buy things from all over the world sitting right here.

I went to my merchant and let him know I was here and would rent or buy us a warehouse. This end of the wharf was the oldest or looked like it. It had fallen into disrepair and needed a lot of work. There were warehouses on this end, but they were in the same shape as the wharf. I found who owned the buildings and the land. I paid more than they were worth, and he was glad to sell them to me.

That night I went under and repaired the wharf, the piers, and the warehouses I now owned. The next morning, I went around to my other tenants and introduced myself, as the merchant next door and the new owner. They said right away they could not afford more rent.

"Your rent is not going up. I wanted you to know that I have hired a Mage to repair the buildings and make them new. So, don't be surprised when you come in and see it." Now they were really expecting their rent to go up. In the warehouse we were using I put in a basement vault, and nice living quarters upstairs. I also gave them enough money to furnish it.

It was the next day before the local "Boss" showed up. "You the man who just bought these buildings?"

"I am."

"Then you owe me rent."

"Are you the only man I'll have to deal with, or will your boss be coming around later."

"There ain't no other boss, I own this area."

"Good. You now work for me, and I will pay you a lot of money." He and his four men laughed.

"And what if we don't want to work for you?"

I dropped them all into the ground up to their necks. "Then I'll kill you and hire the next guy who comes around." I said drawing my sword.

"Tell me, Sir Mage, what will our duties be?" This guy was cool under fire. I raised them out of the ground.

"I don't want any trouble from anyone on the docks. I want to operate with no shakedowns. You will protect my interest, and I'll pay you for it."

"We can do that."

"If you fail me…" I looked at the leader.

He nodded, "Understood."

I handed him a purse of gold. "We'll make sure your business runs smoothly, at least from our side." I nodded, they bowed and left.

I made sure they were fully funded before I left. I closed my pavilion, collected my two studs, and two bulls. I opened a portal home and walked them through. I gave them to my wrangler to put them to work; I went into the earth to rest, and recharge.

CHAPTER 23

I was in my pavilion, looking at the map table. "Show me a map of the whole earth." A flat global map came up. I had never asked this before; all my problems had been local. I compared the map table to the map from Dunwich. they were much the same. I felt the table was more accurate. It showed more landmasses and more detail.

I lay my notebook on the table, "Update the map table with the locations of Dunwich forces, and posts." The table updated and now showed all my notebook showed. "Update my notebook with the more accurate table map." My notebook updated.

There was a lot of land out there that was unclaimed, according to these maps. But I bet there were people there, there usually was. "I wonder? Show me the world's nautical maps." The map view changed to nautical maps. "Update my notebook maps to include nautical maps." My notebook now had global nautical maps, something I bet very few others had, if anyone. I would have to send some ships out to check a few of these landmasses and see what was there.

I looked at the maps west of us. There were mountains, that was our border, but it showed no other Kingdom past that. I needed to go check that out. I needed to see who, and what was out there. I may have to block a pass and extend our borders west. I could put a fort out there and start a town to support the fort and vice-versa.

***

I had to sit in on another court session as we had an envoy from my father. When his turn came to speak, he stepped forward and bowed.

"Your father, the King, invites you to visit for a time to discuss your duties."

I stared at him. "My duties? What duties would that be?"

"I'm sure I do not know, King Aaron. He was most insistent that you present yourself at court."

"Do you think my father thinks you are an idiot?" He didn't answer. "Do you think my father thinks I am an idiot?" No answer. "What is this we are holding now at which you speak?"

"Court." He finally answered.

I nodded, "As we have our own, we will not be using his."

"He will not be happy."

I laughed. "I am long past worrying about what makes him happy or doesn't make him happy." The envoy didn't look happy. "Was there anything else?"

"No, King Aaron."

"Have a safe trip home." He bowed and left.

***

We were sitting down at our evening meal; the twins had been put to bed. This was "our" time to catch up or have alone time. Reggie always caught me up on Kingdom business, and I'd tell her about our other businesses.

"I think I will look at what is out west. I know we have the mountains there, I'm sure there are resources for us to mine. I just wonder who else is out there, and..." I froze.

"What's wrong?" She asked.

"The children."

I grabbed her arm and teleported us into their room. There was a fight going on in their room. Amor had the twins in the corner behind him, he was facing out, tearing someone to shreds. Six assassins were stabbing and shooting arrows into him. His armor flared stopping everything they sent at him. Reggie and I attacked. I hit the Mage tearing his head off taking his knowledge and power. I never slowed as I slashed my way through to meet Reggie who had burned three of the assassins to smoldering ash heaps. She was so mad that someone had attacked her children; she was a pillar of Mage Fire.

Armor whirled around to check the twins, once he saw they were ok, he whirled back around growling, and snapping at the bodies. I teleported us all down to my cavern to our pavilion.

"Go inside and seal the pavilion."

Reggie nodded, "be careful." They went inside.

I knew from the knowledge I had taken from their Mage, there were three more hit teams in the castle. I was in no mood to be merciful. I went up through the walls of the castle. These three were blocking teams for the one we killed. It had been their job to take the twins. *"Thank God for Armor."* I had to smile at that, I always wondered why he had been named Armor.

I found the first group blocking the path from the guard's barracks. I pulled the Mage into the wall and took his power and knowledge. I came out of the other wall behind them daggers in hand. I stabbed up through brain stems, and through their backs into their hearts. They were dead before they hit the floor.

The next group was inside the main doors. They were spread out along the door with bows. I pulled their Mage under and took his knowledge and power. I now knew what Assassin's Guild house they were hired out of. I struck from the wall pulling each one into the wall and leaving them there to die, drowning in stone.

The final team was guarding their escape route. I needed to bleed off some power that I had built up taking theirs. I stepped out of the wall and with a thought, the Mages' head came off his body and flew into my hands. I took his knowledge and power; at the same time, I snapped the other five assassin's necks they fell dead where they stood.

I concentrated and sent all the bodies, equipment, and blood down to my cavern. I teleported there and searched the bodies. I didn't think I would find anything of use, and I didn't. The Mages had some runed jewelry, a staff, and a blessed bag. All of which went into my pouch. Nothing incriminating. I really didn't need anymore; I knew that they had come out of the

230

assassin's guild house here in the city. One that I had not known about. After tonight, there wouldn't be one.

I went into the pavilion. Armor was sitting in front of the door. "Good boy." I patted him and scratch him. His tail was wagging, he knew he had done good. He went over and stayed by the twins. They seemed to take it all in stride.

"Are we all clear?" Her hands were shaking, not from fear, but from the adrenalin in her system.

"We are, and no one the wiser. Hot tea." I said to the pavilion. It appeared on the table.

"Who were they?" she poured our tea.

"Assassins from a guild house here in the city." I took a swallow of tea.

"In our city?"

I nodded, "for a few more hours. I will go pay them a visit. When I leave there will be no Assassins' Guild in our city. I need to go; their Guild will expect them or some word from them. I'll give it to them in person."

She kissed me, "be careful." I nodded.

***

I was under the Assassin's Guild house looking it over. I knew they would have traps, both mundane and magic. I started with the magic ones. I erased the rune that would activate the spell. I was hoping by doing it that way, no alarms would be set off. So-for, so-good.

Once I had neutralized the magic traps, I found and neutralized the Guild lookouts around the neighborhood. I stayed below the house. I concentrated on the sleeping assassins and teleported them one by one into the earth. The only sound that it made was like someone taking a small sip of tea. Their Guild Master, who was asleep, I put in a deeper sleep. I'd save him for last. Next, I teleported the assassins that were awake, and alone down into the earth. They drowned in dirt.

The only one left was a Mage, and he was glowing like a

torch in the darkness. I started toward him; a memory stopped me. He was standing in the middle of a runed circle. I made my Mage signature small, then sent an illusion up into the wall with enough magic around it to make it look like a Mage trying to sneak in. Unless you looked closely, you would think a Mage was in the wall.

I waited not moving, me or the illusion. He blinked first. "At least come out and face me." I moved the illusion to the right, he struck. A huge ribbon of lightning erupted from the floor through him and into the wall. That section of the wall was blown out of existence.

The light was blinding but my helmet blocked it out. I teleported up behind him and drove my hand into the back of his skull and into his brain. I took his knowledge and power. It was like grabbing a high voltage line. All I could do was hold on. He was dead, and if I let go, I would be too. I pulled him down into the earth and fought to stay conscious.

This was the strongest Mage I had ever faced, and the strongest any of my memories knew about. I held on absorbing all his power. All his power was finally drained into me. I felt like a sun burning in the darkness. I let go of the Mage and looked around. I could see farther than before and knew of things further away.

I pulled the Guild Master down to me; I drained him of his knowledge. I sealed all the doors to the guild house. Fortunately, I had accounted for all the assassins, and they were dead. I now knew the names and faces of everyone who worked for the Guild.

Two were Royalty and members of court. A few were in the army. A couple in the city watch, and various others around the city. None were close to us, or in the Red Cloaks. All the ones named apparently had bad hearts, as they would die of heart attacks, as soon as I could get to them.

I concentrated and opened a cavern below the guild house. I concentrated on the guild house and brought everything inside the house down into the cavern, including their library and their treasury vault. They had other businesses and vaults around the city I would get to them later.

The best bit of information I had was, the attack was ordered from Norsewick, but carried out locally. I needed to burn some Mage power off; I was way too hot. I paved a road from our south gate, toward the Volwick. I stopped at the river dividing our two kingdoms but built a bridge over it.

I teleported to Norsewick, but well away from the castle. I went deep under the city to the Assassin's Guild house. There were six mages here. I pulled them all under at once and ripped their knowledge and power from them. I pulled the Guild Master under and took his knowledge. I was burning up with the additional Mage power. I concentrated on the house and with a thought killed everyone in the house, by breaking their necks.

I opened a cavern and moved everything in the house down into the cavern like I had done in the other Guild House. I left the naked bodies where they lay. I now knew it was Cain who had given the order for the kidnapping of my children.

I teleported to Dunwich, then to Port City, then Dunwich, then back to the Norsewick to burn off some Mage power. I felt better now. I didn't feel like I was about to burn up. I was still carrying a lot of power. I shrugged; this might be my new norm.

I went to every assassin's business in the city and emptied their vaults, bringing it all back to the cavern below the Norsewick's Guild House. I put everything gathered there into a crystal.

That's when I had an epiphany. The assassins had Mages. They were not Royalty; they had to be the illegitimate offspring of Royalty. Why hadn't I recognized this. This made us reaching them before the Assassin's Guild, an imperative. Once the assassins had them, they were lost.

I closed the cavern and teleported back to the Shornwick's Guild House cavern. I put everything gathered into a crystal. I had a lot of stuff to sift through, and a lot of it was Mage stuff. I closed the cavern under the house and teleported back to the pavilion cavern.

I put everything I had gathered from the fallen attackers into a crystal and went into the pavilion. The twins were asleep. "You are well husband?"

I smiled. "I am. We won't have any more trouble from that bunch. But I need to go to Norsewick to follow a lead, to see who ordered the attack."

"How long will you be gone?"

"A week may be less. You may go back up into the castle, we are safe."

"I will in the morning, the children are finally asleep."

"That's probably best." I kissed her, "I'll see you in a week."

"Be careful." I nodded and teleported back under the Norsewick assassin's guild house. I concentrated and opened all the outside windows and doors in the guild house. I waited, every assassin that came to check in, or see what was going on, I killed. I put their naked bodies in the main hall. I had either killed them all, or they got smart and quit coming in. I thought the later was the case.

***

Because my power was so bright at the moment, I went deep and opened a cavern and opened my pavilion. I ate a big meal of steak, and potatoes.

I went outside and opened one crystal from the guild house. Most was useless to me. I discarded clothes, there were very few personal items. There were a few runed items, which I kept. I destroyed the poisons, and I kept all the valuables. I did the same to the crystals from the other guild house, and the attackers. Most of the valuables went into the pavilion vault, some went into my pouch. I again destroyed the poisons.

It was now mid-morning up top. I lowered my power output as much as possible and went up to the guild house. There was nothing going on now. I went to the castle but stayed under. Amos, Cain, mother and father were there. Nothing had changed as far as I could tell.

They had gathered for breakfast. No one was talking, one big happy family. I was about to leave, when a servant came in with a note for Cain. He read the note crumpled it and hit the table with his fist. I guess he knows his assassins are dead, the ones here anyway.

Father looked at him, raising an eyebrow. Cain passed him the note. He read the note. "No further information?"

Cain shook his head, "That's the first information I've gotten."

"We need more. Was this an internal fight, something other than us? The timing is suspicious and concerning."

"This couldn't be Aaron, not this soon."

"I'm learning not to put anything past that boy. If it's a choice between Aaron and someone else who has wiped them out. I'm going with Aaron, just in-case."

"If it is him, then he knows it was us, and is taking revenge on the guild."

Father nodded, "He'll be looking at us next."

"Then we should move against him now before he can hire anyone to send against us. Or raise his army to come against us."

"I don't think he will raise his army against us. He might hire it done, but he won't come himself."

"We should hit him now. That Kingdom is a ripe plum, ready to be picked."

"Yes, but it will have thorns around the fruit."

"Our army out numbers his two-to-one."

"Yes, but they are behind a wall which make us equal and gives him the advantage. We must call up the rest of our armies. From the Midwick and Klemstovel. That will give us almost 80 thousand troops. If we do that, it will take us a month to raise them, and he'll know we are coming."

"Maybe he'll fold when he sees our army."

"He won't fold. If we call up the army, it will be a fight to the end. One side will be finished. This may be the time to take control and expand our Kingdom folding in all five kingdoms into one. While we are down there, we'll take Volwick as well."

Amos had said nothing this whole time, neither had mother. He just shook his head. "I don't understand," Amos said.

They looked at him. "You don't understand what simpleton?" Cain asked.

Amos smiled, "You are trying to control three Kingdoms now and their infrastructure is falling apart. Now you want to take 80 thousand men south to take two others. One of which belongs to Aaron. Not a wise move. Moving the army alone will bankrupt us. And if you take 80 thousand troops south, you may come back with 20 thousand. There is also the real possibility you yourselves will not come back. Good luck."

He got up and left the dining room. "He's right you know," mother said. "You should listen to him. Fix what you own and leave Aaron alone. You tried to take his children. I'm guessing that note said they failed, and they are all dead. He will have no mercy on you as the ones behind it, and I will not blame him if he does. Why did you do that, anyway?"

"To force him back into the fold, to force him to pay tithes, and to fix and expand our infrastructure like he has done in the south."

"Did it ever occur to you to ask him to fix our infrastructure rather than forcing him?" She got up and walked out.

"And that is why women and children don't run Kingdoms." Father said. "Let's go look at some maps before we decide." They left to go to father's office.

If I killed these two, I would save 80 Thousand of their troops and an unknown number of my troops. Besides, they tried to kidnap my children; I was in no mood to be merciful. I went to father's office. They were studying the maps.

Father finally nodded deciding. "Call up the troops, we march at the new moon."

I shook my head. I cast the beguiling spell. "He no longer needs you. He will betray and kill you, kill him now." They surprised me at their reaction, it was immediate. They both drew their daggers and started stabbing each other.

"You think you can take my Kingdom, you ungrateful

child?"

"Just die, old man, your time has ended. It's my time now."

They died in each other's grasp. Odd they never used magic to fight, no matter, dead is dead.

CHAPTER 24

I flew under my city spot checking to make sure all was well. I teleported into the wall in the castle, all was quiet. Reggie and the twins were having lunch. I came out of the wall in the hall and walked into the dining room.

"Da" They shouted and ran to me.

"Hey guys." I said.

Reggie came over and kissed me, "You are well husband?" She asked smiling.

I smiled," I am."

"Is it finished?"

"I believe it is. It seems the Crown Prince, and my father were behind it. They wanted to use the children to force us to do their bidding. Apparently, they got greedy and killed each other over who would be King."

"Amos, and your mother?"

"They had advised them to leave us alone, they didn't take their advice. Last I saw Amos and mother they were fine. I think they'll be ok. They'll be too busy fixing their Kingdom to worry about us."

She nodded hugging me. "Good, now maybe things can get back to normal."

I laughed, "I doubt it, but we'll handle whatever comes together."

***

I visited the people left from the Assassin's Guild list, there would be no second visits. Hopefully that was the last of the vipers in this pit. Well, until some migrated in, but now I knew what to look for. I went to the businesses the guild had around the city and eliminated them. I loaded all their vault's contents into crystals. I then went to their secret storage vaults and emptied them into crystals.

While I was out, I checked on my businesses; they were running smoothly and making money. Dov-ees sent me a message that he had news from the northern Kingdoms. I knew what it would be, but I wanted to see what they reported.

We talked business until we were completely done. "You have news from the north?"

"I do, reports from Norsewick is that there is an apparent war going on among the Assassin's Guild. The Norsewick guild house was wiped out. I'm sure you have already heard the guild house here suffered the same fate." I nodded. "There is also news of the death of your father and older brother." He waited for a reaction.

"Killed by the guild?"

"They are not sure; reports say they killed each other. A power struggle perhaps."

"That would be just like them. They were never happy with what they had, they always wanted more. Any news from Dunwich?"

"Nothing new, the business is doing well. No large troop movements."

I nodded, "good, maybe things will be calm for a change."

He laughed, "calm before the storm."

"Usually."

I stopped by the school and checked in with the Head Priest. "All is well?"

He bowed, "It is Sire."

"I wanted to let you know that I will create a new rank equal to a knight. The new rank will be 'Sir Mage', we will recognize them the same as a knight. With this new rank come responsibilities. When needed they must fight for the kingdom and help when their help is called on."

"Will they be required to appear at court?"

"No more than a knight would, unless specifically called

upon."

"Will they be taxed?"

I laughed, "no more than anyone else of their rank. I'll be honest with you. I have recently found out that the Assassins' Guild has Mages. I'll give you one guess where they come from. The assassins are probably using the fact that they might be killed if found out as a way to get them into the guild. More than likely threatening them with turning them in if they don't work with them. As far as I'm concerned, that is a dangerous waste of talent. We need them on our side. So, if you would, spread the word. I'll not force them, but the assassins might."

"That is a danger, I'll make sure the word is passed."

***

I made shield bracelets, both wrist and ankle, and circlets for the twins. I also made them teleportation rings, including one for Reggie. They just had to think of teleporting to the pavilion and they would teleport. We practiced with them and told them it was for emergencies only, not to be played with. I also upgraded the wards around the castle, especially around the Royal apartments.

I also started teaching them hand-to-hand. We started with two days a week. Once we were started, we increased to training every other day, then every weekday. Once word got around other Royal's military children wanted in on the training. We started a special training class for them and brought in trainers to do the job. I'd take over later once they were ready to escalate to my type of combat. I would teach them to fight with magic, steel, and MMA.

"The children are really enjoying the hand-to-hand."

"I know, and we needed to channel that energy into something constructive before they found something to do with it." I laughed remembering my youth.

We got a report that the Volwick had started a road building project in their city and had started on a road headed to the new Southgate road and bridge I had built. Prince Roman was helping with the Southgate road, practicing his earth magic. He was getting stronger with age, and practice.

***

I was still curious about what, or who was out west, beyond the mountains. I knew of no caravans that came from that way, well, no major ones. My map showed no cities, but that didn't mean there wasn't one. It just meant no one had updated the map.

I took a piece of iron with me when I teleported out to the mountains, landing underground. I felt the earth around me and found the highest concentration of iron. I put the drawing runes on the iron to make a trap like I had done for the silver and gold. That would attract the purest iron.

I flew under and along the mountains. The mountains went all the way to the sea in the south with no breaks. I flew under to the north. I knew where one pass was; it was steep. I kept following the range north; it ended in Norsewick.

I made the mountain sides into sheer cliffs at the border. I opened a crevasse 50 feet deep and 100 feet wide from the mountains to the King's road. That would force anyone to use the King's road, at least from the north and west sides.

I teleported back to the mountain pass. I went up to the highest peak and looked west. I saw nothing, not even the ocean. This would be a good place for a fort. I could put a few hundred men in the right kind of fort, and they could hold the pass forever. I could build farmsteads and offer the land to those would move out here and farm the land and support the fort. I could even build a town, for shops, and businesses, and they could support each other. I'd build a King's road to here and maybe out to the coast. I wanted to spread our Kingdom out. We could put one of the Royals in charge of the area to oversee it. We'd just have to choose carefully.

I flew under straight west heading for the ocean. Under

rivers, forests, and fields. It was good land. I was pretty sure the trees here were the type used in shipbuilding.

I found no towns, farm, or ranches. When I reached the coast, I followed it north until I found where a river met the sea. There was a ship anchored off store, and a longboat was hauling fresh water back to the ship. It was a Dunwich cargo ship. There was evidence of ships stopping here to replenish their fresh water. This would be a good place for a harbor.

I'd follow the same pattern. Fort first, then farms, then a town. Actually, I'd build this before the mountain fort. I liked this idea better. I flew under up the coast to the north. I stopped at about a few weeks travel time by horse. I found nothing. My advantage was I could raise a fort, harbor, and city pretty much overnight. It would take anyone else years. The more I thought about it the more I liked it.

I flew all under the area as fast as I could to update my maps. Once I arrived back at the mountains, I teleported home.

***

I updated all our maps and talked to Reggie. "So, this would double the size of our Kingdom?"

"More than double it and would cover our western flank. Moving our Army and Navy out there is the easy part, the harder part is who would we send to govern that area."

"And the population?"

"Free land, farms, housing, and a year's supplies to get started. People will line up to take the deal once the fort and castle are in place."

She thought about it. "You are probably right. But as you said, who do we send as governor?"

"I've been thinking about that. How about General Samuels?"

"A Military Governor?"

"To start with, if he does well, maybe keep it when he retires. We appoint him, he sets everything in place. He protects our western flank, keeps law and order. If he is not the man for the job long term, we replace him."

"How large a force?"

"1000 troops, and 2 Navy ships to start, then families, farmers, and tradesmen. We'll work up from there."

"I like it, let's draw up plans, then invite the General to a meeting."

***

The General was not slow on the uptake; he saw this for the opportunity it was. He was all for it from the start. "What we'd like you to do General, is to make a deployment plan, and supply requirement. I'll be opening a portal for us to travel there. The ships will meet us."

"Timeline?"

"You tell me. How long will it take to gather supplies and prepare for movement?"

"I'll have a plan for you in three days."

"Make it a week, I want a full plan, not an emergency plan."

He nodded, "In one week then."

I nodded, He bowed and departed.

***

A letter was waiting for me when we came down to breakfast. It was from my Mother.

It read:

Aaron,

It is with a heavy heart that I must tell you of the death of your father and brother Cain. They killed each other in a fit of greed and rage. Amos is now King, and I am acting as his advisor. It is in this capacity that I'm writing you. King Amos has inherited a mess. We need your help to repair the infrastructure of the city and the castle. We can't afford to pay or to wait for people to repair these things as we are almost bankrupt. Please come.

The Queen,
Mother.

"I'll be back," I told Reggie. I teleported into the wall of the family dining room. It was breakfast time and mother, and Amos were there. I stepped out into the hallway and walked into the dining room.

I bowed, "Mother."

She nodded, "Aaron."

I looked at Amos. "Brother." I smiled.

He smiled back, "Brother. Come, share breakfast with us."

"Thank you." I fixed my plate and sat down.

"How are the twins?" mother asked.

"Fine, growing like weeds."

"I would love to see them." She said.

I nodded and opened a portal, "kids." I called the twins and Armor came through. "This is your Grandmother."

They both looked at her. "Grandmother," they bowed. Reggie came through and stood behind them. The portal closed.

Mother went around the table, "come here, children." They went right to her. She was hugging them with tears on her cheeks. She took them back to her seat and started asking them questions to get them talking. That was all it took; they took off with stories. Reggie fixed their plates, and we sat down to breakfast.

I sat next to Amos. "I understand you have a few problems and need a hand."

He laughed, "You could say that, yes. Father and Cain made a right mess of things through their neglect."

"We'll work it out, what are brothers for." We laughed.

As we ate, we talked about their problems. Most of which were money related. There was very little left in the treasury, and the Crown owed everyone except the army. They had paid the army through the end of the month.

"Father and Cain were so focused on forcing the four kingdoms to become one under their rule they destroyed this one trying to make it happen. I have a proposal. Norsewick is bankrupt, I propose we join all kingdoms under your banner, your Kingdom. I would inherit nothing, anyway. I will be your governor here. You assign another to Midwick. Let's end this wasteful fighting and live in peace, and hopefully prosperity."

I looked at the Queen, "mother, what are your, thoughts?"

She nodded, "I'm of the same opinion. Your father would not listen to reason. Greed blinded him, and Cain was worse."

I looked at Reggie, "My Queen?"

She looked around the table. "I am for peace. This is a better way to achieve it."

"What will the other Royals say?" I asked.

Mother harrumphed, "They are so scared they are about to lose everything, anything that stabilizes the Kingdoms they will agree too."

"Then we shall combine the Kingdoms into one for the betterment of us all. What needs to be done first?"

"Money," mother said, "The Crown owes half the businesses and shops in the city. You want a peaceful transition, pay them what we owe them. They will follow right along."

I nodded. "Call your accountants, send word to all we owe money too. Have them present their bill to our accountants; we'll pay our debts in full. At the same time we'll let them know about the joining of the three Kingdoms into one. Word will spread quickly."

***

We held Court and paid our debts. I as King, Reggie as Queen, Amos as Duke of the Norsewick, and mother as the Queen Mother and advisor. I opened crystals in the castle vaults as needed. I put the assassin's guild gold to good use.

Once our debts were settled, we called for the Commander of the Army. He approached and bowed.

"General, send half of our army back to their homes, with one month's pay. Keep your best troops active. Send 1000 troops to Midwick to maintain peace. We will meet you there to settle all outstanding debts and install a Governor. Do you have any urgent matters that I need to take care of?"

"None, Sire."

"Very well, you have your orders." He bowed and left.

We restocked the castles supplies, paying in advance. Reggie and the twins went home, I stayed to finish some repair work. The clerks gave me a list of things that needed fixing right away, and I took care of them, I repaired castle walls, bridges, wells, and numerous other projects. I left the lower priority jobs undone and hired them to be repaired. We also put people to work paving the street. That would get money in circulation. I set my silver and gold traps out. Might as well make the land pay for itself.

We did the same thing in Midwick. Mother suggested one of the Royals she trusted for Governor and we installed him there. We paid our debts and started putting people to work. I made sure the treasury was fully funded. Calm was returning to the kingdoms, as lives got back to normal.

I went to see Dov-ees, "I need Master Shipwrights, and Shipwrights. We have the correct types of trees, what I don't have is the expertise."

"The only ones I know of are the ones in Dunwich, and their King will not let them leave."

I smiled, "We'll see."

***

I teleported to Dunwich, under my warehouse. It seemed like a business as usual day. I came up out of sight and went into the office.

The office manager rose, "Sire," He bowed.

I nodded, "All is Well?"

"Yes, Sire. No problems."

"Good. I'm looking for a Master Shipwright. Have you had any dealings with any?"

"I have not, but the shipyards are across the harbor, they should be easy to find."

I smiled, "thank you." I went outside and around the corner. I dropped underground and went over to the shipyard. I went under a few offices listening to conversations. There were several projects ongoing, employing a lot of shipwrights. Inside one office three men were arguing.

"You have to pay guild dues. And your shipwrights must pay guild dues. They have no choice. if they don't belong to the guild, they don't work. If you don't belong to the guild, you are out of business. That's as plain as I can make it."

"So, we buy our work now do we? Then we buy our Jobs?"

"Call it what you want, but them's the rules." The two men left, leaving the third alone in the office.

I came up out of sight and went in through the door; He looked up. "The guild bothering you too?" I asked.

"They bother everyone, it must be part of the job."

I nodded. "I have a proposition for you. One where You won't have to bother with the guild."

"It must be in another country because here, you have to deal with them." I didn't answer. He looked at me for a moment. "Another country?" He asked frowning.

I nodded. He sat down, staring at me. "Just for conversation's sake, what do you need built?"

"Several ships. Some cargo, some fishing, and some Navy. I have forests of ship's wood, I need Master Shipwrights, and shipwrights to build my ships. We have no Shipwright's Guild."

"How many people are you thinking of hiring?"

"How many do you need, and how many can you get?"

"Again, just for conversation's sake you understand, I'd like to have 50 Shipwrights and 50 apprentices. Another couple of masters wouldn't hurt."

"If you were starting a yard from scratch, and could have anything, what would you want?"

"People and facilities?" I nodded. "Four dry docks, six Master shipwrights, 50 shipwrights and 100 apprentices."

I nodded thinking, "I will hire that many, provide housing, and transportation, to the shipyards. If you can get them, you can run the shipyards."

"Wages?"

"You tell me, but more than they make here."

"How soon do you need them?"

"Well, I could take them right now, but… This will cause a fuss in the shipyard and Dunwich. So, let's say I wanted to hire you to build a ship here. You have a business; you just need to hire people. People who will leave the country willingly in an instant. That will be the tricky part, I don't want you in trouble here in your Kingdom."

Staring at me, "you're a Mage" I nodded. "Can you take me to this shipyard now?"

"I can take you to the place I will build it."

He harrumphed. "Come back in ten years, when you have it built."

I smiled, "I could have it finished in a week, but I'd like your input on the design." I raised a table up from the floor with a relief model of the area where I would build. "I will use this river as one side of my harbor." A harbor appeared. "A fort will go here, the town here. The shipyards will go over here. You said you wanted four dry-docks." Four drydock rose on the model. "What else do you need?"

He looked at the model. "Warehouses." They appeared. "A lumber yard." one appeared. "Housing for the workers." They appeared. He nodded his head. For the next hour we talked logistics, and support until it satisfied him. "Take me to the site."

I teleported us to the site where we would build it all. I had to steady him until the dizziness passed. "Thanks."

I nodded, "it gets easier."

He looked around, "show me the trees." I teleported us to the forest, where the large trees grew. He looked around, nodding. "Yes, this will do nicely. I'll need gold to start. The men will want to see that we can pay them." I nodded. "Come back in two weeks, and I'll give you an update on how many men I have, and what trouble we are having."

Nodding, "I'll leave you finances, and check back in two weeks."

I teleported us back to Dunwich and left him a small chest of gold. I walked back to my merchant's office and sent a message to my local muscle to come see me. They arrived in less than an hour.

"Sir Mage," he bowed. I nodded handing him a large purse of gold.

"I'm going to be doing business with Master Shipwright Guy. I don't want him to have any labor troubles."

"We may need more bribe money for the guild and officials." I gave him two more purses of gold. "He will have no troubles."

I nodded, He bowed and left.

CHAPTER 25

The General was ready to move his troops and supplies to our new western location. All I needed to give him was three days' notice and we could go. I gave him his notice, and the Navy their notice, and went to Westport.

I lowered the seabed making an actual deep-water harbor. I deepened the approach for ship traffic. I made the whole harbor stone lined, with stone docks and wharfs. I raised the castle-fort that would protect the harbor and the city. I put a guard chain across the harbor mouth. I raised the shipyard, warehouses, and workers housing. I raised a wall around the whole area. I raised a wall between the wharf and the city. I would raise the actual city later. When I had finished the first phase, I rested in the earth to restore my powers, and strength.

***

I opened a portal, and the General moved his troops and support trains through. They moved straight into the castle and assumed duties. I stayed there a few days insuring we had everything we needed. The Navy ships arrived before I left. I raised a trade road from Westport through the forest to the mountain pass, then joined it to our trade road east of the mountains.

Reggie announced that we were opening farmsteads on shares to any who wanted to go to Westport. We made the same offer to shop owners and merchants but would give them the buildings for their shops on shares. We were already getting inquiries about them. We also hired loggers to cut trees for the shipyards, they took the trade road west to get started on their contract.

The Kingdoms now had many moving parts, and it was taking more time to manage. I expanded my office to include the map room, and map table. I kept changes noted on the maps.

We received a message from our trading house in Dunwich. It had been two weeks since I talked to Master Shipwright Guy. The message said, "trouble, danger waiting." Anymore my normal dress was my armor, so I was ready to go see what trouble we had.

I teleported outside the harbor city, underground. I moved slowly toward my trading house. I saw nothing out of the ordinary. I moved under to Guy's office, Nothing out of the ordinary there either. My gut, which I always trust, said something was off, I was missing something.

I went to my local muscles bar, nothing unusual there. I came up in a back room and went out and sat down at a table. The serving girl came over, "Ale." I told her.

Her boss brought an ale back to me with one for himself and sat down." An unexpected twist has come up. A Mage from court has been sniffing about. He's not after money, he's after information. Your Trading house, and Master shipwright are being watched."

"What kind of information?"

"He suspects that you are connected to the trading house, but he's not sure. They are watching both places. He wants to catch you to see what's going on with the shipbuilder. I'm guessing they want to know who is paying to have the ship built. Your builder has been hiring men but not putting them to work. That made the Crown suspicious."

"Anything else?"

He shook his head, "As far as I can find out he just wants to talk at this point."

I nodded, put a small bag of gold on the table and left through the back room. I toned my aura down and went under. I moved away from the bar and came up in an alley in the market district.

I bought a sweet roll and walked toward the shipyard. I had

my senses open to see who, if anyone, was following me. I picked up a tail when I entered the shipyard.

I walked like I didn't have a care in the world straight to Guy's office. I opened the door and walked in. He seemed nervous." Master Shipwright, I have brought another payment for the purchasing of supplies and instructions to lay the keel for my lords cargo ship."

I saw him relax, "Excellent, I have hired men for the job as you asked. We are ready to start anytime."

I felt the approach of a Mage. I turned slightly toward the door. "Once you start," the Mage opened the door and stepped inside. "How long until completion?"

"If all goes well, about a year give or take a few months."

I nodded. "That will be satisfactory." I looked at the Mage. He was dressed in nice clothes but not flashy. "Sir Mage." I nodded in greeting. He returned the nod.

"Sir Mage," Guy said, "This is the Mage I was telling you about. He represents those who want the ship built."

The Mage nodded. "I represent the Crown, and we wish to know who you represent, and what type of ship you want built."

"Ah, I see my ploy did not work."

"What ploy?" he said frowning.

"I came straight to the shipbuilders, rather than the Crown. I thought to save some cost of the ship by doing so."

He smiled, "and those savings would go into your pockets."

"Of course," I said smiling.

He nodded. "What type ship?"

"A medium-sized cargo ship. And as to who I represent, that would be Merchant Master Dov-ees in Port City."

"A Royal working for a merchant?"

"Sadly yes, I'm a fourth son. My father, and my brothers for that matter, think I should work. They allow me little in the way of family income."

"You dress like a fighter."

I laughed, "hopefully I'll never be tested. I bought it for the look, and the protection of course,"

He nodded, "ten golds." He held out his hand. "What you charge the merchant is your affair."

I nodded giving him ten golds.

He pocketed the golds and left. I fit in his pigeonhole. I was no threat to him. Guy started to speak. I put my finger to my lips. He nodded.

"So, you can start when?"

"Once supplies arrive, we can start, I'd say in a fortnight."

"Good, order the supplies, I'll return in a fortnight." I said nodding, making sure he understood what I wanted.

He nodded in return, "I'll do so straight away."

I gave him a large purse of gold and left. I walked back toward the market district. I found a nice place to eat and had a meal. I hadn't been followed, as far as I could tell. I'd let Guy start on a cargo ship. I'd come back later to talk to him, then we'd make our move.

I went by the trading house and told the master merchant what our cover story was. "If they question you, just say your master does not share all information with you. Let them make up their own minds about the rest."

He nodded, "Simple stories, are the best."

***

I kept harvesting my gold, and silver traps. I deposited the proceeds into the respective treasuries. I returned the gold I had liberated from the wagons to Amos' treasury. To keep peace in the family I changed the chests they were originally sent in.

I harvested the iron from the mountain traps and formed them into ingots. I put them into a crystal and took them to Dovees. "These are to be sold to blacksmiths, and artisans in the city. If they don't have gold, put them on an account."

"And if they default?"

"We'll work something out. They may have to work for the Crown." He nodded. "Any new news not in your report."

He shook his head, "All is quiet at the moment,"

"That's worrisome," I said laughing.

He smiled, nodding. "You've been busy."

"Yeah, like juggling... Torches." I almost said chainsaws. "But we're making money."

"Yes, we are, we are doing quite well, I'd like to, with your permission, move into a larger house."

"Sure, find one you like, and buy it. If you can't find one you like, draw some plans and I'll raise it."

"Thank you Sire. I think I have found a place. It backs up to the wall separating the wharfs from the city, right behind our warehouse. Once we buy it, I'd like to make modifications, including a tunnel to this warehouse."

"Sounds like fun. Let me know when you are ready."

***

I teleported under Guy's shipbuilder's office. Nothing seemed amiss. I went a few blocks away and came up. I walked back to Guy's office. "Sir Mage." He greeted me.

"Master Guy, our supplies are in?"

"They are we started laying the keel two days ago."

"Excellent, perhaps you could show me around?"

We talked as we walked, "I thought it best to start work. I'm sure we are still being watched."

"A wise choice. I want you to continue your work. Use this time to choose who you want to take with you. Get rid of troublemakers, and those who will not want to leave their homes. I can always use a cargo ship, so plan on finishing it. We'll move after it's completed."

"I was going to suggest that." He nodded.

"When you need more gold, go to my trading house, he will pay you. Keep good accounts, the Crown may check you at some point. If you have any other problems let them know, they can help. I'll check in every few months." I gave him a large purse of gold. "For expenses."

He bowed, "thank you, Sir Mage."

I nodded. I headed toward my trading house. No one followed me, I guess they knew where I was going now that I had told them I worked for the Merchant Dov-ees. As I approached, I felt there was a Mage waiting inside, but not the same one from before.

I glanced his way when I entered; he carried two daggers strapped long way along his back. "Sir Mage, you have a visitor who would like a moment of your time."

I turned to the Mage. "Sir Mage, how may I help you." I could tell he was not used to being called "Sir Mage" but covered it well.

"I wish to offer my services to you as you do for your master. I know you have hired muscle, and I have done some work for them in the past. I'm seeking more steady work."

I nodded, "have you eaten?"

"I have not."

"Master Merchant, have two lunches brought into the office."

"Yes, Sir Mage."

"Let's talk inside," he followed me into the office. There was a sitting area with a coffee table, we sat there. He was dressed in sturdy, decent clothes and boots. "What services can you offer us?"

"I'm an earth Mage, like yourself, though not as powerful. So, you know some things I can do."

"Let's pretend I don't, and you tell me what you can do."

"I can manipulate earth, and stone. I can move through earth, I can hear through earth, and I can move through walls. To name a few."

"Have you tried moving through water?"

He thought a moment, "honestly it never occurred to me. I can't swim, but now that I think about it, the concept is the same. I should be able to."

"What kind of work did you do for muscle?" He didn't answer. "Have you been following me?"

"Not really, I was the one that told your muscle that the

Royal Mage was asking about you though."

I nodded, "I guess not all the non-Royal Mages work for the Assassin's Guild."

"Not all of us, hard life that."

"Are you looking for contract work, or full time 'in my service' employment?" Before he answered lunch was brought in. We started eating, I waited for his answer. I could tell he was weighing his options.

"I want to be more than a 'Gutter Mage'."

"Is that what they call you?"

He shrugged, "among other things." He said smiling. "What would you advise?"

"If you work on a contract, you'll make good money while working, but how often you work is not known. If you come into my service, you'll be paid all the time, and have support, equipment and other benefits. Can you read and write?"

"Some. I'm self-taught, and what I have been able to pick up on the streets."

"One benefit would be a tutor to teach you to read and write. We'll build on that, including Magic. Can you use those daggers?"

"When I have to."

"Another thing to consider, if you come into my service, you must be loyal to me, and me alone. Not this country, not this King, only me. In return for your loyalty you will have mine. When you have a need, I'll be there for you."

"Will I be going to your Kingdom?"

"You would stay here for a time. But you would start your training right away. I will hire a tutor, and you will start improving yourself." We finished our meal while he considered. He had manners and kept himself manicured and clean.

Nodding to himself, he started to speak. I stopped him before he could. "There is one last thing for you to consider. If you enter my service, and betray me, I will kill you." I held him with a lifeless stare.

He nodded, "I would expect no less. I would like to enter

your service."

"Your Name?"

"Toll-ess, Sir Mage."

I concentrated and teleported a small keg of nails to the floor in front of me. I opened the keg and cast a tracking spell on the nails. "Your first task is to place one of these nails in the keel of every Dunwich ship that comes into this harbor until you have every Dunwich ship tagged." He looked at the keg of nails and nodded.

"You will want somewhere to live that is safe and secure. Use your powers to make yourself an apartment under this warehouse, you need not make an entrance to it. That way only you have access to it. You will have a safe refuge." I placed a large purse of gold on the coffee table. "Furnish it as you like."

I reached into my purse and took out my extra "purse of holding". "This is a 'purse of holding' anything that will fit into its mouth will fit in it." I took the purse of gold from the coffee table and dropped it into the purse. He watched closely. "And it weighs nothing. Well, you can fill it, but it holds a lot." I handed it to him.

He took it testing its weight. He reached in and took out the gold purse. "Amazing." He dropped the gold back inside and fastened the belt around his waist.

I took out an armor bracelet set, including a circlet. "These are runed armor bracelets. They are magic armor, shields, and helmet. They will automatically activate when you are attacked, protecting you from both physical and magical attack. Once you put them on, they will go under your skin and be hidden from view. You never take them off. Put these on your wrists, and these on your ankles. This one goes on your head like a crown." He put them on as I explained.

"Let me see your daggers." He gave them to me. I examined them. "Do you like these, the way they feel and move, or were these the best you could afford?"

"They were the best I could afford."

"Find some good quality ones that you like the feel of, and

the way they move. I'll show you how to make them better." I gave him his daggers back. "I'll be back in a few weeks; I'll want an update on your progress. I also expect that by that time you will have hired a tutor and have started classes. Check in with Master Merchant every few days to see if he has anything he may need your help with."

My last gift to him was a guise ring. "You are known here, this is a guise ring, it will change your appearance. Just in case."

Nodding he took it and put in on his finger. "Thank you, Sir Mage."

"Leave through the floor, it's best if no one knows you are working for us."

He stood, bowed, picked up the keg of nails, and dropped out of sight. I felt him move away. I briefed Master Merchant on our new Mage and our arrangement, just in case he needed some Mage help.

CHAPTER 26

Dov-ees bought the house he wanted, and I renovated it to his specifications. I added the tunnel he wanted between the warehouse and his new house. He and his wife were happy with the results. I was glad for them.

Since my shipyard was on hold for a while, I opened a lumber mill there to cut and season the lumber for the ships.

Toll-ess was working out well so far. He was tagging every Dunwich ship when it was in port. I could now track where every tagged Dunwich ship was. I did the same to ours, in case I needed to find one.

He had hired a tutor, and his studies were going well. On one of my trips I gifted him a notebook to help him with his studies. I showed him how to hide it inside himself. He loved that. The notebook would also allow me to know where he was as long as it was with him.

He bought a nice set of daggers; we made them an awesome set of daggers. He hid them in his forearms, like I did mine. I gave him a Mage Cloak, and a Mage Staff for him to practice with. I told him he needed to be able to fight with magic and/or steel. Both at the same time would be better.

All my maps, and map tables showed where all the marked ships were. Dunwich showed up in red, ours in blue. Everything had been running smoothly for the last six months... Then it wasn't.

Dov-ees' message just said, "Trouble."

I teleported down to his office. "We have trouble?"

"We just received a message from Dunwich, they have seized the ship you are having built, and the merchant house."

"Our people?"

"Toll-ess got them out and is hiding them in his

apartment."

"It's always something." I teleported to Dunwich, under the warehouse. Toll-ess had his apartment there, and they were inside. I looked up into the warehouse, the doors were closed, and guards were posted. I stepped through the wall. "Everyone all right?" They all nodded their heads. "What happened?"

Toll-ess stepped forward, "I heard that the Crown was going to seize your ship and came to warn the Master Merchant. On the way here I passed troops coming down the wharf. I assumed the worst and brought them down here. If I was wrong, no harm done. Turns out, I was right."

I nodded, "Well done. Did you hear why they seized the ship?"

"They found out you were from Shornwick, they've lost a lot of ships and troops to you. The King's not happy with you." He said smiling.

"What about the people at the shipyard, anyone hurt?"

"No, they were told that the ship now belonged to the Crown, and to continue to build it."

"Gather your belonging we are closing up shop for a while and going home. Toll-ess, you are welcome to come too." He nodded gathering his things. When they were ready, I opened a portal to Port City. "Tell Dov-ees I'll be back as soon as I conclude my business with their King." They nodded and stepped through the portal. I closed it behind them.

I lowered my output and masked my power levels. I travelled under to the castle. Parts of the castle were warded, I erased the activation runes. The Throne room was also warded, enchanted, and had Mage traps. I erased their activation runes as well. Everything looked and felt like they would do their jobs, they just wouldn't activate.

I would be as peaceful and as diplomatic as they would let me. I came up out of sight and approached the main gate of the castle.

"State your business," the guard said.

"I am the Mage from the Shornwick Trading House. The

King sent a message for me to come see him."

"Wait there I'll send for an escort."

Before long, I could sense a flurry of activity in the castle. Mages were gathering, so much for being diplomatic. I continued to wait.

My escort, a single soldier, finally arrived. They were trying to put me at ease. They took me straight to the throne room. As I suspected it was full of Mages.

I stood before their King waiting. One Mage stepped forward, "you will bow before the King."

"Kings do not bow to other Kings." That sent a ripple through the assembly.

"King you say? Name yourself."

"My Name is King Aaron, King of Shornwick, and the Northern Kingdoms. You have seized the ship I paid to have built, and my Trading House, I have come to ask why."

"You did not have permission from the Crown to have a ship built. You did not pay the fees."

"Oh, but I did. I paid ten golds to the Mage to your right. He gave me the go ahead to build." All eyes shifted to him. He looked daggers at me but nodded.

"That does not matter," The King finally spoke. "You have sunk, or stolen 20 of my ships, and killed or captured thousands of my troops. You will pay me for them all."

"Are these the same ships and troops that invaded my lands? The ones you hired out as mercenaries? Are those the ones you are talking about? Because if they are, that was war. You knew the risk when you sent them, or you do now." His face was getting red.

"You will pay me, or I will land 50 thousand troops on your shores and take everything you have. You will pay me a yearly tithe, or I will come take it. I have you here, and here you will remain until they pay your ransom."

I stared at him; he sat there so sure of himself. "The only thing worse than a bully, is a bully with power. Here is my counteroffer. I'll forget you tried to steal my ship. I'll close my trading house and leave you in peace. Once my ship is complete, I'll pay for it and you send it to me. If you attempt to stop me, I'll burn your harbor to the ground and every ship in it to the waterline."

"Kill Him!" He screamed. I threw my shields up. Every Mage in the room attacked. Through my feet I felt the strength of the earth powering my shields. I took their attacks of fire, lightning, ice, steel, whatever they fought with, I absorbed it all. I felt my power expanding. I sealed the doors and windows shut. I melted seams in the stone walls. No one was leaving this room. As my power expanded, it would envelope a Mage. I would take his power, which grew my power. They saw this and were panicking.

"Kill him before he kills us all!" The attacks intensified. lightning strikes multiplied, as did the fire and ice attacks. Some at the rear were trying to escape but could not.

The power, the raw power was intoxicating. I could feel the whole city. I melted the road from the castle to the harbor, turning it into lava. Then I turned the stone wharfs into lava. Ships started burning because of the intense heat, it was a chain reaction after that. Ship after ship caught fire.

The Mages and the Mage King of Dunwich were no more. I had absorbed all of them and their powers. My power still grew feeding off the magic in the castle. I felt the forts around the city I started melting them like lava. People were fleeing to get away from the fires and lava, still my power grew. I laughed at the small Mages who thought they could stop me. I was the sun, who can extinguish the sun? I felt the castle melting around me, my power grew. I felt myself expanding, consuming, becoming more powerful.

A distant memory surfaced. "Be careful of that spell, it's dangerous, and addictive... dangerous, and additive... Addictive..." It echoed through my mind.

Survivors of that night told of a giant fiery warbird that rose above a melting castle. Spreading its great wings, it screamed a challenge to the world. Then like a sun exploding, it turned the night into day, and was gone.

It took a week to put all the fires out. The harbor had melted into the earth. Every ship that had been in the harbor was burned to the waterline. It would take years for Dunwich to recover. They called all their ships and troops home to help rebuild.

***

"Ron in Chopper Five News is on the scene where the collapsing cliff face has closed the interstate. Ron what can you tell us?"

"Bob this was a terrific explosion. Initial reports said it was a single car, but they are now saying a fuel truck could have been involved. It's hard to believe a single car could have caused all this damage and fire. Emergency services are on the scene, fire fighters almost have the fire under control. It will take a while to recover any remains from the vehicles, if they can find any. They tell me the intensity of the heat has probably consumed any remains. This is Ron Chipley Chopper Five News, back too... What the?..."

"Stand by Bob, something is happening at the crash site. There seems to be more explosions, oh my God, look at that. Bob a huge explosion has just happened. Flames are reaching hundreds of feet into the air. Oh my, what in the name of... What is that? A Phoenix? Are you kidding me? Are you getting this Bob? There is a giant Phoenix rising above the crash site. There must be a fireworks truck involved in this. That would explain all the damage to the cliff face. That was a heck of a display, it must have cost someone a fortune for that one. Look at that, it's flapping its wings, and screaming. I have never seen anything like it before. I hope they had insurance." It blazed bright then faded out, sparks twinkling to the ground. "Firefighters are pulling back; they are going to just let this one burn itself out. You saw it here folks, Ron Chipley Chopper Five News, back to you Bob."

***

"He's kind of a strange one," one waitress said.

"Are you kidding? This close to San Francisco he doesn't even make the top 100. As long as he doesn't bother anyone and pays his tab, I don't care. He can sit there eating his meal and read his paper all day long. I don't care if he is wearing a lizard skin cloak." The older waitress replied.

From the TV in the corner, "continuing our reporting on what has got to be a strange news week," the News Anchor said. "New information has come out about the break-ins and vandalization of libraries around the city. Well, they weren't really vandalized, just broke into. Numerous books were stolen, but the thieves left gold coins to pay for what they took. It started at public libraries then college libraries, now bookstores. Books taken, but they always leave gold coins to pay for them. We are told the value of the gold far exceeds the cost of the books taken. We aren't talking about a few books either, they say there were over 3000 books taken. I guess someone is starting their own library. In national news the FBI is investigating a break-in at the U.S. Patent offices, no word yet on what was taken."

"More tea Sir?"

"No thank you, I have to be getting home, my wife and kids will be worried about me."

She nodded, "I'll get your ticket ready." She returned to the table with his ticket, he wasn't there. She looked around to see if he might have gone to the restroom. Two gold coins lay on the table. She picked them up and put them in her pocket. "For that kind of tip, you can be as strange as you want to be Mr. Lizard Cloak."

***

I flew under, back up to the cliff where I had challenged God to a fight. No one else was there. I emerged from the ground and stepped over to the cliff's edge. I looked at the reef below where waves crashed.

"Thank you, Father, for my family, and all you have given me. Help me make wise decisions and be a wise ruler of the people under my care. Give me strength to resist my weaknesses, and to control my anger. And, as my LT used to pray, don't let me screw this up." I smiled, "Amen."

I felt the world around me; I centered myself and concentrated on Reggie's location. She was far, far away. I smiled. This would be a long jump. I gathered my power and opened a portal. It took a few seconds to fully form.

"Da's home!" I heard the twins squealing from the other side. I saw Reggie standing there, I stepped through. *Yep, I was home.*

OTHER BOOKS BY
JAMES HADDOCK

The Derelict Duty

Prologue:

The Blaring klaxon jolted me out of a sound sleep. I threw my covers off and was halfway to my Vac-suit locker before I was fully awake. It felt like I had just fallen to sleep having just finished a long EVA shift. It would be just like Dad to have an emergency drill after an EVA shift to see if I had recharged my suit. I had, I always did, both Mom and Dad were hard taskmasters when it came to ship, and personal safety. Vac-suit recharging was top of the personal safety list. If you can't breathe, you die, easy to remember.

Donning a Vac-suit was second nature for me, after 16 years of drills and practice exercises. Having literally been doing this all my life, but I loved life on our Rock-Tug. I was reaching for the comms when I felt the ship shutter. "That can't be good," I said to myself.

Mom's voice came over ship-wide, "This is not a drill, this is not a drill, meteor strike, hull breach in Engineering". Mom's voice was just as calm as if she was asking, what's for lunch. This was a way of life for us, we trained and practiced so that when the reality of working in "The Belt" happened you didn't panic, you just did your job. You didn't have to think, you knew what you needed to do, and you did it.

I keyed my comms, "Roger, hull breach in Engineering, where do you need me Mom?" "Get to Engineering and help your Father, I'm on the Bridge trying to get us in the shadow of a bigger rock for some protection." Mom answered. My adrenalin was spiking but Mom's calm voice, helped to keep me calm.

I sealed my helmet and left my cabin heading for Engineering. The klaxon had faded into the background, my breathing was louder than it was. I kept telling myself "Stay calm, just do your job, stay calm."

I had just reached Engineering, when the Tug was rocked by a succession of impacts each one harder that the last. The hatch to Engineering was closed and the indicator light was flashing red, telling me there was hard vacuum on the other side. I switched my comms to voice activated, "Dad? I'm at the hatch to Engineering it's in lockdown, I can't override it from here." "Dad? Dad?, Dad respond!

"Mom, Dad is not answering, and Engineering is sealed, you are going to have to evac the air from the rest of the ship, so I can open the hatch." Mom's steady voice replied, "Understood, emergency air evac in 10 seconds."

Those were the longest 10 seconds of my short life. The hatch indicator light finally turned green and the hatch door opened. The Engineering compartment was clear. No smoke, no fire, some sparks and lots of blinking red lights. I looked over to the Engineering station console, there sat Dad. He had not had his Vac-suit on when the hull was breached.

Hard Vacuum does terrible things to the human body. I suddenly realized that I had not heard Dad on comms the whole time, just Mom. She probably knew what had happened but was sending help in the hope that Dad was all right and that maybe the comms were down.

I heard Mom in the background declaring an emergency and calling on the radio for help. Her voice still calm somehow, "Mayday, mayday, this is the Rock Tug Taurus, Mayday, we have taken multiple meteor strikes, have multiple hull breaches, please respond."

"Come on Nic, think! What do I need to do?" I asked myself. I closed the hatch to Engineering, to seal the vacuum from the rest of the ship. I turned and started back toward the bridge.

There was an impact, a light flared, and sparks; time seemed to slow, there was no sound, we were still in a vacuum, just shuttering vibrations and sparks. Holes seemed to appear in the overhead and then the deck, it was so surreal.

The meteors were punching holes through our ship like a machine punching holes on an assembly line. "Meteor storm"

Duty Calls

Duty Calls continues the story of Nic, Mal, Jazz and Jade as they fight to hold what belongs to them. The Corporations are becoming more aggressive in their effort to steal their inventions. Our four friends are matching the corporate's aggression blow for blow. The fight has already turned deadly, and the Corporation has shown they aren't afraid to spill blood. Nic has shown restraint, but the gloves are about to come off. They've gone after his family and that's the one thing he will not tolerate.

From Mist and Steam

Searching the battlefield after a major battle Sgt. Eli finds a dead Union Army messenger. In the messenger's bag is a message saying the South had surrendered, the war was over. Along with the Union Messenger was a dead Union Captain carrying his discharge papers, and eight thousand dollars.
Sgt. Eli decides now is a good time to seek other opportunities, away from the stink of war. While buying supplies from his friend the quartermaster, he is advised to go to St. Louis. Those opportunities may lie there and a crowd to get lost in. Sgt. Eli, becomes Capt. Myers, a discharged Union Cavalry Officer, and strikes out for St. Louis.

The war has caused hard times and there are those who will kill you for the shirt you are wearing. Capt. Myers plans on keeping his shirt, and four years of hard fighting has given him the tools to do so. Realizing he must look the part of a well-to-do gentleman, he buys gentleman clothes, and acts the part. People ask fewer questions of a gentleman.

What he isn't prepared for is meeting an intelligent Lady, Miss Abigale Campbell. Her Father has died, leaving the family owned shipping business, with generation steam-powered riverboats. They have dreams of building steam-powered airships, but because she is a woman, there are those who stand against them. Capt. Myers' fighting is not over, it seems business is war. They decide to become partners, and with his warfighting experience, and her brains the world is not as intimidating as it once seemed.

Hand Made Mage

Ghost, a young Criminal Guild thief, is ordered to rob an ancient crypt of a long dead Duke. He is caught grave robbing by an undead insane Mage with a twisted sense of humor. The Mage burns a set of rune engraved rings into Ghost's hand, and fingers. Unknown to Ghost these rings allow him to manipulate the four elements.

Returning to the Guild to report his failure, everyone thinks he has riches from the crypt, and they want it. While being held captive by the Criminal Guild, Ghost meets Prince Kade, the fourth son of the King, who has troubles of his own. Ghost uses his newfound powers to escape from the Guild saving the Prince in the process.

Spies from a foreign kingdom are trying to kill Prince Kade, and Ghost must keep them both alive, while helping Prince Kade raise an army to stop an invasion. Ghost finds out trust to soon given, is unwise and dangerous. He is learning people will do anything for gold and power. As Ghost's power grows, his enemies learn he is a far more deadly enemy than anything they have ever faced.

Wizard's Alley

Scraps, a gutter child, is sitting in his hiding place in a back alley, waiting for the cold thunderstorm to pass. Suddenly, lightning strikes in front of him, and then a second time. The two lightning bolts become men—two wizards—one from the Red Order, the other from the Blue.

The Red Wizard, chanting his curses, throws lightning bolts and fireballs. The Blue Wizard, singing his spells, throws lightning bolts and ice shards. So intense is their fighting, they become lightning rods. It seemed as if God Himself cast His lightning bolt, striking the ground between them and consuming both wizards in its white blaze. Scraps watched as the lightning bolt gouged its way across the alley, striking him.

Rain on his face awakens Scraps. The only thing left of the fighting wizards is a smoking crater and their scattered artifacts. He feels compelled to gather their possessions and hide them and himself. The dispersed items glowed red or blue, and he notices that he now has a magenta aura. Magenta, a combination of both red and blue, but more powerful than either.

Scraps then does what he has done all his life to survive. He hides. And unknowingly, he has become the catalyst for change in the Kingdom.